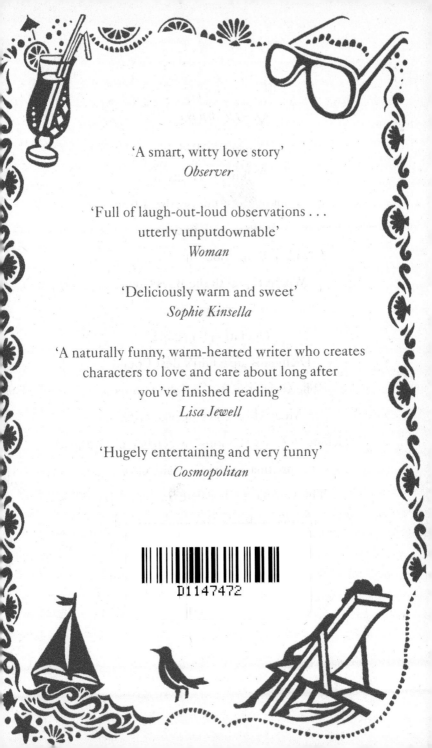

'A smart, witty love story'
Observer

'Full of laugh-out-loud observations . . .
utterly unputdownable'
Woman

'Deliciously warm and sweet'
Sophie Kinsella

'A naturally funny, warm-hearted writer who creates
characters to love and care about long after
you've finished reading'
Lisa Jewell

'Hugely entertaining and very funny'
Cosmopolitan

D1147472

Novels by Jenny Colgan

Amanda's Wedding

Talking to Addison

Looking for Andrew McCarthy

Working Wonders

Do You Remember the First Time?

Where Have All the Boys Gone?

West End Girls

Operation Sunshine

Diamonds are a Girl's Best Friend

The Good, the Bad and the Dumped

Meet Me at the Cupcake Café

Welcome to Rosie Hopkins' Sweetshop of Dreams

Christmas at the Cupcake Café

The Loveliest Chocolate Shop in Paris

Christmas at Rosie Hopkins' Sweetshop

Little Beach Street Bakery

Summer at Little Beach Street Bakery

The Little Shop of Happy Ever After

Jenny COLGAN

Operation Sunshine

sphere

SPHERE

First published in Great Britain in 2007 by Sphere
This paperback edition published in 2008 by Sphere
Reissued by Sphere in 2013

5 7 9 10 8 6

Copyright © Jenny Colgan 2007

The moral right of the author has been asserted.

*All characters and events in this publication, other than those
clearly in the public domain, are fictitious and any resemblance
to real persons, living or dead, is purely coincidental.*

All rights reserved.
No part of this publication may be reproduced, stored in a
retrieval system, or transmitted, in any form or by any means, without
the prior permission in writing of the publisher, nor be otherwise circulated
in any form of binding or cover other than that in which it is published
and without a similar condition including this condition being
imposed on the subsequent purchaser.

A CIP catalogue record for this book
is available from the British Library.

ISBN 978-0-7515-5106-8

Typeset in Caslon by M Rules
Printed and bound in Great Britain by
Clays Ltd, St Ives plc

Papers used by Sphere are from well-managed forests
and other responsible sources

MIX
Paper from
responsible sources
FSC® C104740

Sphere
An imprint of
Little, Brown Book Group
Carmelite House
50 Victoria Embankment
London EC4Y 0DZ

An Hachette UK Company
www.hachette.co.uk

www.littlebrown.co.uk

For someone due out the same week as this book –
we cannot wait to meet you.
Well, two of us can't wait to meet you. The other one would
probably prefer a new bicycle and some apple juice.

Acknowledgements

Huge thanks and respect to Ali Gunn, my sensational agent, of Gunn Media, and Jo Dickinson, my brilliant editor. Both of you were right about everything, as ever!

And thanks to everyone at Little, Brown, especially Tamsin Kitson, Antonia Hodgson, Helen Gibbs, Alison Lindsay, Louise Davies, Peter Cotton, Hannah Venn, Ursula Mackenzie, and all the sales team who've done so much and worked so hard – thank you.

To all the yachties who have been so friendly and kind to me over my years of hanging about and getting in the way, particularly the crews of *M/Y Golden Cell, M/Y Leander, M/Y Jo* and *M/Y Deniki*.

Jonny Popper, whose excellent and lucid poker game was too long to make it in here, but will somewhere else; AME-LISA and Roni for being such great friends during our year abroad, and Jojo Moyes for chocolate and sanctuary on so many occasions; Mrs Doctor Karen, Katrina, Wesley, Dan and, of course, everyone on the board, as well as a big shout out to Feb Mums.

Huge thanks to Marina, and the staff of Kozie, de Drukkery and Zeeuwse Bibliotheek.

Thanks to my wonderful family for everything, and special thanks to Mr B & wee B, my two favourite people in the whole wide world.

Chapter One

'Holidays suck,' Lydia was proclaiming loudly, stabbing her straw into her drink to make her point. We were in a new West End bar which had been recommended in *Time Out*. Places like this normally intimidated me, but Lydia loved them; her dark eyes flashed at the cheesily good-looking barman, and her movements got more emphatic. You'd notice her.

'They SUCK!'

'Well, that's your opinion,' I said, a little stiffly under the circumstances. But I was the one who had brought up the subject of holidays, and now I was being told that, therefore, my dreams and desires were effectively a big pile of steaming dog turds that I'd just deposited between us on the bar.

'It's not an opinion,' she said. 'It's a fact. Everybody

knows. You've got to fly in a shitty plane, which is always shit, sit on some stupid bus for nine hours, sleep in some stupid room that's nothing like as nice as your own, listen to other people shouting all night, get sunburnt, get hungover, spend all your money, have a shit time, get knocked over by a car, remember you forgot to buy travel insurance, get your leg amputated and get flown home on a cargo plane to face three years in debtors' prison.'

'And that's what always happens, is it?' I said.

'Pretty much.'

I sighed. This wasn't going exactly as planned.

You always see, don't you, other people's holiday snaps, where they're patently having the most fabulous time somewhere incredibly exotic, and you ask them about their holiday (if you have a lot of time on your hands at work, which I do) and their faces go all slack and dreamy and they get a faraway look in their eyes and say something stupid like, 'Well, we'd get up early in the morning and go running along the surf on the empty pink sand, then pick coconuts and fruit for our breakfast in the hammock.' And you think, Eh? How come I got vomited on by a child all the way from Gatwick to Fuerteventura and ate chips every night for a week?

Or they organise massive gangs of chums.

'Oh, yes, thirty of us are going sky hiking in the Peruvian Andes, then we've taken a luxury villa for a month in a cloud forest.'

How do people do that? Do I have the wrong friends? I

can't get any three of mine to commit to going to the cinema on the same day without two cancellations, one cancellation retraction, one falling out between two people who then refuse to sit together, a skirmish over the M&Ms and nobody paying me for the booking fee.

'My last holiday,' said Lydia, tossing back her long black hair, 'I copped off with a bloke who lives two doors down from my mum. Ten years of my life getting away from that place, and then what happens?'

'Well, if you knew that, why'd you cop off with him?'

'Durr! Because ON HOLIDAY they make you drink big goldfish bowls full of spirits until you're nearly unconscious, that's why. Chalk another one up to "why holidays are shit" by Lydia Li.'

'Well, THAT is why you have to listen to me,' I said.

I was doing my best to be assertive, whilst not being blinded by the retro disco lighting. It's important to be assertive with Lydia. Not that she's the most insanely competitive woman that ever lived. OK. She's the most insanely competitive woman that ever lived. If *you've* broken your leg, *she* was once skiing in St Moritz with Prince William and she did the world's highest ski jump and broke her neck and the doctors said it was a miracle and they gave her the Nobel Prize for prettiness.

You never ever wear new clothes if you're going to see Lydia. If she likes them she'll say, 'Oh, I like your outfit – very WAG.' (Even if it's, like, a grey sack made out of plasticine.)

3

And if she doesn't, she'll say, 'Oh, that was seventy per cent off down the King's Road – is that where you got it?'

We work next door to one another. We're receptionists on Harley Street in London, where all the plastic surgeons reside.

Lydia is 50 per cent convinced that one day a rich man is going to come and pick his wife up from surgery but instead get blasted by a lightning bolt and fall in love with her instead. I've told her this is both unlikely – rich men NEVER bother to pick up their wives, and their wives wouldn't want them to – and immoral, but she won't be moved. Her other 50 per cent is convinced that she's going to pull a young doctor. She doesn't date very much. No wonder she went mad on holiday.

So being assertive, my friend Bailey says, would help me no end. Growing up with three evil brothers in a very small house meant I had to develop a very loud mouth to even get fed, or rescued when the horrid beasts I had to share a home with, also known as John Jr, Patrick and Cassandro (Mum went a bit mental at the end), had alighted on some new form of torture involving holding me down whilst they shut the automatic door of the garage on my head, or setting fire to one of my pigtails, or threatening my pet rabbit with dire dismemberment whilst tying me to a tree. It wasn't what you'd call idyllic. I'm only stunned (and occasionally disappointed) that they're all now rational adults roaming free and not in some prison somewhere.

We didn't go on foreign holidays when I was young, partly because we didn't have much money for all six of us, but mostly because Mum and Dad knew the boys would behave so unbelievably badly that we'd all end up getting deported.

So we always ended up in a caravan park in Wales, where the boys would instantly turn feral and run free, returning only for frequent top-ups of sausages and ice cream. We always stayed one week in one place and one week in another so that the boys didn't get enough time to form an international criminal conglomerate with all the other children on the site.

I'd sit inside with my parents and we'd eat crisps and play card games as the rain beat against the window whilst I indulged my fantasies of being a cosseted only child. It wasn't bad, but it wasn't the same as returning to school sporting a suntan and ankle bracelet with ribbon braids in my hair, and talking about mysterious dark waiters and romantic young men on motorbikes and staying out all night, like the other girls in my class.

When I was seventeen and just about to start college, I had my first all-girls' holiday, to Malaga. I looked forward to it for months. I stuck the tickets above my desk and fantasised solidly with my friends about the gorgeous boys who were going to fall madly in love with us, and spent every Saturday going in and out of Dolcis and Ravel choosing exactly the right pair of white stilettos. Tanya and Claire

5

promised that we'd get free drinks everywhere and that it would be sun, sea and snogging all the way. I pored excitedly over letters in *Jackie* that said, 'I fell in love on holiday but now I don't know if I'll ever see him again,' and vowed to take the problem page's wise advice, and not put too much hope into a holiday romance when it probably wouldn't work in the rainy days back home (although I was sure mine would).

So it did come as something of a disappointment when it turned out that our one hundred and twenty-nine pound special was a room in a grubby white building next to a small pool filled with pissing children and surrounded by bull-necked families who'd brought their own packets of lard and deep-fat fryers.

This wouldn't have mattered if we weren't chased around by tragic-looking reps effectively begging for a huge share of our holiday money to take a 'party cruise', which we duly did. Tanya pulled one of the reps, who it then turned out Anne-Marie, another, slightly plumper girl, had a thing for, precipitating an enormous row which split the camp and lasted the whole of the rest of the holiday. Which hardly mattered to me, I was so shivery and shaky with sunburn (I had covered my mousy locks in Sun In and sat out through the heat of the first two days) I couldn't think straight, and Los Animalo's only disco, the Slutty Slug, gave me a pounding headache the first five thousand times they played the 'Macarena'.

Between hugely intense levels of secretive bitching, dirty

looks, Anne-Marie showing how over the club rep she was by snogging a different bloke every night, until they started hanging around outside our apartment like stray dogs, it was not what you might call the holiday of a lifetime, particularly after I got home and my finkish brothers developed a new game called 'Peel the Skin Off Evie'.

Since then I'd kind of sworn off holidays. At college, whilst other people went off Interrailing and trying to make it through Italy on five quid a day, I worked in the local pub and tried to look interested when people showed me pictures of the lions they'd seen on safari in Namibia, or of the Tuscan villa they'd hired, or of them falling hilariously off a big yellow banana and I'd think glumly about the night Anne-Marie got sangria sick on Tanya's new coat and they went for each other's hair.

And now, well, I was older, Bailey had got me a job in London working for some very grumpy doctors on Harley Street, which sounds a lot more important than it actually is, and I have some new friends, which, post-holiday, seemed the best thing to do under the circumstances.

And I wanted a holiday. I hadn't been away for two years, apart from to visit friends who were working overseas which was less of a holiday (they never wanted to take you to the tourist attractions) and more of an extended piss-up. I'd been single for eighteen months. Eighteen months. I felt like a born-again virgin. It was a desert out there. Or at least it was if you didn't have tiny thighs and a modified nose, like the clients I saw every day. They seemed to do all right.

And it hadn't exactly been wine and roses before then. My last boyfriend, Bill, had . . . well, it had never really progressed to the right moment to go on holiday. There isn't really a right moment, sometimes. With Bill I always felt like I was saying, 'Fancy going on holiday?' and he'd hear, 'Fancy getting a mortgage and getting married tomorrow and having nine children and you're never allowed to go out ever again and I'm about to put on four stone?'

He once condescended to take me on a long weekend barge trip with his unpleasantly sporty friends. It was the most boring thing I've ever done in my life. Travelling at two miles an hour whilst getting up and down to open locks isn't a holiday, it's exercise for a sixty-year-old recovering from a heart attack.

Maybe it's me. Maybe holidays and me are just not destined to go together. Maybe I'm designed to spend the rest of my life waking up at 7.40 a.m. and eating Weetabix for breakfast, even though I hate it, because apparently it means I won't feel hungry again until lunch, even though I always do and have a KitKat at eleven. With four fingers if it's raining. I'm not allowed to eat them in front of the clients though, we do a lot of liposuction, and they might turn wild and tear the wrapper out of my hands.

Back in the bar I toyed with my white wine. The rain was lashing down outside. I wasn't sure it was just about a holiday. I think I need more excitement in my life. I shouldn't get so excited, for example, when a new flavour of Pringles comes out. I'm twenty-seven. I feel I should be exploring the world; having mad passionate love affairs; dancing in the surf.

The city is fine, but it's hard to feel truly free with an Oyster Card. There must be more to life than magazine day (Tuesday – my favourite day. I especially like it when the stars tell you their diet and exercise secrets when we've had them in two weeks before).

'What if . . .' I said to Lydia. She really is intimidatingly beautiful, which makes the clients think they'll end up looking like her. I'm 'approachable-looking' according to Dr Bennet, which I think means they hired me so that even if an operation goes horribly wrong, the patient will still come out thinking, Well, at least I still look better than the receptionist. 'What if I organised a holiday so fantastic, you came back totally relaxed and had the best time you'd ever had and it was in paradise?'

Lydia looked at me sceptically. 'What, and it's free?' she said.

'No, of course it's not free. What are you talking about?'

'Oh. The way you're talking about it made it sound like it would be free.'

'No. But I'd organise it and do all the legwork.'

'Who's going? It'll have to be somewhere fancy.'

'Like all the really fashionable places,' I said casually, as if I was totally au fait with where those might be.

'They don't have to be fashionable.' She sniffed. 'They just need to have rich people in them.'

'Which makes them expensive,' I said.

'Well, duh.'

'OK, so do you have a secret trust fund I've never heard of? Are you not really a receptionist, but actually an heiress slumming it for a reality TV show?'

She shrugged. 'You asked what it would take to make me go on holiday with you, when it's a given that all holidays suck. And I'm telling you – somewhere posh and full of rich blokes but not too expensive for us.' She looked at me. 'Actually, I'm not sure we should go together after all.'

'What's wrong with me?'

Lydia didn't say anything, just played with her glass. 'Nothing. Oh, I don't know. Maybe I should take a busty blonde, you know? For contrast? Enhance my prospects?'

And she wasn't even joking. Proximity makes you some funny friends.

I wasn't downhearted. Yet. Next stop Bailey. I've known Bailey for ever. We grew up on the same street, and spent a lot of time hiding from my brothers.

His mother, in the manner of a zookeeper feeding fish to sharks, kept throwing him together with the beasts in the hope that they'd all become friends, rather than Bailey becoming Chump.

I think of Bailey as my backup. He's not gorgeous, but he

is funny, well off and really smart. Lydia keeps going on about wanting to meet him. I do my absolute best to keep them apart; I don't want her getting her talons into him.

It didn't help that he was very small and very clever and absolutely refused to know when he was beaten – even the time John Jr buried him headfirst in the sandpit he still came out spitting mud and threatening to curse them unto the third generation (he was going through a *Lord of the Rings* period at the time).

To escape the sheer brute force he took to hanging about with me, even when I made him spend an entire summer as a patient whilst my girlfriends and I played *Casualty*. I was always fascinated with medicine. It was one of the biggest disappointments of my life when I entered my third year of physics, chemistry and biology, hoping to romp into a fabulous career as an emergency doctor (this was pre-*ER*, but nonetheless I think I already had George Clooney in mind before he was even invented), only to discover to my shock and horror that I didn't understand a word of it. Not wave forms, not Boyle's law, not photosynthesis.

How I was ever going to perform emergency transplant surgery when I couldn't even remember the parts of the flower I did not know, so I switched to business administration instead. Mind you, there's not a lot I don't know about healing times for bhleroplasty (that's your upper eyelid). Sometimes I think if I work at the Saint Harley Clinic for long enough I'll become a plastic surgeon by osmosis, another scientific concept Mr Gahery failed to explain adequately to me in Year Nine.

Still, I do get to do quite a lot of interesting stuff at work – I've sat in on various ops, so I'm not the least bit squeamish, even for pus. And I run the back office too, all the paperwork. Well, most of it; Dr Bennet has a secretive streak. It's a more prestigious job than Lydia's, which drives her crazy.

Bailey came and found me a couple of years ago when I was drowning in a hospital basement on this ludicrous temp job I'd picked up, coding people's injuries in their medical files. So: hit on head, 310. Hit on head with brick, 310-12; hit on head with fish, 310-96; hit on head by flying saucer, 310-977, etc. It was doing my brain in.

'I've found a job for you,' he'd said, observing me over the top of his lunchtime hummus sandwich. 'It's got windows and daylight and everything.'

I liked it when Bailey did things like this for me. Made me think he cared.

'Oh, yeah?'

'Harley Street.'

'I don't believe in private medicine,' I'd said snootily.

'Do you believe in . . .' and then he'd mentioned a figure nearly twice what I'd been gritting my eyes up for.

'I also have very flexible moral standards,' I added (unnecessarily), thinking about Top Shop's new collection. Bailey briefed me for the interview too, to make me appear a bit classier than I actually am, and I was in.

Anyway. Bailey, being a mini-genius – he really plays up this angle, too much I think – wears shirts with buttons on the collar that he gets in America, and John Lennon glasses, like he's in the Geek of the Month club. Anyway, he took to the summer of *Casualty* too, and is now head of development for a cutting-edge hospital design company who build really big things, and he's always flying all over the world with a briefcase chained to his hand and being extremely important and constructing the world's largest MRI scanner or something. I always make sure I mention it to the beasts at Christmas time. Patrick says, 'Well, it's no wonder he's building big things, he's such a tiny fellow,' and John Jr pretends not to remember who he is, even though he hit him with a spade every day for nine years.

I met Bailey near his office in Fitzrovia two nights after I saw Lydia. There were lots of other zippy people in the pub looking clever and explaining things to each other using rulers. I know it's nerdy, but I secretly think it's also quite cool. Plus, lots of blokes work for Bailey's company. I think it's very rude of him not to devote more time to finding a man for me.

'Let's go on holiday,' I said, almost before we sat down. Bailey looked up at me, blinking in surprise behind his glasses. When we were sixteen we snogged in Clissold Park. For four hours, even though up until then I'd only ever thought of him as the brother I could push around. It was a really mild night in early spring. The next day neither of us said a word about it. But it's nice to think it's there. I often think we should have one of those Julia Roberts 'if we get to thirty without meeting anyone . . .' pacts. Just to formalise things.

'Why?' he said. 'I'm always on a bloody plane and you hate holidays.'

'Well,' I explained patiently, 'I hated asparagus too, until someone made me some in butter sauce and told me not to eat the bottom bits.'

'So you think you'll like holidays if you just avoid the bottom bits?'

'Exactly!'

'Well,' he said. 'What kind of holiday are you going to have?'

'A *good* one,' I said emphatically. 'With lots of nice people all having fun together.'

'Are your brothers coming?'

'Are you listening to me or what? I said nice people. People we like.'

'Is it going to be a sun, sea, sand, paperbacks kind of holiday? They're quite boring.'

'No, they're not! That's my dream!'

'Sounds boring.'

'OK, well, what if it were a sun, sea, sand and lots of interesting activities holiday?'

'Hmm. Cambodia's very interesting right now.'

'The place with all the skulls?'

'It's interesting. It's a country in transition.'

'I don't want a country in transition! I want a completely stable country with sun, sea, sand and cocktails.'

'Wouldn't you rather do something that helps indigenous peoples and increases your cultural understanding of our planet?'

'No, because that would be annoying and make me feel guilty and I spend my life being annoyed and feeling guilty. That's why I need a holiday.'

'So you're going to spend a lot of money on the holiday of a lifetime but endeavour to make it as banal as possible? Where are you going? Does it matter?'

'Not to you,' I said grumpily. 'You're not coming.'

'Oh, come on, Evie!' he said. 'I'm only teasing. Anyway, I know what this is about.'

'What do you mean?'

'This sudden push for a holiday.'

'What?'

'You're jealous.'

'Of what?'

Bailey just drummed his fingers on the table and waited for me to catch up. 'Well, all your brothers got married in the last two years ... you're just feeling left out, in need of adventure.'

I stuck my lip out.

'Well, it's not fair, is it? John Jr is a big fat bastard, Patrick thinks he's God's gift ...'

'Well, his marriage only lasted four months.'

'Yes, and that bronze bridesmaid's dress monstrosity will take twenty-four thousand years to decompose on a landfill . . . I can't believe he chatted up the lady vicar.'

'Mmm.'

'And Cassandro . . . I mean, he's younger than me.'

He'd married a girl from my year at school. They'd disappeared to the Caribbean on holiday and called us when the deed was done.

But I'd seen the photos – the pink, clear sky, the soft yellow sand and Jilly and Cassandro looking so absolutely blissed out and beautiful and tanned. Jilly had a simple white cotton shift on and a huge flower tucked behind her sun-bleached hair, and she looked radiant. Cassandro had pale trousers rolled up over bare feet which made him look not quite as much a dick as it might have done. They looked like they were part of a perfect, romantic world, miles away from the grey streets and the everyday and the commute and the dirt I had to put up with. Why couldn't I get a bit of that?

I was jealous. I was jealous of their obvious, sun-kissed happiness. They looked part of a scene straight out of a movie, and I wanted a bit of it.

'Is that the rain again?' said Bailey, sighing heavily and staring out of the window.

'What happened to this drought we're supposed to be having?' I asked moodily.

'Well, no, it still rains, but it all runs off people's decking because nobody can be bothered to cut grass any more, so it doesn't soak into the soil and therefore people use more water to . . .'

'Yawn, yawn, yawn,' I said. 'Glad you're not coming on my luxury holiday. I'd say it was girls only, but that wouldn't necessarily rule you out.'

'Doesn't matter,' he said infuriatingly. 'I'm off on a big luxury secret junket anyway, and it's all paid for, and it's somewhere gorgeous. So there.'

I walked into work the next day downhearted but determined not to be put off by a few negative reactions and, well, the fact that my credit card statement had just arrived.

I'd left it on the mat, jumping over it quietly as if it were a poisonous snake I was praying hadn't noticed me. It's my fault, of course: in a moment of impassioned clarity I decided to transfer my balance onto one of those zero interest credit cards, the way you're meant to. Then, of course, I didn't either pay it back or transfer it onto *another* credit card, which meant 3000 per cent interest or something kicked in and I realised I'm the sucker who's funding everyone else's free credit cards. Which I wouldn't be, I suppose, if I didn't leap over my credit card statement as if it were a poisonous snake.

Anyway, I'm not exactly sure what's in there, but I know it's not pretty. So the absolute last thing I should be doing at the moment is planning luxury holidays. Or planning anything, in fact, apart from, obviously, getting a night job and moving into a shed until I've paid the damn credit card off, which I suspect, unless I win the lotto/marry a millionaire (not likely until I, at the very least, get my roots touched up) or invent something great (like, for example, the way to tell the difference between black and navy tights when it's dark and cold in your bedroom first thing in the morning and you've still got sleep in your eyes), is a very, very long way off.

So, I thought, heading into the office. Just to recap. I want to go on a fabulous holiday with my friends, except nobody wants to go with me and I don't have any money.

'Good morning,' said Dr Bennet. He's very handsome and smooth and he makes all the ladies fizzy. Doesn't do much for me; I've seen his toupee flap in a high wind and met his terrifying wife, but he smells nice.

'Dr Bennet, where would you go on holiday if you wanted to go somewhere nice?' I said.

He tried to wrinkle his brow thoughtfully, even though he can't: it's shot full of dead cow stuff and doesn't move.

'A nice holiday?'

'A fabulous holiday.'

'Aha. Well, you don't have a private jet, do you?'

'I do actually,' I said. 'I just park it in the mews.'

'Well, you should fly with British Airways first or Virgin upper class. Obviously you would think first would be better, but, you know, I don't always like the stewardesses, and the food is a little frilly for my taste. And, in fact, now you mention it, somewhere I visited for a wedding, Necker. You know, Richard Branson's island? He has a private island in the Caribbean; nobody there except people to look after you. Oh, it's beautiful. It's in the Balinese style, and it's so quiet, and the food, oh my God, I can't even begin to tell you about the food . . .'

His large brown eyes looked a bit melty as he stared out of the window into the grey and red-brick surroundings of Harley Street.

'Of course, it's expensive, you know? It's forty-five thousand dollars a day.'

'OK.' I said, sitting down at my desk. I did some quick addition in my head. 'Uhm. Can I have a raise of three hundred and fifteen dollars?'

Dr Bennet smiled. 'Well, OK. But you did ask me for fabulous. That is fabulous. Maybe I should be a plastic surgeon in America. It annoys me that I can't afford Necker myself.'

'I'm really, really sorry too,' I said as sincerely as I could manage. He can't be that far off, anyway, the amount of loaded old bruisers that march through the doors. And I'm not calling them that to be mean. Well, I am, but trust me, they are *really, really* mean to me first.

'Yes,' he said, picking up his case list for the day. 'Well, anyway, if you have not got much money, Venice is always nice.'

'Oh, yes?' I said, but without enthusiasm. I did want to go

to Venice, madly, but I had a secret life plan for Venice which involved, ideally, a flashing-eyed lover who would call me *cara* and we would run over picturesque bridges together and fall madly in love and feed each other spaghetti, like in *Lady and the Tramp*. So Venice was out. For now.

'Spain?' he said.

'Oh, no.' I shuddered, remembering my teenage Spanish experience.

His mouth twitched. 'Really? You have seen all of Spain? Much of it is very beautiful, don't you think? Have you been to Bilbao?'

'I don't like Spain,' I said firmly.

'Oh, well. There is only one place. The South of France, huh? Beautiful, warm sunshine, expensive Orangina . . . you would like it.'

The bell pinged, and one of our regulars, Zephyr, an ageing model (she calls herself a supermodel in the press, but I don't think there's anything terribly super about getting your tits out for *Nuts* magazine twice a week), came in for a top-up of fillers. It's not Dr Bennet's fault, he only does what she demands, but she's getting very weird-looking. Her top lip is now so pronounced she has to drink through a straw, and the very top touches her nostril, which can be extremely off-putting while she's talking to you.

'Hello, my dear!' Dr Bennet launched himself at her, charm personified. 'I'm terribly sorry, we don't treat under-eighteens here.'

Zephyr attempted what might have been a smile, but, hampered by the thick layer of plastic that now made up her face, came out more like a twitch.

'Hello, Yuri,' she hissed in a bad transatlantic lisp. Really, knowing your plastic surgeon by his first name. Is that sad or what? 'I need you to get to work.'

'Indeed, my dear. Although I am weak in the presence of beauty,' said Dr Bennet. I rolled my eyes. 'My dear, why don't you come through for a cup of herbal tea?'

'Got any champagne?' said Zephyr. It was ten past nine in the morning.

'But of course. Evie,' said Dr Bennet, 'see to our guest, will you?'

Zephyr didn't even bother glancing at me as I led her into Dr Bennet's office and made her comfortable with a copy of French *Vogue* on an armchair that cost more than my annual salary. I didn't think much of her shiny tight skin, but I couldn't help myself admiringly glancing at her long giraffe legs, carelessly clad in skinny white designer trousers. What must it be like to be able to wear tight white trousers? If you had legs like that did you think about them, or did you not even notice the elegant way they folded up under you without spilling out at the sides? The first and last time I tried on a pair of 'skinny' jeans, my legs looked like parsnips.

'There you go,' I said cheerily. A sniff came from Zephyr's suspiciously hollowed-out nostrils.

'Tell me,' she said as I reached the doorknob, 'what's Dr Bennet's wife like?'

I considered telling her she was ninety and had no teeth, just to see if she would try to seduce him, but I'm not a horrible person. Well, I have horrible thoughts, but I don't *think* that's the same thing, is it?

'She's absolutely bloody terrifying,' I said kindly.

Zephyr nodded her head a fraction – gratefully, I think – and went back to her magazine, as Dr Bennet entered the room.

'Now, my beauty. How can I improve on perfection today?'

Zephyr sighed. 'Oh, God, I have to fly to Barbados *again*. Sort me out, they don't even run Concorde there any more.'

'It's a scandal,' said Dr Bennet seriously. And I think he meant it.

I knew I hadn't got long to check holidays online, because Fanny Eleanor Moncrieff was coming in at 9.30, and she always brought her four tiny yappy dogs. Naturally dogs aren't allowed in a health centre, even one as lax as ours, so guess who has to take them out and round the block regardless of the weather? I wouldn't mind, I like dogs, but these aren't dogs, they're rats wearing coats, and they hate me, and each other, and spend their time getting their Chanel dog leads wrapped up with one another. Fanny Eleanor Moncrieff is ninety but, thanks to the wonders of Dr Bennet, looks eighty-five.

The door pinged as Dr Maitland marched in, head down as usual. He's not one for good mornings. In fact, I've worked here for three years and Dr Maitland's lack of interest in the niceties borders on the completely weird. He's not interested in charm, but he's unbelievably good at what he does. I can tell the difference between his work and Dr Bennet's in a minute – not that Dr Bennet is bad, but he gives a definite plastic surgery 'look'. Which, weirdly, some women actually prefer, in the same way platinum blondes don't really expect you to think their hair is that colour.

Anyway, if I needed anything done (ha ha, ha ha! More like, if I decided to start to tackle, over a period of some years, the pug-nosed freckle factory that is my face), it would be to Dr Maitland I'd go. Which is why he annoys me so much. It's OK for Dr Bennet, he's got family to support (as well as a sports car habit). But I don't understand why Dr Maitland is wasting his time, and his talent, injecting goo into stupid women who park their SUVs in the middle of the street then shout at me when they get a parking ticket. Why isn't he at Great Ormond Street repairing burns victims, or working in a plastics unit for people who get their faces eaten by dogs or something? Even helping kids who get teased at school for their huge ears would be more worthwhile than this. Which is just my opinion, obviously. And I realise the money is good – for all I know he's supporting ten thousand orphans through university. I just can't help feeling it's a bit of a waste of a very good doctor.

Anyway, he walked through the outer office, grunting as usual, and taking off his hat. He isn't old – not older than forty anyway – but he dresses like he's about a hundred. He always wears a hat and a bow tie. I asked Dr Bennet about the bow tie and he said it's so your tie doesn't drop into the mucky stuff when you're operating, which makes sense I suppose. Despite Dr Maitland's complete lack of personal charm, he's always busy because he's so good. In fact, he gets more celebrity clients than Dr Bennet, because you can hardly notice his work and because he's extremely discreet, or, possibly, lost his tongue in a climbing accident (I imagined once in a dull moment).

'Morning, Dr Maitland!' I said in a friendly way. Technically, you were meant to call him and Dr Bennet 'Mister' as they were so eminent, but I always called them doctor (secretly, I think they preferred it. What's the point of swotting for all those years if you can't impress total strangers on the street). I know to make him a cup of very strong coffee very quickly. That's one thing we've all caught off Dr Bennet – I can only drink coffee now if it comes in a tiny cup with the spoon standing straight up out of it.

'Hello,' said Dr Maitland, rustling his *Telegraph*, grabbing his coffee and rustling past as quickly as possible. He makes the ladies fizzy too, actually – God, what is it about women and doctors? They've seen your guts, for goodness' sake. Do you really want to sleep with a man who spent his formative training years sticking his fingers up old ladies' bottoms?

'Ocean Consortium rang again,' I said, reading off from his messages list.

'Oh, bloody hell,' he muttered, almost to himself. 'This thing just doesn't quit . . .'

I had no idea who Ocean Consortium were, except that they kept phoning, that it was secret, and that Dr Bennet was always delighted to hear from them, and Dr Maitland was always pissed off. Sometimes I heard them arguing about it in the consulting suites.

'Who are these people?' I said. 'They're incredibly persistent.'

'Don't ask,' said Dr Maitland, disappearing into his office. 'Nothing good.'

That sounded interesting. I was just about to look them up on the Internet when I realised Fanny Eleanor Moncrieff, with dog entourage, was already standing right in front of me, and I hadn't even helped her up the steps.

God, it was freezing out there walking those bloody rats. I stomped around the block, calling in on Lydia to see if she wanted to join me. She laughed, pointing out that she was sitting in a nice, cosy, centrally heated office. Her place is much posher than mine; she works for three brothers from Tripoli who specialise in lunchtime lipo. But she has less to do – they have a practice manager for the docs; she just smiles and answers the phones. She's always pretending to be sympathetic about my horrible workload though. Plus, she added, she was getting her sneer ready for when the new girl band turned up in five minutes' time.

'Do they get a discount for doing all five at once?'

'Yeah, course. That producer sends all of them here. The only thing is, they don't get to choose what they get done, he does.'

'Yuk.'

'Oh, they're so desperate. You could say, "OK, we're just going to graft an extra ear on, here, over your tits," and they'd say, "Awesome! That's hot!"'

'You're very harsh.'

'I'm just a bit stressed out.'

'You need a holiday.'

She narrowed her eyes at me. 'I NEED you to close the door and stop letting the heat out. What are those things you're walking anyway? They look like mops.'

'Psychotic mops.'

'OK. That's enough. Shoo. Shoo!'

Back at the office Fanny Eleanor Moncrieff was being ushered out by our nurse, and I took over pronto to make sure her driver was outside to pick her up.

'Thank you, my dear,' she croaked through the white bandages. She peered at me suddenly, her eyes sharp, even though she must have been well under the cosh of the painkillers Dr Bennet doled out with a liberal paw.

'You know, you really are very helpful. Are you looking

forward to Cannes . . . ?' Her voice trailed off as her long-suffering driver opened the back door for the dogs, firstly, then helped her in.

'Am I looking forward to what?' I said. You never know, sometimes people get a bit woozy and think they have to tip me. Dr Bennet's warned me very seriously about it, but I don't see the harm.

'I love the place, you know,' she said, going a bit misty eyed. 'Lost two husbands' fortunes on the Riviera. Great days. Life on the ocean blue . . .'

And before she had the chance to go any further, the big black doors of the Mercedes had closed behind her, and the huge vehicle simply slipped away.

Chapter Two

'That's strange,' I said, pulling my cardigan tightly around me as I bounced back into the welcome warmth of the office. Dr Bennet was ticking off the charts.

'What?' he said. 'You weren't soliciting for cash again, were you?'

'I do not "solicit for cash",' I said. 'One time that Arab princess offered me a small gratuity just for mentioning you couldn't even tell she'd had surgery.'

'While she was wearing her veil.'

I tried to look contrite. 'Well. That wasn't it. Miss Moncrieff mentioned something.'

'Did she indeed?' Dr Bennet raised one of his perfectly plucked eyebrows.

'About Cannes.' I pouted. 'Are you going on yet another jolly and not taking me?' It wouldn't be the first time.

Dr Maitland entered the office, silently as ever.

'The FDA turned it down again,' he announced gruffly. 'Now there's a surprise. A sensible decision.'

'Wilf, come here a second,' said Dr Bennet. 'I was just thinking about discussing Cannes with Evie here.'

Dr Maitland barely raised an eyebrow.

'Well, she'll have to know sometime.'

'What do you think? We could divert the phones, have a bit of a human face. And she was just telling me how much she needs a holiday.'

'I was.' I nodded emphatically. I didn't know what they were talking about, but it sounded promising.

'What would you think about her joining us in Cannes? We could do with the help on the paperwork.'

'That's hardly a holiday,' said Dr Maitland, running his hand through his thick hair. 'There's masses to do.'

'Well,' said Dr Bennet. 'It could be time we got some extra help involved, don't you think? For "Operation Sunshine"?'

Dr Maitland squinted a bit and lowered his voice. 'Whatever you think. Won't everyone else be taking those daft model dolly birds though?' He looked at me apologetically. 'I wouldn't want you to feel out of place.'

I was slightly insulted that he didn't think I'd be mistaken for a six-foot dolly bird, despite evidence to the contrary.

OK, so I don't look like Lydia and most of the other girls up and down Harley Street. But I'm not a gargoyle; if you saw me coming you wouldn't throw your hands up and shout, 'For the love of heaven, cover it up!' then light torches and come and burn me out of my house.

In fact, boyfriends have on occasion called me pretty. It's not my fault that at some point in the last five years freckles went from being cute to being considered a vile mark of global warming, or that curls are out and all hair must be straightened and ironed until it's as flat as a sheet of metal.

But this was just insulting. I knew that the docs didn't really see faces as faces per se – just as problems to be looked at, imperfections to be fixed. They had a picture in their minds of a woman's face: long, high of cheekbone, pointed of chin, tiny of nose, peculiarly flat of forehead, and anything that deviated from this presented itself as a series of problems to be fixed. *But I was standing right here.*

Dr Bennet leaped in, anxious to pour oil on troubled waters, as usual.

'No, we don't need any slutty types,' he said. 'Just someone friendly-looking to help people if they're feeling nervous.'

Dr Maitland raised an eyebrow. 'I don't think anyone in Cannes is ever nervous.'

My heart, which had been beating too fast at the insult, suddenly skipped a beat. Cannes? South of France?

'Well, I think it's a good idea. You know this thing is about to go huge.'

'I suppose,' said Dr Maitland grudgingly. Gee, thanks boss.

Dr Bennet turned round to face me squarely.

'OK, Evie. Would you like to help us with Operation Sunshine and come with us to Cannes?'

Would I? My head filled immediately with visions of palm trees; red carpets; great big yachts; beautiful actresses dancing on the sand; sunshine and blue skies.

Dr Bennet smiled as he noticed my reverie.

'Now,' he said, 'it's not a holiday.'

'Of course not,' I said, shaking my head seriously. Dr Maitland rolled his eyes and went back to his office.

'It's this practice's latest project. We'll be working with and talking to some of the best doctors and richest financiers in the world.'

I nodded, but my brain was doing a little dance to 'holiday holiday holiday holiday'!

'I was going to use the admin company from the conference organisers, but Miss Moncrieff might just be right ... why shouldn't it be you? You could make sure everything runs smoothly ... book the flights, the hotels ... take minutes.'

Ooh. Business-class seats were de rigueur when the docs travelled ... I wonder, maybe we should book a private jet? And as for hotels, wasn't there a really famous one there?

Where George Clooney always stayed and you had to pay in cash even though it was a million pounds.

'I think separate accommodation for doctors and administrative staff,' said Dr Bennet hurriedly.

I nodded.

'Good. It's settled. We're quiet in July anyway. We'll just divert the phones. Now, come here.'

Dr Bennet handed me a thick file. On it was a picture of a beautiful woman in a striped bathing suit. TOP SECRET was stamped on the cover. Ooh! In big letters across the bottom it said: OPERATION SUNSHINE.

'Looks exciting,' I said. Then I opened it and saw it was full of boring-looking legal documents. Hmm, maybe later.

Anyway, just then the door pinged to admit Hank, an American actor who always comes by whenever he's in London, despite the fact that he thinks, correctly, getting stuff to make his face freeze is doing absolutely nothing for his emotional range (bloody doctor/patient confidentiality kills me; if my friends knew who I'd been having cosy little chit-chats with, and how gay he was, no way would they keep blowing me off for holidays). Dr Bennet slipped off to his consulting room, before I even had a chance to say thank you.

'Aha ha ha,' I messaged Lydia, who I could see was online. 'You know what you were saying about free luxury holidays? Well . . .'

Infuriatingly, the message came back almost immediately.

'Oh, that. Yes, my docs are going. I didn't want to mention it in case you weren't invited.'

I couldn't believe this. What kind of a work-based acquaintance was she, not filling me in on all the juicy trips? What else was I missing out on?

'So you're going then?' I messaged. 'Business class?'

This time it was my turn to receive the laughing smiley.

'I booked my ticket two months ago,' the message read. 'All the seats have probably gone by now. But the coach only takes thirty-six hours.'

Wow, Lydia really does kid around a lot.

'So, anyway, I won't be able to come to the all-night horror show at the NFT,' I casually dropped into the conversation, as Bailey and I sat with our noses in the trough at Wagamama. I didn't really like horror films, but Bailey liked someone to grab at creepy moments, and I didn't mind.

'I'm going to be in . . . oh, let me see, where was it again? Oh, yes, the South of France!'

Bailey looked up from his udon noodles. His glasses were steamed up.

'No way! Yuri's taking you?'

Yuri is Dr Bennet. Him and Bailey are thick as thieves; I've never really understood why.

'Don't sound so surprised,' I said. 'Can I have the last dumpling while you're staring at me with your mouth open?'

'You know I'm going to be there?' he said. 'It's my project.'

'Operation Sunshine?' I said, to make myself look in the know.

'Yes! What do you think?'

'Oh, fabulous.' I must read the brief. 'Amazing.'

I changed the subject as quickly as I could.

'So, everyone's going. It's going to be a proper jolly. Lydia's coming too. There you go, I asked for a holiday and look what's arrived. I think Noel Edmonds is right about that cosmic ordering.'

'Is Lydia the one who wants to meet me?'

'Oh, yes, I forgot.' I frowned. 'I think she wants to do it with you like they do on the Discovery Channel.'

'Charming.'

'I mean it. I think beneath her elegant exterior lies a sex-crazed maniac.'

Hang on, wasn't I meant to be putting him off her?

'You can see the tension in her ten-inch fingernails.'

This was a high-risk strategy to keep him away, all right. I wondered if it would work.

'This isn't a jolly, you know,' said Bailey. 'It's a big serious development.'

'Yes,' I said, slurping the last of my apple and ginger juice. 'Do you think polka dots are still in this year?'

'Who am I, your gay BF?' said Bailey crossly. 'Talk sensibly or I'm taking out *Practical Mechanic* and reading at the table again.'

*

34

I'd tried – and failed – not to eat too much as Mum and Dad had invited me round for tea – I'd agreed to go only if the beasts weren't invited too. I called in on them and told them about the trip. At least Mum sounded genuinely pleased, even if she thought that meant I might be getting a promotion of some kind. I don't know how to tell her there's not much in the way of promotion in the medical reception field unless, like Lydia's evil plans, you get lucky and marry the boss and/or a client.

'I'll look out your old French book,' she said. Oh, yes. Suddenly something that had been niggling at the back of my mind jumped to the forefront. Well, have you ever met anyone who *doesn't* put 'French' on their CV? No, you haven't, have you? So maybe, just maybe, under 'other languages' on my application form, I'd written 'French' quite proudly because, 1) how often was I going to have to use that in Harley Street and, 2) if required I could order a cup of coffee with pretty much no problem at all. (Although was it *un* or *une* *café*? I could never quite remember.)

'So, the boys are coming round . . .'

'They're not, are they?' I said, looking around our beige sitting room like a caged animal. Mum and Dad got so used to all their nice things being destroyed or broken that they'd never got out of the habit of buying the absolutely cheapest of everything, and the room looks like it's been entirely furnished from the back of the Sunday supplements.

'Evie Esme, don't be silly. You've got to stop thinking like you're nine again.'

'That's like saying to a victim of torture that they can't go through life looking over their shoulder,' I grumbled, picking up a fruit scone and removing all the raisins from it in one practised move. 'I've got post-traumatic stress disorder.'

Sure enough, as I was doing this my mum quickly set eight places at the table. Why I hadn't noticed the size of the stew pot she was stirring I don't know. And then the doorbell rang.

'I can't believe this,' I said. 'You lured me here under false pretences.'

'We've got to welcome Cassandro's new wife,' said Mum. 'It was the only way I knew you'd turn up.'

'By telling lies to your only daughter?'

'Hello, hello.' John Jr's loud tones rang through the house. His horrible bullying ringleader ways when we were children have made him a highly successful manager of a car show-room, and he's got the trophy wife, Kelly, to prove it. Kelly's thirty-one and weighs about six stone, most of that gold jew-ellery and lip gloss.

'Just parked the new Lexus outside. Hope it won't get stolen, huh huh. Evie. How's it going? What are you driving these days.'

John Jr knows fine well I can't afford a car in London, but he always asks people what they're driving the second he meets them. It's like some knee-jerk thing he can't help, if I'm being charitable. If anyone (a man, usually) is foolish enough to venture an answer he will suck in his teeth and go,

'Oh. Happy with it?' Then, if they say yes, he'll raise his eyebrows, as if he can't believe they're such an idiot for driving that car, but he wouldn't like to mention it in polite company. Usually he'll work his way round to bragging about Lexuses (Lexi?) for hours. I don't know anything about cars but I do know that if I ever buy one it will never ever, ever be a Lexus, not even if it was free and delivered by George Clooney carrying a year's supply of jam.

'Hello,' said Kelly. Despite being incredibly pretty (if you like the bleached-blonde aerobicised look, and in my experience blokes really, really do, even if sometimes the girls are a *teensy* bit difficult to tell apart), she was incredibly insecure about her looks. She was always on at me to find out the latest procedures and peels, then went home and got her unqualified beautician to do them for her. I really wished she wouldn't, but she won't be told. 'What's new?'

I thought for a bit.

'Well, there's Radoflux 9000. Gives you baby skin apparently. But it keeps getting turned down by the FDA in America, and the BMA won't look at it. That means you can't use it. It's driving Dr Bennet demented. *Don't* try and buy some off a dodgy website.'

'Would I?'

'Remember that chemical peel?'

'It smelled like Cillit Bang.'

'Remember what we said? If it looks like Cillit Bang, and smells like Cillit Bang . . .'

'Don't use in the under-eye area.'

'Don't use in the under-eye area, that's right.'

She was all right Kelly. I don't know why she was so insecure; John Jr was unbelievably lucky to have pulled her in the first place. It would never strike twice.

'Ooh, what's for dinner, Anne? Smells gorgeous.' Kelly always says this, but never eats anything, and we all pretend not to notice.

'Stew,' said Mum. 'How are you doing, JJ?'

John Jr sat down on the best armchair and spread out his big beefy legs, like a visiting king.

'Yeah, great, Mum. We're thinking of building a swimming pool onto our conservatoire extension, ain't we, Kell?'

Kelly looked pleased. I wasn't surprised: wow, a swimming pool.

'Well, we thought what's the point, right? What's the point of even *having* a conservatoire if it ain't got a pool? Doncha think?'

As soon as John Jr made some money they moved out to Essex, and they live on a gated executive estate, or, as I like to think of them, wanker zoos. My mum blinked. Her and Dad have struggled all their lives – he's only a cabinet-maker, a good trade nobody wants any more, and she spent her life bringing us up, but they wouldn't dream of asking John Jr for a helping hand now and again, and he wouldn't dream of offering. Or me, of course, not that I give a shit. I just wish he wouldn't keep pointing out exactly how much money he makes, and asking me about my salary all the time.

The door crashed open and Patrick burst in, without a girl in tow for once. He's extremely good-looking, or so my female friends have always insisted. At least, he doesn't have a face like a burst pudding, like John Jr. He has a bad-boy swagger that's made the girls go all wobbly since I was twelve – he's also got a motorbike, wears leathers and sneers. It's amazing that still works these days, but it does. Anyway, by night he drinks cider and plays the bad boy, by day he goes to work in a surveyor's office with his hair combed down.

'All right,' he said sulkily, throwing himself down.

'Hiya, Patrick,' Kelly said. Patrick ignored her like he does all women, which usually makes them worse. I rolled my eyes and pointedly asked Mum if she'd like any help in the kitchen.

'Where's Mr Ball and Chain then?' said Patrick. 'I can't believe he got caught by a bird like that. Is she up the duff?'

'Patrick,' said Mum. 'It was very romantic, that's all. They just got carried away on a beach.'

'Yeah,' said Patrick. 'And then they had to get married.' He and John Jr sniggered. 'Got any beer, Mum?'

'Are you on that motorbike?' asked my mother. 'Because if so, no.'

Patrick tutted as my father came in and patted me

comfortably on the head. He's at least a head shorter than the boys and always looks slightly puzzled as to how on earth he could have produced them.

'All right, boys?' he murmured.

'Yeah,' said Patrick. 'Mum was just getting me a beer.'

'Dad, you going to get that wreck through its MOT?' said John Jr. 'You really want to think about upgrading, you know.'

My father muttered something and took his seat at the head of the table, looking around for his stew. My mother looked at the brown clock on the kitchen wall – it has birds that are meant to chirp every hour but they haven't chimed since 1978, when John Jr had a spectacularly high-reaching tantrum. In this case, I'm glad.

'I wonder where they are,' she said nervously. It can't be helped; Cassandro, by virtue of his being as slippery as a snake and not actually evil, is her favourite, and I could tell how nervous she was about meeting his new bride, even though she'd known Jilly since her knees were permanently skinned.

'Probably still at it,' sniggered Patrick.

'Stop that!' said Mum. 'I won't have that kind of chat at the dinner table.'

'Well, I'm not sitting down at the table yet, am I?' said Patrick.

'It's romantic though, innit?' said Kelly. 'A beach wedding. Just you and the one you love. Simple and gorgeous.'

Which is a bit rich, because they had three hundred

people to a sit-down in the world's most floral hotel and Kelly wore a dress so wide people had to brace their feet and heave to get her into the toilet.

'And cheap,' said John Jr. 'Nice one.' He heaved his fat bottom onto one of the creaking kitchen chairs. Because Kelly isn't interested in food, she doesn't much care about John Jr's diet, and I think everything that enters his body has to come wrapped in pastry. I sometimes think Kelly wants him fat and lethargic so that he won't have the energy to chase other women; and possibly so he'll have a heart attack.

My mother sighed and started dishing out stew and dumplings. Patrick tried Cassandro's mobile, but didn't get an answer. He then started texting someone at the table, until Dad gave him a very hard look.

'So,' said Mum. 'Anyone else got any news then?'

'Best February sales in three years,' said John Jr through a thick mouthful of stew. 'I'll be getting some kind of prize.'

'Oh, JJ, that's wonderful,' said my mum, genuinely pleased.

'Yeah, well,' said John Jr. 'Takes bloody thirteen-hour days, but it's worth it.'

'I've got news too,' I said. Everyone turned to me with concerned-looking expressions on their faces. Oh, for goodness' sake. Why do they assume my news is automatically going to be terrible, like I've been arrested or something?

'I'm being sent abroad on a business trip,' I said. That sounded pretty good, actually.

'Where they sending you then?' said John Jr. 'Timbuktu? Is it a one-way ticket?'

'No. The Côte d'Azure actually. That's in France.'

'"That's in France",' mimicked Patrick. 'Why are they sending *you* to France?'

'To administer to a major conference, *actually*.'

'Why, have doctors medically discovered a cure for farting, Evie?'

'No, it's about how to make surveyors more interesting. No cure's been discovered yet, sadly.'

Patrick went back to stuffing his face. I was just about to elaborate on my glamorous trip, now I'd got a word in edge-ways, when the doorbell rang.

'Here they are!' sang my mother, her face lighting up. And in swanned Cassandro and Jilly. Even on this dull rainy evening, they seemed to emit a glow – not just their light tans; their happiness and love seemed to light up the whole house. As they chatted excitedly about dolphin-spotting, barbecues on the beach and yacht parties, I felt my mood get lower and lower. Everything I wanted – excitement, change, adventure, sunshine. It was right here at the table, and none of it was mine. I got quieter and quieter and, as soon as I politely could, left to catch the tube, after swallowing a Battenberg cake that tasted like ashes in my mouth.

'Everything booked?' said Dr Bennet, bowling into the office the next morning. I'd got in early too. Three business-class

42

seats (not for me, sadly – Dr Bennet's scary wife was accompanying him) was going to cost over two thousand pounds. For a two-hour flight and a sandwich! Despite my gloom, it felt fun to spend that much money. Yes, those were the circles I was in now. Two thousand pounds? No problem! Now, hotels. Christ, there were thousands. I didn't trust myself not to stick them in some underground dungeon by mistake, and decided to ask my supportive friend and colleague for advice.

'Oh, for goodness' sake. Just as well I didn't want to go on holiday with you. We'd have ended up at the Birmingham Novotel, but paying five times the rack rate.'

'What's rack rate?' I said to be annoying. Lydia was bringing me back down to earth.

'If I tell you, do you promise not to follow me around like a little puppy dog when we get to Cannes?'

'Well, I thought I could be your wingman.' I had, actually. I didn't mind pulling the good-looking guy's best friend; they're normally more fun anyway. Just call me Ms Brightside.

'Is that what you thought?'

'Yeah, you know, pinpoint the hot young docs . . . check out wedding rings . . .'

Lydia sighed and named two hotels.

'One for them, posh, lots of other docs there. One for you, not quite so posh, lots of PAs there so I won't be the only person you turn to when you need your shoelaces tied.'

Wow, Lydia was lucky my brothers had already softened

me up for lots of insults. Anyway, I'd already started dreaming about suntan lotion . . . large oversized sunglasses (except they didn't make me look all weeny and young and fragile, like an Olsen sister, they made me look legally blind), acres of white sand and young Frenchmen with pert bottoms and a widespread knowledge of history, art, literature and the erotic arts.

Chapter Three

The Saturday before we left I went to the drawer under my bed where I keep clothes I've bought by mistake, or for a special occasion, or that don't fit quite as well as I thought they might when I bought them. It's a big drawer. Normally I stay away from it as it just serves to remind me of stuff I've spent money on but haven't got around to wearing. Yet.

I pulled everything out one by one. OK, the ethnicy kaftan might be a bit last season (and made me look like one big square box from my shoulders to my thighs, where it cut off at a ridiculously high point) but surely it would be just the thing for pulling on after, let's say, a swim to the pool bar?

So yes, the kaftan was in. Now, swimwear. In my knickers drawer I had my swimming costume, which I'd had since school, and although it gave me a bit of hungry bum these days, it was still wearable. It was also, however, a plain black Speedo and did make me look like I was about to cover myself with goose fat and have a shot at the Channel, whilst wearing a nude-coloured skullcap.

This was no good. I needed at least one fancy bikini – Coleen McLoughlin always looks like she takes about fifteen on holiday. Mind you, her job is going on holiday. Why didn't I fall in love with a footballer?

I added to the pile an ill-conceived bright orange skirt, bought during that peasant frills fiasco we all went through a couple of years ago – maybe in Cannes they'd think it was retro chic. Anyway, from what I remembered from our school exchange, all French people wore skin-tight white denim and those women that didn't all wore black suits whilst smoking furiously and talking about pudding, and I wasn't going to be able to manage any of that.

Buying bikinis is such a hideous affair but it was either that or spend my weekend reading the briefing notes, and I didn't think I could take it. Also, I had forgotten it was half term and thus found myself in a department store with about a million unbelievably skinny teenagers moaning to their mothers. I wish my mum had taken *me* shopping for clothes when I was a teenager. But no, she was taking the boys to casualty while I was working in a handbag shop. Why didn't these moony whingers work? Then I wouldn't have to wait two hours to get into a changing room and feel sweaty and hot before I even tried anything on, then wondering how sweaty other people had been whilst trying on bikinis. Yikes. I was *not* in the holiday mood.

'Oh, for goodness' sake,' I exclaimed to myself, trying to turn around in the minuscule cubicle. I felt like a dog chasing its tail.

That reminded me, it was one of the few conversations Dr Maitland and I had had. Geneva Pitt, a horrid society stick woman who calls everyone 'girls' and pretends she's some kind of a dizzy lassie but is actually the most ruthless witch ever, had come in howling. Her face is so stretched and shiny it looks like she's made of pink chewing gum.

'Wilf!' she'd hollered, ignoring my greeting. For goodness' sake. He's your doctor. Just call him 'Doctor'. What, you think we're impressed that we bill your poor husband for tens of thousands of pounds a year?

'I've got cellulite!' she screamed. 'My life is over!'

Seriously, she was in tears. Must have nicked them off a spare crocodile she'd passed on Wimpole Street. Then, right in the middle of the waiting room (there was no one else there except me, and I'm invisible), she pulled down her incredibly tight leather trousers to reveal, just under her absurdly tight bum, one tiny, tiny bump which was only visible when she scrunched up her arse. Honestly, sometimes I realise how men can be completely confounded by women.

'There, there,' he'd said gruffly. 'Follow me, err. Mrs . . .'

He'd forgotten her name! What a boor. I quickly jotted it down in big letters on a piece of paper and held it up behind her back.

'. . . Pitt,' he finished. 'Come right in.'

Afterwards, he came up to me whilst picking up his hat.

'Thank you,' he said quietly, in his dignified way. He was right to thank me; the whole business relies on making women feel pampered and special, and it's hard to feel special when someone is calling you Thingy.

'That's OK,' I said. Then I added, 'Can I ask? Cellulite . . . What is it? I mean, really. Will it go away if you stop drinking coffee?'

'Oh, God,' he said. 'Professional ethics forbid me from talking about it.'

'OK,' I said, trying not to sound sniffy. Professional ethics seemed to stop him from talking about a lot of things, up to and including a 'How are you, Evie?' once in a while.

'Well,' he said. Then he looked around again. 'Can you keep a secret?'

I nodded heartily, regardless of the fact that this wasn't perhaps 100 per cent true.

'It doesn't exist,' he whispered.

I almost jumped. 'What do you mean it doesn't exist?' I said. 'I've got bloody masses of the stuff.'

He shrugged. 'Well, it's simply an aesthetic term. What you've got is fat deposits on your bottom and hips.'

'Thanks very much.'

'That's where fat deposits in females. And that's what it looks like. End of story.'

'But . . . aren't we supposed to be able to get rid of it with brushes and stuff.'

'You can get rid of it by stripping all the fat out of your body. Paula Radcliffe doesn't have any. Nor does Ms, ahem, Pitt, once you suck it out. Otherwise, well, that's it.'

'But all those creams, and potions . . .'

Dr Maitland shook his head. 'You think a cream can penetrate your skin and specifically dissolve fat?'

'I would like to think that.'

He almost patted me on the head.

'Bless you,' he said. 'I don't think you'd like liquid-permeable skin. Certainly not after the first time you took a bath. And, I promise, there are many, many more important things in the world to worry about than cellulite, a made-up money-spinner for the beauty industry.'

Then why, I thought, for the nine thousandth time, as he left to hop into his little MG, quietly closing the door behind him, don't you worry about any of them?

Reassuring though this had been at the time, well, it wasn't bloody helping me *now*, was it? I wrestled myself into another pair of 'boy cut' bikini bottoms. I'd asked all the men I knew (apart from the beasts) what they thought about cellulite and none of them knew what the hell I was talking about, except for Bailey and he said it didn't bother him, though what would he know about it seeing as he only dates supermodels? Or, at least, better-looking girls than I'd think he'd get without the platinum corporate Amex and the access to cheap boob jobs.

Then I turned around and saw 'it'. It was just hanging there, on the shelf full of stuff to be taken back into the store. Obviously one of the Keira Knightley-esque teens had tried it on and nearly drowned in it . . . but for me . . .

It was a dark red dress: not an in-your-face tomato juice colour, but a deep, shimmering silk that slipped on like a second skin. I wondered for a moment if it might look a bit like a nightie but, when I tried it on, it didn't. It looked like someone had sat down and designed a beautiful red summer dress, just for me.

Shopping moments like this almost never happen. When they do, your only choice is to grab them and run with it. Terrified in case the person who'd orginally tried it on realised they'd made a terrible mistake and came running back, I whipped it off, grabbed the first bikini that came to hand and charged to the checkout.

It's not that I didn't have anything to do that Saturday night *at all*. I would have had loads of offers, probably. It's just I happen to really, really like my mum's cooking, especially when she's doing lamb, that's all. My mother's roast lamb is so good it makes it worth sitting next to a bunch of disgusting animals in a zoo. Which is just as well.

I'd spent the afternoon curled up in my old bedroom with the pictures of ponies still on the wall, immersing myself in a guidebook on the Côte d'Azure and occasionally jumping up to try on my new dress again. I didn't want to show Mum; she had conniptions about anything that cost over £15.99, and this had cost quite a lot over £15.99.

Cannes looked incredibly thrilling. Miles of palm trees and golden beach, huge yachts tied up in the harbour at sunset; pictures of Chanel and Louis Vuitton shops. It wasn't actually that crucial for me to know the whereabouts of the Louis Vuitton shop. I suspected I may have bought the wrong guidebook – *The Côte d'Azure Guide For the Skint and Non-Beautiful* wasn't in stock, but *The Glamour Guide to Cannes* was.

Don't miss, it enthused, *the many glamorous parties and premieres of the film festival. Some prefer the Splendid to the Eden-Roc, overrun as the latter is at this time with movie stars and wannabes.*

Movie stars and wannabes sounded all right to me. And I would be delighted not to miss the many glamorous parties, if someone would only tell me where and when they were; I had the dress for it.

Or of course just moor the yacht (but make sure you've got mooring sorted well in advance – tel: 06 55 43 32 10).

I had definitely bought the wrong guidebook. Although I was tempted to call the number. 'Hello, *bonjour*, yes, I just need to reserve my yacht parking space. For the film festival, yes. My name . . . uh, it's Jennifer Aniston. A-N-I . . .'

Dressing for dinner in Cannes is very dressy indeed – now is the

*time to wear your couture, and break out your family jewels. View the
setting sun from the terrace of the Hotel Belles Rives, which shimmers
nightly with crystal champagne glasses and diamonds.*

'Evie!' my mother yelled up the stairs. 'I need a hand
chopping cabbage.'

I sighed.

'OK!' I shouted down. 'I'll just back up the yacht,' I
added to myself.

Downstairs, sitting *right there* was John Jr, watching the
sport.

'Oh, it's all right,' I said. 'You've already got John Jr to
chop the cabbage.'

'Yeah, yeah,' said John Jr. 'Some of us are actually recovering from a hard week's work where you don't just sit behind
a desk reading magazines.'

'I would do it, Anne,' said Kelly. 'But, you know.
Fingernails.' She held up her hands apologetically. Her nails
must have been three centimetres long.

'You do that on purpose!' I said.

'It's just grooming!'

'It's chore avoidance!'

'Because she's a lady,' said John Jr proudly.

I wielded the knife grumpily, wondering if he'd fancy the
cabbage if I stuck some lipgloss on it.

'So, Anne,' Kelly was saying, examining her cuticles.
'Apparently in Cannes the champagne glasses and the diamonds shimmer in the setting sun.'

'That sounds lovely,' said my mum, who was sweating slightly, pulling huge trays from the oven. 'You're going to have such a lovely time.'

I turned round, shocked.

'What are you talking about?'

'In Cannes, you know?'

'Yes, I do know. Are you going there?'

'Why?' said Kelly in a teasing voice. She knew how I felt about John Jr. 'Scared we'll show you up?'

'Other way round more likely,' said John Jr.

Thing is, I do like Kelly – it was her choice to marry an unmitigated baboon, but she has to share an en suite with him, so it's her that's suffering. But I really, really didn't want them barging in on my holiday. This was my trip; my chance to be whoever I wanted to be. I didn't need someone creeping up behind me making farting noises while I was talking to Dr Maitland or, well, anyone really.

'I thought you said the French had arseholes for mouths, hated fighting wars and ate their own shit,' I accused John Jr, whose sentiments on the peoples of the world were often expressed.

'What my darling wants she gets,' he said, not taking his eyes off the television.

'Apparently it's really, really classy and lovely,' said Kelly. 'Chanel shops everywhere and that.'

'Yeah,' I said.

'Evie don't know what that is,' said John Jr.

'It's clothes,' said Kelly. 'And they do skis, like what Posh Spice has.'

'I *know* what Chanel is,' I said.

'Don't worry,' said John Jr. 'We're going high style, so I don't think we'll see much of you.'

Then he leaned over.

'But Kelly wants you to introduce us to all your doctor friends,' he said.

I looked at Kelly. 'No way. Really?'

She shrugged. 'Well, I was thinking of getting some more serious work done . . . I am nearly thirty-two.'

'Don't do it,' I advised immediately. 'I could tell you some stories that would curl your GHDs.' Actually, most of what we do is pretty safe, but even so, it's still a bit dumb that someone as pretty as Kelly would submit herself to the knife. And I can always tell.

'Not your guys, though,' said Kelly.

'No,' I conceded. 'My guys are very good. But you're gorgeous, Kell. What do you want to go messing with that for?'

Kelly leaned back, looking mollified. But she didn't take her eyes off the French brochure I'd noticed earlier in her lap.

'Any news from Cassandro?' I asked loudly, trying to change the subject. My mother's brow furrowed.

'Yes,' she said. 'He called to tell us they loved Antigua so much they're thinking of going back and opening a beach bar and living happily ever after.'

Oh, God, that sounded blissful. I could just imagine it – clear blue skies, soft blue seas, rum punch every day. Oh, God, I so needed to get away.

'Lazy bastard,' said John Jr. 'He should come back and get a job. In the rain,' he added.

'You never tell John Jr off for swearing,' I immediately pointed out to Mum.

'Cos I'm not a lonely spinster like you,' said John Jr.

I mouthed 'bastard' in the direction of his beefy shoulders but carefully, so Mum didn't see.

Heathrow early in the morning is a fearsome sight. The airport was so huge, mobbed with people and slightly imposing, what with the policemen carrying machine guns and everything. I looked at my scruffy green rucksack. It was inherited from the boys' turns at the Scouts, and smelled like it too. And it hardly had anything in it: a couple of suits and my orange skirt; my not-bad bikini, which wasn't too disastrous if you half closed your eyes and repeated very loudly 'cellulite doesn't exist' three times whilst tapping your heels together (it also struck me that the South of France might be somewhere you'd be expected to wear high heels with your bikini so I'd thrown in my party shoes too); one sun dress, slightly faded, bought the year I said I really was sick of never going on holiday and was going to go and tour India all by myself, then I'd crapped out at the last minute; and of course the new red dress. I'd caressed the material packing it. It felt so full of possibility. It was a pulling dress, if you were being vulgar. A romantic dress, if you weren't.

Lydia came striding towards me. She looked chic and striking in a black trouser suit and white shirt that you could tell was really well cut and expensive, rather than the white shirt I own, which make me look like a pregnant man painting a house. She was also wearing a positively gigantic pair of sunglasses.

'Did you know you've got two coffee cups stuck to the front of your eyes?' I asked by way of greeting.

'Nice jeans,' she replied. 'Are they those loss leader ones they do for five pounds in Tesco?'

'No.'

'Oh, how funny. I could have sworn the waist was elasticated.'

'OK, OK, truce,' I muttered. 'Shall we go and check in?'

She sniffed loudly as we made our way across the concourse. She was trailing a chic black bag with a completely indiscreet large gilt label on the top, just in case it got mistaken for the million other identical black bags out there.

I wouldn't have minded but, looking round the queue, there were certainly a lot of very slim-limbed women, and none of them was wearing jeans. They were wearing Gillian McKeith-style trouser suits in pale shades, or, occasionally, mini skirts. There was one girl in 501s, but as soon as a smart mother shouted, 'Magda! Toilet the children, please!' it became patently obvious she was the hired help.

'Well, this isn't right.'

I tuned in from my sulk to hear Lydia remonstrating with the check-in woman, who looked scared.

'I send a lot of business your way, and I have to say, it doesn't seem too much to ask.'

'Yes, but we have to keep those seats . . .'

'Yes, but I checked in online six weeks ago.'

The woman looked pink. Honestly, sometimes I don't know why Lydia's working on reception. She should be marshalling troops somewhere.

'I'll just go talk to . . .' the woman scuttled off. I forgot I was meant to be sulking.

'What's up?' I said. In reply Lydia looked at me like I wasn't there.

The woman came back from her secret office at the back. 'I'm going to be able to upgrade this ticket,' said the woman. Lydia bestowed a beatific smile.

'*Thank* you.'

'If you'd just follow me.'

Fantastic! Upgrade! Lydia was bloody marvellous! I'd never travelled swish class before. I looked at the rest of the queue with pity. So long, suckers! Enjoy the cheap seats! I picked up my bag to follow them. At that precise instant, they both turned to look at me and the expression on their faces was almost identical. It said, 'Not you, you moose.'

Crushed, I put my bag back down slowly.

'Well, nice to run into you, Evie,' said Lydia casually. 'See you later, yeah?'

I think it was at this point that it started to occur to me that Lydia maybe wasn't all that great a friend.

'Magda! Tell Jacintha to stop kicking,' came the voice behind me for the millionth time.

'Stop keecking, pleece, Jacintha,' said a low, tentative voice that I could already tell would have no effect on Jacintha, because Jacintha was right behind me and it was me she was kicking, and had been for an hour and forty-five minutes.

'NOOOOOOOO!'

When I'd seen the family group I'd wondered why on earth you'd take your nanny on holiday. Having become well acquainted with the feet of Jacintha, it was no longer such a mystery. Certainly didn't help me focus on the briefing notes, anyway. I couldn't read a thing.

Sighing I turned towards the window. We were descending – I'd had my breath taken away earlier, both by a Jacintha boot to the kidneys and the sight of the snow-topped Alps just below us, continuing on for miles. Now, though, I was looking at a long swathe of bright buildings lining the shore and glistening in the bright sunlight, framed by dark forbidding mountains rising up above.

As I watched, looking for the airport, we continued on past the beach and out into sea. This was odd, as we were definitely getting lower and lower. I could see the white wakes of the boats out on the open sea . . . now I could see their sails. Uh, I didn't want to cause panic, but was no one else aware that we were about to all crash into the water and drown?

I looked around for a stewardess but there was none to be found. Oh, no! They must all be up the front, huddling! Or maybe they'd all bailed out already. I found my fingers making a clawing shape as the wings tilted and nearly hit the water. Bugger! I was going to die before I had the chance to go to Cannes! I was going to be a terrible loss just as my life was beginning! I couldn't help it; even though my heart was pounding, I had a momentarily satisfying flash of my brothers all crying and being miserable and wishing they'd been nicer to me, and my mother would say, 'I knew we should have bought her that pony,' and they'd all be very sorry I was dead and would think about me all the time. I hoped I'd get to come back like that girl in *The Lovely Bones* and watch them all being sad and talking about how fantastic I was and how they wished they'd told me when they had the chance, and Bailey would throw himself onto my coffin and say I was the only girl he'd ever loved and now his life was practically over too.

I was just closing my eyes to prepare for impact – and hoping it was quick – when the plane wheels bumped down onto something solid. I realised, with a sense of mild disappointment, that we'd landed, and that the airport seemed to be in the middle of the sea.

My spirits perked up, however, when I heard the captain say, 'Welcome to Nice, Côte d'Azure, ladies and gentlemen... where the temperature is twenty-seven degrees Celsius.'

The terminal building looked, frankly, too clean for my manky old bag. It was last out too – maybe they'd temporarily mistaken it for a duster of some kind. God, Lydia better have waited for me. She would know how to get to Cannes, surely? Otherwise, if she'd left me on my own ... well, maybe I should have prepared slightly better for when I got here, but obviously I'd had a lot of very difficult bikini issues to work out and simply hadn't had the time.

Oh, thank God, there she was, standing with her gigantic sunglasses on, next to a short man. A man with sticky-up hair. A man who looked incredibly familiar, in fact.

'Oh, there you are,' she said. 'I thought you'd got completely lost. Anyway, I just wanted to tell you, I'm getting a lift in this lovely gentleman's helicopter, OK? So I suggest you get the train or a taxi, if you can afford it. *Adieu!*'

'Hello, Bailey,' I said. Lydia's eyebrows shot up.

'*You're* Bailey?' she said, as Bailey came up and gave me a hug. '*Bienvenue*,' he said. It didn't seem fair to be annoyed with him because a) he'd not yet thrown himself on my grave in the event of my imaginary death, and b) he'd not got to know Lydia yet.

'I certainly do,' I said. 'What's this about a helicopter?'

60

'They've sent a helicopter for me,' said Bailey, half apologetically, half obviously unbelievably delighted. 'I am the chief designer, I suppose.'

'Oh, how boring. Helicopters again,' I said. 'Why don't you ask for the space shuttle like all the fashionable people?'

'Shall I see if there's room for you, too?' he asked.

'They do have quite strict weight limits,' said Lydia. Then she turned round. 'We were sitting next to each other. In business.'

'Oh, did you go business?' I said, trying to sound airy. 'I thought they'd led you off to put you in the hold.'

'Well, this is going to be fun,' said Bailey. He turned to a smartly dressed man and spoke a few words to him in rapid French. Lydia made a big show of widening her eyes and nodding her head along to show she understood, though I bet she didn't.

'OK, no problem,' said Bailey to me. 'I promise not to throw your horrible kit bag into the sea either.'

'Yes, I must swap it for a handbag, like you have,' I said. In fact, it was a man bag, but I smiled to show him I was genuinely pleased to see him.

Ooh, and I was. What a thrill. I instantly realised that this was the way I was born to live. The speed from which I could get from a manky high street changing room to going *flip flip flip flip flip* (helicopter noise, as experienced first hand by me) over the deep blue Mediterranean sea must mean something. It must register a change in my life; a fresh start, a new beginning. As I sat back in the (not very comfortable) seat and stared into the sun, it certainly felt like it.

Chapter Four

Well, this wasn't exactly what I'd been dreaming of. A huge black car had been waiting at the helicopter pad (hurrah!) and, after whisking us through busy traffic, it had dropped Bailey off at some huge five-star joint on the front, where three little flunkies, actually wearing hats and white gloves, hopped down to take his luggage.

Then the car had dropped Lydia off at a nice smart white-washed place that looked more house than hotel, with bright green shutters, wisteria growing up the walls, overflowing window boxes, a lawn, a pool and a nice fat lady who'd greeted Lydia by name and with a kiss. 'Why didn't you recommend I book here?' I'd asked. 'Well, I can't give the name and address out to just anyone, can I?' said Lydia, as if this were reasonable.

Anyway, it was now forty minutes later and the driver was circling what looked like a housing estate in the back end of nowhere, looking grumpy and muttering to himself under his breath. *I hope I wasn't meant to tip this guy.* Well, even if I was, I only had twenty-euro notes, and not that many of those, and he certainly wasn't getting one.

The driver said something which sounded like 'vlah vlah GarRUMPH' and stopped the car, pointing towards a grimy-looking apartment block. I thanked him, considered offering him a pound coin but then scarpered before he had the chance to say anything to me I wouldn't understand. *Hmm, maybe my French wasn't just 'rusty'. Maybe it was more like 'non-existent'.*

This couldn't be right, though. It was just a big block of flats, and all the windows were covered in metal grilles. I turned round, but the driver had already whizzed off, obviously affronted that his beautiful car had had to pass through such upsetting surroundings.

Hoisting up my rucksack, the sun suddenly felt like it was beating very warmly on my head – I looked at my watch. It was noon, the hottest time of day. I moved to what had to be the front door. Sure enough, there written next to a bell was *Hôtel de Cannes (deux)*.

I sighed. Well, Hôtel de Cannes had sounded such a good bet. You know, like the best hotel in Cannes, thus the title. The fact that it was so cheap in the middle of conference season was simply a bonus. Now I suspected that the *deux* might actually be quite important, some kind of legal requirement from somewhere. I rang the buzzer, which sounded deep inside the building, and sighed.

There was no answer. Actually, after a couple of minutes my heart lifted a bit. If the hotel was shut I'd just have to move – maybe to that place Lydia was in, that looked nice. Or maybe Bailey would have a spare bedroom in his luxury bloody hotel or something. But just as I was wondering where I could get a cab, the door creaked open. A small woman stood there. Very slender and with her hair fiercely tied back she did not look a single bit like the friendly woman with the rolled-up sleeves who had greeted Lydia.

'*Oui? Qu'est-ce que c'est?*' she barked at me, and various other sentences stuck on the end. I looked at her blankly.

'Uh, *bonjour*,' I said, my brain searching for the set phrase I'd learnt off by heart to ask for my room. But I wasn't going to get that far.

'Ah,' she said. 'Hell-OH.' She said it in a deliberately slow and simple way, I reckoned, as if by not being French it was clear that I was mentally retarded. 'Yes? What do you want?'

'Uh . . . the hotel?' I said, as if *she* wouldn't be able to understand more than a few simple nouns.

She raised her eyes to heaven and then pointed out some numbers under the sign, which I'd assumed were the address or something.

'*Fermé 12–14h*,' it said.

'*Fermé*,' she said. 'Closed. Until two o'clock.'

Closed? I didn't know hotels could close. I thought that was the entire point of why something was known as a hotel rather than, say, a youth hostel where you had to do chores.

'I can't get in till two o'clock?' I said.

'No,' she said. Then she turned her back on me and clip-clopped off down the road.

I love it. France. I do. I love travelling and going away and visiting new countries and having holidays in lovely places such as France.

These are a few of the thoughts that did NOT go through my head for the next two hours, as I sat on my gigantic bag. I thought about trying to go somewhere – anywhere – but I couldn't move the damn thing and I could only see apartment blocks in both directions. I called Bailey but got no answer and I couldn't bear to phone Lydia – after that little conversation about the hotel I didn't really trust her to help me, rather than, say, come and run me over with her hired car.

So I had to stick it out, listlessly reading *Heat* magazine for the ninth time and trying to work out what horrible thing I could do to this hotel room to get my own back. By the time I'd got to jamming up the plug sockets with egg sandwiches (a favourite trick of Patrick's, particularly when I had friends round at that awkward stage in my early teens, who very quickly became not my friends when they realised my room smelt funny) I was ready to scream.

Nobody passed me in the street at all, apart from a curious

fat woman who stared at me rudely. Where was everybody? Were they all getting ready for super-fancy cocktail parties? Asleep? I was in the middle of the buzzy Côte d'Azure. Puff Daddy comes here to throw Beyoncé into the sea. I'd arrived by bloody helicopter, for goodness' sake, didn't that stand for anything?

Nineteen hours later, at two minutes to two precisely, there came a clip-clopping up the road. I regarded the woman through narrow slits for eyes.

'*D'accord*,' she said. She didn't ask if I'd had lunch or been for a swim or even had a glass of water, simply eyed me as I heaved my enormous, stupid, smelly bag and traipsed wearily after her.

The Hôtel de Cannes (deux) was . . . well, it was cheap. It was up a flight of stairs and seemed to be built around an apartment block, which was a new concept in hotelling to me – I'd expected a swimming pool. It smelled of disinfectant, which failed to mask the odour of old cigarette smoke and cheap coffee. The walls were a horrible brown, with mirrors reflecting back more dismal brown.

The woman checked me in grudgingly, as if my sit-in outside her hotel was some kind of ruse to scam her out of a room. Finally, after laboriously photocopying my passport, and amidst many weary sighs – how could she possibly be expected to fill out these forms after a mere two-hour lunch break? – she handed me a slightly sticky key card and nodded me up to the third floor.

Here was a long corridor of brown once again. There wasn't another soul in sight. I stomped along, pulling the bag behind me like an errant dog. At room 317 I stopped and inserted the card. The cheap, brown Formica door swung open. It really did look quite a lot like the kind of room someone would get murdered in in an exploitation movie from the seventies.

Brown, stained lino. Shutters closed on a small window, rendering the place wreathed in gloom. Chipped cabinet with yet another brown-reflecting mirror.

I figured I'd have a shower and that would make me feel a bit better, but the water was brown and dribbly and lukewarm. I had to get out of here.

The hotel woman grudgingly pointed me in the direction of the promenade ('It is water. You just go *downhill*.' '*Merci*,' I said. We really were talking to each other like idiots) and I headed out into the bright afternoon light.

It was lovely. Fresh and clean under the bright blue sky and I slipped on my sunglasses as I walked down towards the harbour. The air felt warm on my skin and I began to forget all the indignities of the last couple of hours. There was street after street of apartment blocks, painted yellow and blue, with wrought-iron balconies draped with swimming trunks hanging out to dry, mixed with the high gates and walls of whitewashed villas whose driveways curled up into the hills. Coming further into the town there were indeed the promised lines of shops: Louis Vuitton, Chanel, Gucci. Here it was absolutely thronging with people; emaciated women of a certain age, with huge powdered hairdos and tiny little dogs, picking their way through the cobbles on heels. Suave, Italian-looking men with slicked-back hair and pink shirts took telephone calls as sullen-looking model-y girls with Russian accents looked at incredibly over-the-top dresses in Nancy Dell'Olio colours.

Baby girls in big puffs of pink fluff were being pushed around in baby carriages that looked more like small convertibles, and gorgeous, tanned teenage girls showed off flat stomachs over low-slung jeans and Hi-Top Converse, chattering loudly all the while. Quite obviously set apart from the colourful locals mooched groups of tourists: Brits, Dutch, German, all made obvious by their sloppy sports gear and bad posture.

At last I emerged at the water's edge. The soft Mediterranean waves – now with a hint of early evening pinkness on them – shimmered into the endless distance, whilst the boats bobbed up and down along the quay. There were huge white boats; huge blue boats; little boats that would look grand if they weren't tied up next to the huge boats. There was a massive grey boat that looked like a warship but, judging by the chandeliers, it was a big gin palace too. There was the easyJet cruise ship, stuck out in the bay miles from shore, looking like a big orange blob. Young, hunky men cleaned the sides of the boats while others carried crates of champagne on board. Huge Bentleys and BMWs purred up and down the road. I liked it. A lot.

I watched the most absurd little yellow sports car with a million-decibel engine roar by. People were congregating at pavement cafés and ordering carafes of wine and I suddenly felt a distinct desire to be one of them. I decided to go and get Bailey. I could do with a friendly face to go with the rosé.

Bailey's hotel was set right on the palm-lined seafront, past carousels and ice-cream stands and immaculate-looking couples strolling hand in hand, accompanied by their clean and beautiful children. It didn't remind me much of home.

The hotel looked like a cake that had been spun out of icing sugar for some ridiculous billionaire's wedding – layer upon layer of scallops and frills which resolved themselves, as you got closer, into balconies and crenulations. It was wildly over the top, there were turrets everywhere. I loved it.

As I clopped up the stairs into the huge lobby I started to wonder if I should have just thrown on the red dress straight away. That, actually, it was a little subtle. If the women on the street had been dressed up, the ones here were positively festive. Millions of sparkling lights from the chandeliers bounced off huge mirrors and onto glinting ear lobes, huge rings and heavy necklaces.

This was serious jewellery, and it all looked real. I tried not to stare too much, but I couldn't help it, and anyway, why would you wear this stuff if you didn't want people to stare at it? And they were all so thin. This wasn't just in shape, or gently toned, Coleen McLoughlin style. This was full on I-will-never-not-ever-eat-a-meal style. It was amazing their tiny wrists and necks could even take the weight of the precious stones. It looked like just wearing them would be all the exercise they would need that day. I saw some pretty high-glamour women at the practice, but even they weren't like this. This was a different realm altogether; it wasn't millionaire's wives looking for bigger tits. It was billionaire's wives looking to float away, and only the rocks were keeping them tethered to earth.

'Oh, my,' I said, out loud.

'Can ah 'elp you?'

I did find it mildly dispiriting that the beautiful young man in the smart designer uniform could tell I was English before I'd even opened my mouth or glanced in his direction. Damn you, Topshop, for making us all so completely identifiable from thirty metres or more.

The receptionist was beautiful, though he had a look in his eye that implied that if I was only in here for a quick sniff around, he'd rather I left.

'Bailey Arnold, please,' I said in my best imperious tones, which aren't that imperious, frankly, and make me sound constipated.

'Ah, Monsieur Arnold. Of course.'

He nodded his head and made a quick call.

'Go right up – room 801, on the top floor.' I wondered if that was penthouse good or servant's quarters bad as I got into the incredible panelled lift, which had a small red chair and a

71

small red man who pushed the button to '*numéro huit*', as deftly rehearsed by me.

The lift slid smoothly up and deposited me on a bright landing, with large windows at either end and thick, lush carpet spreading out in both directions. There were only two doors visible on the entire floor, which went on for miles: 801 and 802. I figured it probably wasn't the servant's quarters.

There was a proper old-fashioned bell outside the door so I pushed that. Bailey opened it immediately as if he'd been waiting for me.

'Come in!' he said. 'Come in! Learn why it was, in fact, worth getting my head kicked in by the beasts every day because they knew to lie in wait for me outside the technical library! Learn why, yes, CAD physics is worth giving up every Tuesday night for a year for. Yes, why—'

'Shut up, boffin-oh,' I said. I wanted to take in my surroundings in peace because, quite frankly, I'd never been anywhere so nice in my entire life.

You entered the suite via a parquet-floored hall in which stood a coat rack and various large pieces of marble art, until the room opened out into a vast living area. It had a vast, spotless cream carpet that felt like it could curl up to my ankles; it was like walking in moss. Three huge windows overlooked the pale blue sea, sails bobbing up and down in the distance. A huge fireplace had a fire dancing in it, even though it was hot outside, but the room still felt temperate. There was a glass table set for dinner with an enormous bowl of fruit on it, and several huge and comfortable-looking jewel-coloured sofas. In the corner was a fully stocked drinks cabinet with proper-sized bottles, none of your minibar nonsense (I didn't even have a minibar in my 'hotel'). Panelled doors led off either side of the living area, presumably into more rooms.

'*Mon dieu*,' I expostulated.

'*Mais oui*,' said Bailey.

'Fuck a duck,' I said.

'*Exactement*,' replied Bailey.

'I don't understand,' I said, looking round again. Bailey? Here? It was just amazing. 'I mean, this is for rock stars, or royalty, or . . . or . . . you know, VIPs. Not swots from St Michaels' whose hobby was "getting their head kicked in".'

Bailey sank happily into one of the other sofas.

'My dear,' he said. 'In the world of dynamic changing environments in healthcare, I *am* a rock star.'

I'd always known Bailey was a brainiac with a brainiac job, but this was something else. I'd clearly completely underestimated him. No wonder he went out with supermodels all the time. Imagine, a man in undying love with me having all this.

'Where's your robot butler? Can you have him bring me a gin and tonic?' I said looking round and trying to be casual.

'*Mademoiselle?*' and from one of the panelled doors came, I promise, a man dressed in a black frock coat. For a second I thought he really was a robot and nearly screamed. Bailey looked embarrassed.

'He comes with the room,' he whispered to me. 'I don't know how to make him go away.'

'Uh, a gin and tonic, please,' I said hesitatingly.

The butler glided over to the bar and started mixing drinks, the sound of which made me very happy indeed.

'I knew I should have copied off you at GCSE,' I said. 'Bugger. What have you actually done?'

'Well, you've read the brief?'

'Oh, yes, of course.' Well, I would. I'd hate to look unprofessional.

I opened the balcony doors, to be greeted with a sudden yell that sounded like it was coming from next door.

'You'd think they'd soundproof this place,' said Bailey. 'Seeing as it's a royal palace and everything.'

'Yeah,' I said. 'Can't the robot butler . . .'

Bugger, what was I thinking? I'd completely forgotten he was a real live man, standing there.

'*Immédiatement, mademoiselle,*' he said, and shimmied out of the room as if on wheels.

'That butler thing gives me the creeps,' I announced.

'He's a real person,' said Bailey. 'Do try and treat him like, you know, a humanoid. Now, do you want to see the rest of this place? I have to say, it's the nicest . . .'

But before he could beckon me over, the butler came hurtling back into the suite, looking terrified for his life, closely followed by a leering, menacing – why, it was none other than John Jr.

'Oh, for crying out loud,' I said, almost stamping my feet. John Jr was in full flow.

'So if I say best room in town oi MEAN best room in town and that means, buster, if oi want to have a bust up with the old trouble and strife you better keep your big nose aht of it, know wharra mean?'

The butler had recovered his composure somewhat and gave John Jr a look that said 'You will never order another dish in any restaurant bar or café in this town without someone I know personally peeing in it,' but he said nothing.

'John Jr, for God's sake.'

John Jr turned round at that. He got the shock of his life when he saw me; his already red face turned puce.

'Evie . . . Evie, for fuck's sake. Are you staying here?'

I sighed. 'If I say I am will you move?'

Kelly came out of the suite to see what the commotion was. Now I understood the noise; there'd obviously been some sort of incident with the hair straighteners. A large chunk of her hair looked distinctly singed.

'Ow, hello, Evie,' she sniffed, smiling bravely. 'I hoped we'd run into you.'

'Yup,' I said. 'Well, this was quick.'

'Now, I don't want to push in . . .'

'Uh huh . . .'

Kelly looked towards Bailey. 'But is this one of your fabulous doctors?'

I looked round at Bailey, who was retreating towards the

windows of his huge suite, away from John Jr. It was almost comical to see. He probably didn't realise he was doing it, just vestigial habit.

John Jr narrowed his piggy eyes. 'Hey. I recognise you.'

Bailey's lips twitched and he fussed with his glasses. I'd never mentioned at home that I still saw Bailey. Mum would have wanted us to get married and the beasts would never have let me hear the end of it.

'It's Bailey boy, innit? Ol' Bailey boy, Snaily Bailey.'

I could see the colour rise in Bailey's cheeks. I forgot sometimes, encased as he was in his great job and nice lifestyle, that it had been pretty bad for him too.

'Mnnff,' said Bailey.

John Jr's face broke into a huge smile. 'Well! Fantastic to see you! We had some great times back then, didn't we? Some right laughs. Kelly, this is Bailey, one of the old gang from Leadbetter Road. Come here.'

And he marched up to Bailey and gave him a great bear hug. I don't think I've seen a man so surprised since Will Young won *Pop Idol*. Bailey took a step back as soon as he reasonably could.

'John Jr,' he said stiffly. 'It's been a long time.'

I instantly felt sorry for him; it sounded like he was saying it in a James Bond/*Goldfinger*-type fashion and should be stroking a pussycat and dreaming up shark-related tortures for his lifelong foe. Instead John Jr clearly thought he'd stumbled on a long-lost 'homie' from back in the 'hood'.

'Kelly, Kelly, come meet Bail the Snail. Oh, we had some times in those days, didn't we, Bailey boy?'

'I don't know,' said Bailey stiffly. 'It was quite hard to hear because you kept dunking my head in a bucket of water.'

John Jr guffawed mightily. 'Right laugh, so it was.'

'Hello,' said Kelly. 'Now I don't want to bother you, but I wanted to talk to someone about this freckle.'

She pointed to something invisible perched on top of her cleavage.

'Getting someone to feel your knockers again?' roared John Jr. 'She's a right tart, my wife, eh?'

'I'm not a doctor,' said Bailey. 'I'm an engineering specialist.'

'Pff. That sounds boring,' said John Jr. 'Mind you, you always were a speccy get. Any money in it?'

There was a short silence as we waited for the penny to drop.

'Oh! You're stayin' here, are you? Well, well done, my son, well done. Looks like it wasn't a waste getting all those swot levels after all. Course, I went to the university of life . . . oy, gar-SON!'

Oh, no. Once John Jr got started on the university of life diatribe the evening was well and truly done for. And he didn't go to the university of life at all. He went to the university of misbehaving at school, causing teachers to have nervous breakdowns, then leaving at sixteen and hanging around amusement arcades before falling into second-hand car dealing and borrowing money off Dad to open his own garage, a loan I'm sure he's never paid back. John Jr went to the university of being a complete arse. And now he was hollering at the butler for drinks – we had to do something! And fast!

'Uh, Bailey,' I said meaningfully. 'We're going to be late for dinner. You remember. That *very* important dinner.'

Bailey was still trapped, looking like a rabbit hypnotised by a snake.

'Right. Dinner,' said John Jr. 'That sounds great.'

'It's a private dinner,' I said. 'There won't be any room for you.'

'Oh, we'll see about that,' said John Jr. 'Little lesson, Evie. Money can open a lot of doors. Come on, Kelly, get yourself dressed up.'

As Kelly was already wearing a bustier twinkling with Swarovski crystals, spray on black trousers and five-inch heels, and her hair resembled the crest of a tidal wave, I couldn't imagine exactly what he meant by 'get dressed up', but she instantly shuffled off.

'Right,' said John Jr. 'Where we going? Hope it's not too fucking Frog. They eat horse, you know. Did you know that? Filthy fuckers. Are we going to a horse restaurant? Hope not. *GarSON*. What does horse taste like?'

Defeated, as if taking part in some horrible zombie movie, we headed for the lift. I pressed the polished brass lift button; it pinged, the lift already there.

'Oh, fabulous, you're all ready,' said Lydia, stepping daintily out of the lift and taking Bailey by the arm as if he were her personal property. She was wearing a beautiful, understated, swinging navy and cream cotton-knit dress that I swear I've seen on Sarah Jessica Parker, with a dinky navy handbag to match. As soon as I saw it I knew that instead of buying half a dozen cheapy high-store outfits I should have saved up for something like that and just worn it every day.

'Dinner time? I'm totally ready to go.'

She lowered her voice by about half a decibel and pouted her mouth in the direction of Bailey's ear. 'Didn't realise we were taking the Addams family, though. Ah huh huh huh!'

Chapter Five

I had had a fantasy of how my first night in the South of France would be. The evening light would be soft and sweet-smelling (that at least was true) as we strolled down to the Croisette, home to every film star of the last fifty years, including the porny ones.

Bailey would be handing me a cocktail as we stood on a balcony watching the sun go down; he'd tell me how much he'd loved me all these years and I, looking elegant and graceful and like something out of the twenties, would touch my elegant hand to the top of the balcony, accept the cocktail with sadness and say, in perfect French, 'I'm sorry, Bailey. I can never love you,' as my gaze lingered on the extraordinarily hunky doctor who was waving at me from the beach, where he was running, shirtless, with his black Labrador. A single crystal tear dropped from my eyes with the exquisite pain of *les affaires de la coeur* and . . .

'Steak fwites, that's what it's called,' John Jr was saying loudly, stomping out into the road without looking (the Ferrari swerved to avoid him, worse luck. Mind you, in a fight between John Jr and a small lightweight sports car, my money was on JJ). 'Oh, right, not to worry, we'll just find somewhere with pictures in the window. *Comprendez?*'

We were all marching in a long line across the Croisette, the street which ran parallel to the sea. It was covered in palm trees, and the hand- and footprints of European film stars were embedded in bronze in the concrete, just like in my fantasy. The place was absolutely mobbed with people, none of whom looked anything like as British as us. Bailey and Lydia were behind me, deep in conversation, Kelly was bringing up the rear in very high heels that made her look as if she was trying to perform a circus act by balancing on tiny knives.

'I was thinking maybe somewhere nice and traditional,' I said timidly, holding up my guidebook. 'Somewhere that . . . *"brings alive the freshness of the Mediterranean and the gentleness of the soft Côte d'Azure breezes, wrapped up in the tastes of the Provençal hills and grated with the zest of—"'*

'Steak fwites,' said John Jr.

And so it was that we found ourselves sitting outside a restaurant with plastic flowers on the table, surrounded by several other tables full of lost English people looking at the laminated plastic menus with pictures on them and trying to ignore their badly behaved children. John Jr thinks he likes the finer things in life but when it comes to his stomach he's pretty straightforward.

'Oi! *Garson!*' shouted John Jr. 'How many of us are there? Five? Right. Five bottles of white wine. Sweet.'

The waiter gave John Jr a look he absolutely deserved but one, sadly, he was incapable of noticing.

Bailey sidled in next to me. 'Em, I think we have to—'

'Kill him,' I whispered. 'I know. I thought maybe we could drop his body in the bay.'

Bailey's brow furrowed. 'Um. I was thinking, maybe try and lose him.'

'Oh,' I said, trying not to look too disappointed.

'Obviously, you know, death would have been a good option too.'

'It would,' I said. 'One down, two to go.'

'But really, I just meant . . . please don't think I want to hang out with your brother all week.'

I was shocked by the injustice of this. 'What do you mean? You think I do? I didn't invite him! You're the one that's all "Oh, great to see you John Jr, let's catch up," kiss kiss.'

'I was not,' said Bailey hotly. 'I didn't say anything.'

'Well, maybe you should have,' I said. 'I tried to save you with the whole "fake dinner" thing and you just stood there, wobbling.'

Bailey looked at me and suddenly I had a flashback to him aged eight. Nobody likes being reminded of how embarrassing their childhood was. Also, telling men they're cowards is hardly a guaranteed banker either. I saw he was really hurt, and I felt really bad.

'OK,' he said, and left the seat, heading to the other end of the table where Lydia had saved him a seat. Oh, good. I'd sent him into the arms of Cruella de Vil. I poured myself a very large glass of wine. This was going to be a long night.

'I said a hey-a ho-a wibble-a wobble and a hammy and a bullet to beat.'

Oh, God. Oh, God. How had everything gone so terribly wrong? It was several hours and many, many bottles of wine later. I'd reached that horrible point where I was too afraid to move, convinced that my legs no longer possessed the power to lift me. The wine had definitely seemed to improve the more of it I'd drank. I wondered if this was because it had had time to breathe. Or maybe because it had stripped the tastebuds from my mouth – I wasn't sure.

Bailey and Lydia were buried in conversation down the other end, which pissed me off big time. I didn't know why; normally when Bailey introduced me to some gorgeous girl I could hold off getting jealous for about ten minutes, waiting until she said something idiotic like, 'Isn't it amazing how every sheep born has its own baa? Do you know what I'd really love to do? Go on *Big Brother*,' and then I could relax again. But this was Lydia, whom he'd already seen being not very nice to me. And every time I tried to casually sidle up to their conversation Lydia shot me a look that very clearly said, 'You, go away,' in monkey language.

Meanwhile, Kelly was talking to me about face cream at the most extraordinary length. I was ready to knock myself out with the pepper grinder. Every time I thought Kelly was my ally in the war against John Jr, she'd start doing this; banging on about pentapeptides or fruit acid till I wanted to cry.

John Jr, who I'd been trying to ignore as he snurfed his way through what seemed like several bottles of nasty wine, had decided to get up, lift his polo shirt and expose his pork-red body (no wonder Kelly was always crying). Using the wine bottle as a microphone he started singing along to the piped music whilst the waiters appeared to be entering a superciliousness competition, leaning against the flapping canvas with their arms folded. Oh, God. This couldn't get any worse.

'Hello, Evie.'

There was a funny noise behind me, beyond the plastic covering, and it sounded like it was calling my name. Half nervous, half pleased to be temporarily distracted I slowly turned round.

Oh, God, of course it was. Of course. After all, who else did I know in the entire country?

'A hibby-hobey-hibb,' yelled John Jr, oblivious to Dr Maitland standing on the other side of the plastic, immaculately dressed in a pastel shirt and a pale linen suit which as usual was ludicrously old-fashioned, but somehow looked rather dashing here.

I smiled wanly. Both docs weren't due in till the morning; I was going to collect them from the airport, for goodness' sake. I thought it was a bit rude of Dr Maitland to turn up and witness my embarrassing family before I could safely get rid of them.

'Hello,' I said, jumping out of my chair and barrelling towards him in an attempt to distance myself from everyone behind me and thus render them not even acquaintances. John Jr had taken off his shirt entirely and was hurling it round his head as he came to the emotive finale of the song.

'So, you know everyone in Cannes already!' said Dr Maitland. 'Good networking skills.' Oh, God, please tell me he had another dinner to go on to. Please. I tried to keep him out of Kelly's sight line; she'd ask him to eat with us immediately.

I shrugged and tried to look nonchalant and businesslike and not at all tanked up on cheap wine.

'Was your flight OK? I'd have arranged transport.'

'Yes, I decided to come early. Little bit of groundwork. Big week ahead for us, don't you think?'

I agreed heartily.

'HE-llo,' came a voice. Oh, bugger. I'd only considered

the risk from my end of the table, but Lydia had spotted an opening.

'It's Dr Maitland, isn't it? Want to join us for a drink?'

'Hi.' Bailey waved hello.

'Well, er . . .' Dr Maitland looked at me enquiringly, which was nice of him. Suddenly, John Jr's glazed vision gained focus.

'Oi! Oo are you? You're not after our Evie, are you?'

Oh, Christ on a bike. How mortifying. Dr Maitland went a little pink, which was quite cute.

'No, no . . . we work together.'

'Yeah, didn't think so . . . you're definitely out of her league, ain't he, Eve?'

'Shut UP,' I said. I was used to crap like this from JJ, though, so it didn't harm me that much. But Dr Maitland's head snapped up.

'Excuse me?'

'Don't listen to him,' I said. 'It's just my . . . um, brother. He's a bit pissed.'

'Not as pissed as he'd have to be,' shouted John Jr jovially.

'Don't speak to her like that.'

I had to admit, I was quite impressed. Dr Maitland was tall, but John Jr weighed about three of him.

'Yeah, and oo are you?'

'JJ,' shouted Kelly. 'It's the *doctor*!'

Now I was even more embarrassed. Doctors, lawyers – any professionals – get automatic 'respect' in my family. A bit outdated, forelock-tugging, I'd always thought, but thank goodness, because it worked.

'Doctor?' said JJ, as Kelly pulled at him to sit down and handed him another full glass of wine, perhaps unwisely. All the tables in the restaurant were watching us extremely closely. Dr Maitland took off his glasses and started to rub them with a handkerchief. I bet he was glad he'd stopped by.

'I think I'll get on,' he said. I was burning up with mortification. He must have thought I was a real guttersnipe.

'OK,' I managed to stutter. 'Uh, see you tomorrow.'

'Uh, OK then,' he said.

'Lovely family,' Lydia had smirked, as she'd departed into the night – in the same direction as Bailey, I couldn't help but notice.

'He was just pissed,' I said stiffly. Kelly and John Jr had already departed, John Jr drunkenly insisting on splitting the bill exactly, which then took hours. I mean, I could slag JJ off, because he was mine, but nobody else could. Then I'd trudged the long way up the hill in the dark, conscious that I'd drunk too much, not had any fun and now had to get up at the crack of dawn to fetch bloody Dr Bennet from the airport.

Nice airport was cool and white in the early morning glare as I held up my printed sign. Obviously Dr Bennet knew who I was, but he thought this looked smarter.

I looked around at the women passing through the airport. Oh, they were good-looking all right. But in such a boring way (it seemed to me – of course I know men are relatively simple in their tastes for these things). Tiny bottoms, long legs, tits hoisted up to clavicle level, hair bleached to straw, huge sunglasses balanced on augmented cheekbones – it looked so relentlessly dull, so uniform. We got quite a lot of desperate divorcees at the surgery. Often, their husbands had left them for someone who looked absolutely identical to them but was twenty years younger. Why bother? I often wondered. If you kept trying to look the same way you would get gradually more grotesque, and if your tit perkiness was all your man was after, well, there would always be someone perkier.

Not a single woman looked remotely happy. I bought a croissant to eat at the little coffee bar outside Arrivals and could almost feel them sneering behind me as I tucked in to the refined carbs and sugar.

OK, so I was a midget with curly brown hair next to this lot. But hey! At least I was getting a yummy croissant for breakfast.

The gate started to flood with people – many of them men with that unmistakeable patina of plastic surgeon about them. Maybe I've become a bit of an expert. But their skin is always a little smoother than yours, as if they know about a secret bar of soap you're barred from, and their stubble is always non-existent, as if they've given themselves electrolysis instead of shaving. There was a clattering of different languages – it sounded like German and Dutch – and I got quite engrossed looking at the expensive luggage and loafers and silk ties and . . .

'Hello!' said a friendly voice. Shaken out of my reverie I turned around. There was a man standing in front of me. He had a cheerful face with freckles, and russety hair. He looked very young. I hoped he didn't want money for something.

'*Non, merci,*' I said loudly.

His face looked a little crestfallen at my obvious confusion.

'Uh, you're here for me?' he said. I was what? He looked a bit nervous. 'I know, I look a bit young to be a doctor, everyone says that, ha ha ha.'

I blinked.

'Oh, shit, are you French? I mean, *merde*. Eh, eh. *BON-JOUR. Je m'appelle doc-TEUR Bennet.*'

'I'm not French,' I said.

'Oh. OK.' There was a pause. 'Uh . . . are you *special*?'

'What do you *want*?' I said crossly.

'I'm Dr Bennet. Are you picking me up?'

Oh, for goodness' sake, how could I have been so dense?

'Sorry,' I said. 'Um. There's another Dr Bennet. It's not you.'

Freckle face looked puzzled. 'Oh. Right.'

'Are you here for the conference?'

'Yes,' he said. 'I'm a junior. I don't know why they sent me really. So that's why I thought you were picking me up. I'm not used to all this.'

'Me neither,' I said. 'It's my first time too.'

'As a driver?'

'No. I'm a medical receptionist.'

'Really? Where are the dragon claws and fire coming out of your mouth?'

'Ah, I'm private,' I said. 'If you pay money you get a smile and maybe even a cappuccino. Maybe.'

'Well, that does sound like it's worth thousands and thousands of pounds,' he said, his face looking slightly cross suddenly. 'I'm Tom Bennet.'

'Evie Kennedy,' I said. 'Hi.'

'Hi. I don't suppose you know where the bus stop is, do you?'

'I'd offer you a lift,' I said, 'but . . .'

Just then I saw my Dr Bennet and his wife emerge from Arrivals. As usual, he looked poised, and she looked furious. He'd mentioned looking forward to having a romantic time in Cannes. In my head, the idea of having a romantic time with Mrs Bennet seemed akin to trying to clamber on top of an unwieldy metal chair, but I nodded and smiled hello to her nonetheless. In response she sighed at me.

The effect on Tom was immediate; he got very nervous, glancing from the Bennets to me. I thought he was very embarrassed.

'Not to worry yourself,' Tom said. 'See you around. Is it a big place,' Cannes?'

'Not really.' I watched him go. Under other circumstances, bumping accidentally into a young doctor at Côte d'Azure airport might be construed as rather romantic. This one though had skin that looked like it might burn up in direct sunlight. How disappointing. Still, compared to everyone else I'd seen come off the plane, he was definitely number one.

The Bennets weren't chatty in the cab, which made me think that perhaps I shouldn't have bothered coming and instead kept the probably hundred extra euros it had cost to keep the driver handy in the car park, for all the thanks I got.

They seemed oblivious to the sun glancing off the waves, the girls rollerblading in bikinis on Nice promenade, the real French families unfolding picnic baskets containing golden, sticky-looking roast chickens and whole cheeses and baguettes. I don't know why I got a little thrill when I saw French people with baguettes. I suppose it would be like coming to London and seeing everyone dressed up as pearly kings and queens and saying lor, luv a duck.

When I'd checked the itinerary I'd drawn up earlier my heart had sank – they were in the same hotel as Bailey and my idiot brother. Oh, good, I was so glad everyone was in the very height of comfort and luxury whilst my bed smelled of someone else's deodorant.

'Do you want me to talk you through the schedule?' I said

when we drew up in front of the hotel. Once again the chap with the white gloves was out doing his stuff. I wondered if every so often some plutocrat just dropped him ten thousand euros for no reason.

'Yes,' nodded Dr Bennet. 'I've lost mine,' he added. That was strange. Dr Bennet never lost anything.

The beautiful boy on reception had given me even more of a curled lip today, as if I was some prostitute that followed men up to their bedrooms. Mind you, from what I'd heard that didn't exactly faze people who worked in posh hotels. Maybe he just thought I was a really cheap prostitute. Dr Maitland joined us in the lobby. I was embarrassed to see him again, but he looked even more so, so I didn't mention anything.

'OK,' I announced. 'The backers want to see you first, then there's the Ocean Consortium meeting – does that make sense to you?'

They nodded mutely.

'It's in the DeVere rooms, then the introductory session, then at five it's cocktails for everyone in the Belles Rives American bar, then dinner . . . my God, just as well you're not in surgery this week. You'll all be completely wombated.'

For the first time Dr Maitland looked like he might be about to smile. 'Not everyone,' he said, 'gets falling over drunk just because there's free drink available.'

'Why not?' I said. 'How can you help it?'

His eyebrows twitched. 'Well, you know your limits, so you're careful with top-ups.'

92

'But it's *free*,' I explained again, just in case he hadn't got it the first time.

'It's free,' he said, 'it's not compulsory.'

'Do you do any operating?' I asked. 'At this expo? I wondered if there might be . . . you know, like competitions.'

'Competitions,' said Dr Bennet gravely. The two doctors looked at each other. 'Like, races?'

Oh, God, I MUST read the brief.

Dr Maitland looked at me sternly over his spectacles. 'Evie Kennedy, is there anything else?'

'No, sir,' I said.

'Are you coming to the introduction?'

'Can I?' I nearly squeaked. There was a free bar! Not, of course, that I would be conducting myself with anything other than total decorum at all times.

'Well, you're taking notes, aren't you?'

Curses.

The first person I saw when I arrived at the venue – which was completely gorgeous, I could see why people liked this South of France malarkey so much – was Lydia.

There was the cheering sound of clinking glasses as I approached, trying to look as if I dropped in on these occasions all the time and was thus completely blasé about the whole thing even though I was the only woman in the entire place who wasn't wearing a rope of pearls big enough to drown you if you fell into the sea whilst you were wearing them.

I decided to take the sophisticated adult stance and give Lydia a Kennedy 'cool nod', as I tried to flounce past with my notebook.

'Hey, you.'

Well, it didn't work with my brothers either. They just gave me Chinese burns until I eventually let out some kind of sound.

'Uh-huh?' I said snootily. 'I'm very busy with my important conference.'

'Forget about that,' said Lydia. She looked me up and down. 'You look good,' she said.

I smelt a rat immediately. Lydia never thought I looked good. Lydia usually said things like, 'Don't you need tits to wear those wrapover tops?' and 'Platform soles? How hilarious,' about my new boots, and things like that.

'Uh-huh,' I said. 'How's your luxury B and B?'

'Oh, it's not all that,' said Lydia. 'All that freshly baked patisserie, it's havoc on the figure. *Why French Women Don't Get Fat*; by ignoring the white flour their country is drowning in, that's how.'

I just stood there.

'So,' Lydia leaned over conspiratorally, as we walked into the beautiful room, which overlooked a perfectly manicured garden. She swiped two glasses of champagne from a black-and-white-dressed waitress; I was quite impressed by how smoothly.

'We've been such great friends for *ever*, and I can't

believe you've never told me about your wonderful friend.'

'Kelly?' I said to be annoying. The champagne was delicious. 'Yeah, she's great.'

Lydia did this funny laugh thing. 'Darling,' she said. 'The fascinating Bailey.'

'Bailey isn't fascinating,' I said. 'He's a dork. Although I did think there was something up—'

'Yes?' said Lydia, her eyes lighting up.

'When he sat seven A levels. I thought he was just showing off.'

'Geniuses don't have to show off,' said Lydia knowingly.

'Short-arses do,' I said.

'So is he . . . you know?'

'Quite annoying?'

'Married? Gay? He is terribly fascinating.'

'Do you mean rich?' I asked suddenly, looking suspiciously at Lydia's necklace. Yup. Pearls. 'Because let me tell you one thing. He may be a bit of a know-it-all, but when it comes to women he's a bit of a divot, so if you dare mess him about, you'll have me to answer to.'

'Wooo,' said Lydia, her face changing. 'Ooh, sorry. I didn't realise. Do you want me to back off?'

'Didn't realise what?' I said, suddenly feeling slightly daft for my outburst. Maybe I'd gone in a bit strong.

'That you're, you know . . . in love with him.'

I felt my face go all hot suddenly, the way you do when

you're six stops from home and you remember you've forgotten your wallet. It all suddenly went quiet. I wasn't in love with Bailey. *Was I?*

Lydia gave me a meaningful look and backed away towards a large group of doctors, who all smiled at her and widened their circle to let her in. That would never happen to me. I was left completely alone in the middle of the room, my head in a whirl.

Chapter Six

'Evie? You look like you are a whole world away. Are you dreaming of London, huh? How much you miss its rubbish-soaked streets and shouting young men in hoodies?'

I spun around. Dr Bennet was standing there, immaculate as ever, looking at me kindly.

'No, I . . .' I looked round for inspiration. 'I don't know anyone.'

Dr Bennet looked round. He obviously didn't want to introduce me to anyone himself; it was tantamount to him saying, 'Look everyone, here's the assistant I'm having an affair with,' and even if he dared to have an affair, which I very much doubted, I assumed he'd like people to think it would be with someone a bit more impressive than me.

'Don't you have some kind of secret international secretary's cabal?' he said. Well, I knew one witch, I thought.

I shrugged. 'I'm fine, Dr Bennet, honestly. I'm just ready to take my notes, that's all.'

As I said this my eye was irresistibly drawn to a bright red beacon that seemed to be glowing above the rest of the crowd. It rotated to face me and I realised I was looking at that other Dr Bennet bloke I'd met at the airport. His hair was glinting in the sunlight bouncing off the chandeliers. Our eyes met.

'Hello?' said the other Dr Bennet – Tom, that was his name. He said it tentatively, as if he was prepared for me to completely blank him. Maybe he still thought I had a learning disability.

'There we are,' said the original Dr Bennet, pleased. 'You young folk have a good time.' And he shot off towards the sleekest-looking doctor with the most expensive-looking loafers.

'Hi there,' I said. 'Having fun?'

'Not sure,' he said, looking around. 'I mean, it seems like I should be having fun, doesn't it? Champagne, sunset, lots of shop talk . . . but somehow it's just not coming together.'

'I know how you feel,' I said. 'But they seem to be getting very agitated over there.' I pointed to where a large group of Germans were gesticulating wildly. One did a particularly graphic arm movement, he appeared to be pulling on his vest underneath his shirt.

'What's he doing?' I asked.

'I don't know. Tummy tuck?'

'You really are a doctor,' I said, impressed.

'Hmm,' he said. 'Med student really.'

'Oh, yes? How come you get sent off to five star . . .' I waved my hand expansively, just as a waitress appeared with a tray of caviar things. I've only tried caviar once, at John Jr's wedding, and I'd absolutely hated it, but I didn't want to look unsophisticated in front of Tom, so I grabbed a canapé and stuffed it in my mouth. Yes, just as I thought – revolting. I took a huge slug of champagne to compensate, then choked a bit. I hate it when I do that.

'Are you all right?' said Tom, looking at my red face with concern. I was a bit miffed by that.

'It's OK, no medical assistance required,' I said, when I finally got my breath back. Tears had sprung to my eyes.

'I didn't think so,' he said. 'But, you know. If your lips had gone blue I'd have been right in there.'

'Glad to hear it,' I said. 'It would be very embarrassing to be saved from death, you know. *Too early.*'

He smiled.

'So what are you here for then?'

Tom looked slightly unsettled. 'Well, um. It came up in the department and nobody wanted to go, so they let me go.'

'Although you're only a student?'

'Well, yes. We don't normally get sent on things like this.'

'So they must think you're a scalpel whizz?'

'Mmm,' said Tom. He stuffed about nine canapés in his mouth and didn't choke on any of them. 'God, I'm starving. I don't speak any French and when I point at stuff in shops they just keep raising eyebrows at me and offering me Chanel handbags and things. Which serves me right, I suppose.'

'It does,' I said. 'What were you doing at school?'

' Physics . . . chemistry . . . biology, that kind of stuff.'

'Oh, yeah,' I said.

'Anyway, I deal with burns mostly. I'm not really interested in this end of things. What about you? Do you work for . . .' He nodded at Dr Bennet, who was laughing outrageously at a joke that couldn't possibly be that funny, bless him. He was the world's best schmoozer. Nobody had better introduce him to their clients. Dr Maitland was standing in the circle too, looking miserable. Honestly, if he didn't like the clients and he didn't like his colleagues and he couldn't fake either it was more of a mystery than ever why he was in this line of work in the first place. I waved to him tentatively, and he waved back in, I suppose, a way that didn't scream, 'Get away from me, you of the unbelievably tacky family.'

'Yes,' I said. 'And I know Bailey Arnold, who's giving the talk.'

And who, apparently, I might be in love with, I didn't add. Bailey wasn't here; I suppose they kept him hidden behind a curtain backstage until his time came to be revealed. I bet he pretended to be annoyed by all the fuss but secretly loved it.

I wondered if he still wanted to get off with me. Ten years was a long time. Too long?

Tom looked around. He didn't seem terribly interested. 'Oh. Right. So, you're like the best-connected person here.'

I laughed, which he immediately looked offended by, and I realised I sounded like I was saying, 'Ha ha, yes, if I was well connected do you think I'd be standing here talking to you?' which wasn't what I meant at all.

'I think we're going in,' I said. 'Shall we grab a couple more glasses just in case the speech is very boring?'

'That's not very flattering for your friend,' said Tom.

'He's my friend, that doesn't mean I have to understand *everything* he says,' I pointed out, lifting four glasses from a passing waiter with almost as much élan as Lydia had shown before.

On a stage that had been erected at the side of the room were several orange-backed chairs, as well as pitchers of water and little mikes. Worryingly, it all looked rather like we might be about to have a bit of a lecture.

'This doesn't feel like a holiday,' I grumbled to Tom as we found two seats near the back. I approved of his choice, much easier to snicker and pass notes unseen.

'You're on *holiday*?' he said, with some surprise.

'Not a very good one,' I said, as I picked up the information pack that had been left on our seats.

'You can say that again.'

'But still,' I mused, 'better than most.'

Tom looked as if he felt extremely sorry for me. I leafed through the pack that was given out to everyone. It was full of groovy drawings of palm trees and beaches, none of which made a lot of sense, and phrases like 'facing the future' and 'a brand-new paradigm', which didn't mean much to me either. I'd better concentrate on the speech.

I was about to ask Tom what it was all about when the lights dimmed dramatically and Dr Bennet, followed by Bailey, walked on the stage. My heart beat a little faster when I saw Bailey, standing there with his button-down collar and glasses, a large sheaf of paper clutched in his hands. Something to the side caught my eye. I glanced across, and Lydia was staring at me, arching an eyebrow in a meaningful manner. Immediately I felt myself flushing. She twitched in a 'I thought as much' kind of a way and turned back, looking satisfied. Damnit. And I'd missed Dr Bennet's intro.

Then a distinguished-looking man stood up and, in French, thanked everyone for coming, and then, thankfully, he switched to English and started talking about a great new opportunity for plastic surgery, blah blah blah. I slightly tuned out at this point, and found my thoughts, and my eyes, creeping towards Tom and wondering if he had red chest hair, and if he did, was that really, really disgusting? Or mildly interesting? After all, Damien Lewis had red hair, and he was gorgeous.

Then I looked at Bailey. He looked so sweet and vul-
nerable on stage, his glasses reflecting the spotlight as he
sipped his water, looking hardly older than eight. I blinked
a few times. I mean, I felt so much for him – and you were
always hearing about people realising that in fact they were
really in love with their best friends. I mean, look at Ross
and Rachel, and Chandler and Monica. OK, they were fic-
tional people, and I was never that convinced by Chandler
and Monica anyway, but still . . . people said you should
settle with someone whose company you really enjoyed . . .
who you could spend a lot of time with, who never bored
you, and all those things were true about Bailey. Plus, I
suppose, he was really successful, and although I didn't
like to think of myself as someone who cared much about
stuff like that – mostly because I'd seen an awful lot of the
girls who did, and I didn't think much of them – it was
nice, nonetheless, and fun, to feel proud of him. Which I
was, so much. I hadn't realised until I'd got here just how
well he was doing.

I snapped out of my reverie, realising I'd missed the
entire speech, as someone – something – marched on the
stage. It was a woman (I was reasonably sure), about six foot
tall, and she looked as close to a human Barbie as it was possible to look.

Her hair was huge – surely a wig – and blonde, back-
combed miles into the air and flowing back over her broad
shoulders, with which her tits were nearly level, narrowing to

a waist the size of a pin, amply outlined by the skintight pink leopard-skin jacket she was wearing at least two sizes too small.

A pierced belly button was visible above a pelmet skirt that only just covered her hips – I think if we'd been sitting any lower we'd have seen something one wouldn't ordinarily wish to see – and she had the skinniest pair of mile-long stick legs I'd ever seen, ending in fuschia pink stilettos with needle-sharp heels. I looked at Tom and he made an extremely comical face at me.

The woman approached the lectern and picked up the mike.

'My name is Cindy Linklater,' she said. The voice was a shock. I looked around in case it was booming out from somewhere else. It was the voice of an old lady; an old lady who'd smoked a lot.

'And I am sixty-two years old.'

Amazingly, a huge round of applause broke out throughout the hall. But this women was scary! She was grotesque! She looked like a horrible Frankenstein-esque monster someone had stuck together from Jordan's spare parts!

Holding the mike she marched down the steps from the stage and paraded up and down the aisles so we could all have a good look at her.

'And I'm widely believed to have had the most plastic surgery in the world,' she said. No kidding. On the back of the stage appeared a photograph of a normal, completely pleasant-looking woman with worried eyes and a nice smile, if slightly crooked teeth.

'That,' she said, in a sneering tone, 'was me.'

She was closer now. Close up, she appeared even more frightening. Her face was a pulled-back mask, weighed down with pots and pots of bright orange make-up. Her throat was so tight it looked like she'd have difficulty swallowing with it. I shrank back as she came past in case she invited me to come and take a look inside her gingerbread house.

'And I'm just showing the beginning of what we can do. Growing old is a choice.'

She said this with a curl of her huge synthetic lips and it was eerie to look at. I glanced at Bailey to see if he would say something along the lines of growing old not being a choice if you were born in Sierra Leone or something, like he normally would, but he was watching in silence. That didn't seem right.

'Which is why I'm going to be the perfect face for the opening of New Horizons. Tax free. Offshore. Completely private. And a place for new experimental technologies to begin. To keep us beautiful. For ever.'

All the doctors started to applaud. I looked around. What was this? It sounded like some evil James Bond master plan to take over the world. Why hadn't I read the brief? Were they going to create a race of crone-faced super-zombies? Would it be compulsory?

'So I'd now like to hand over to our elite team of creative construction engineers . . .'

Bailey stood up on the stage. The crone retreated. 'Must be time for her to eat another baby,' I whispered to Tom, who was scribbling stuff on a piece of paper, in true student style, and didn't reply.

'Stay beautiful!' croaked the crone, and opened her mouth widely in what I suppose her withered brain had once considered to be a smile. Her teeth were absurdly white and straight and looked like she kept them in a glass by her bed. 'For ever!' Then she tottered off.

Bailey came to the front of the stage and started talking about timescales, engineering difficulties, water tables and stuff I had no idea what he was talking about. I wish I'd listened to Dr Bennet's intro. Although, I couldn't have listened even if I had understood, I don't think. I was concentrating on him so hard, about seeing him in a different light. Not as nerdy little Bailey, complaining about everything again, or getting his head kicked in, but as a confident if quiet speaker talking about a large project, and clean lines, and vertical-suspended stabilisers and things. I risked a glance at Lydia again. She was watching, purportedly with rapt attention. Well, it was certainly food for thought.

The thing is, I don't want to care about what people do. That's the point of democracy and stuff, right? So when I see people like Cindy, I do think, well, it's her choice. But then when I talk to some of our clients – I mean, they're not all rich. Some save up for years, or take out loans. They're usually the more talkative ones. And it's always the same – their husbands have left them, or they never knew their dads, or they're lonely, or scared of something. And I always want to say that I see rich beautiful women all the time and they're miserable too – maybe even worse. And really, they'd probably be better off keeping their money and taking the kids to Euro Disney or something.

A couple of times – and he doesn't know I know this – Dr Maitland has talked people out of surgery. Maybe they don't need it, or patently can't afford it, or have wildly unrealistic ideas of what it's going to do to their lives. I don't know what he says to them, but they come out of his surgery sniffing hopeful tears, and head off, looking happier than a lot of our ladies.

Dr Bennet never turns anyone away, not even the skinny girls with the hollow eyes who come in asking about spot lipo.

After the speech was over, I glanced at my notes and realised I'd forgotten to take any at all. Oh, no, the docs would be expecting this written up shortly, and I'd been miles away.

'Can I borrow your notes?' I said to Tom as we got up to file over for drinks. He looked a bit uncomfortable.

'Didn't you take your own?' he said.

'Why, are yours covered in pictures of willies and things?'

I asked. 'And doodles of the AC/DC logo, and women's boobies?'

'No,' he said. 'It's just I promised I'd fax them back to my consultant.'

'Right,' I said. 'And the little fax pixies take the paper away and curl it up really small and you never see it again.'

He smiled. 'Let me fax it first. Then maybe you can have them. If you're good.'

'I'm always good!' I protested, following him towards the bar.

'Except at note-taking and paying attention when you're being paid for it?'

'That's a quibble,' I said.

Bailey was standing next to the bar, surrounded by intense-looking docs chatting to him. I caught his eye, and immediately felt weird.

'Good speech,' I said with my nicest smile. I felt nervous suddenly, my hands felt a little sweaty. I felt like I was talking to someone I didn't know at all.

He gave me a very characteristic Bailey grin though. 'Did you understand it all?'

'Yes!' I said indignantly.

'Even the stuff about sea vectors?'

He made his way over to me. I felt inwardly triumphant.

'You're creating a race of terrifying blonde zombies to take over the world from your secret, evil, underwater lair,' I said. 'What's hard to understand about that?'

108

Bailey's brow furrowed a bit. 'You weren't listening at all, were you?' he said.

'It's true, isn't it?'

'No! It's a creative project. It's very exciting.'

'Until all the evil starts.'

'It's a huge challenge. It's going to be amazing.'

'Well, whatever it is, I bet you'll kill a lot of fish.' I think my mind was on undersea villain's lairs.

Bailey looked a little uncomfortable at that, though, and sipped his drink deliberately. He liked to think of himself as a person with values, I knew that.

'I eat fish,' he said finally, just as Lydia dashed over and, with a completely uncharacteristic show of enthusiasm, started to gush madly about what a genius he was.

'That was amazing,' said Lydia. 'You know, I have a lot of project management in my background.'

'Really?' said Bailey to her. I must have let the surprise show on my face, because Lydia said, 'Oh, *sorry*,' in the most exaggeratedly concerned fashion. 'I forgot Evie wanted to get you *alone*.'

And she shot me a look and flounced off to where Dr Bennet was standing. He didn't seem to have quite the same problems making small talk with her as he did with me.

'What did she mean by that?' said Bailey, turning round to face me. His earnest grey eyes blinked, magnified behind his spectacles. We must be, I estimated, almost exactly the same height. I looked at him closely, stared him right in the eye.

My romantic history has been nothing to write home about, much like my holidays. I used to get horrible crushes on my brothers' friends, which they would always manage to find out about (which wasn't hard even for lard brains like them; I would just possibly conspire to be hanging around whenever Miles or Fraser or Mark or whoever it was that day was round kicking a football, playing Tekken or discussing how to pull the trampy-looking girl that worked at the local HMV), and then tease me absolutely mercilessly, including telling the boy, shouting his name in supposed fits of passion whenever I passed by and searching my bedroom for evidence of me writing my first name with said boy's surname.

They made such a good job of destroying my confidence it took a lot of reasonably comprehensive cider drinking and copping off with the easiest, grottiest boys in the neighbourhood (starter snogs I liked to think of them) to work my way up to an actual boyfriend, one who could cope with the reality that he would never ever get invited back to my house.

There was Greg, who already had a girlfriend, which, even though I knew this, didn't stop me making a complete fool of myself; Danny, who I went out with for three years, more for the novelty factor of having a real, live boyfriend rather than any huge love bond on either side; Bill, who was too old for me; and Jingo, of whom – well, I don't want to talk about Jingo. Let's never talk about Jingo. If I were to give advice, though, which I hate to do, it would be to try not to date men who live in trees. And are called Jingo.

Anyway. The older I got the more I was beginning to believe that the difference between the desperate, yearning way I'd felt about my crushes – those tall lanky boys with white grins and feet so big they looked like boats on the end of their legs – and the boys I'd actually ended up with, was a simple fact of life. And at the back of my mind I always liked to think, Well, there's Bailey. My mother would be delighted. And it would be nice to be with someone who liked me for a change, rather than someone who liked racing bicycles with a side order of me.

Even though it was ten years ago – a little more – that we'd had our clumsy attempt at a snog, I'd always considered that it meant he was there for me, and the amount of time we spent together was an indication of that.

And here he was, grown up, successful – so successful I was finding it hard to believe – standing, with a glass of champagne, in a beautiful room overlooking a stunning sunset on the Côte d'Azure. Right in front of me, all mine. Was it time to grasp the nettle?

'What?' he said, looking slightly amused and nervous all at once. I felt reckless, attractive in this room full of men, and suddenly decisive. People always said, didn't they, that you should end up with a friend, with someone you could talk to? That looks fade, but companionship is for ever, blah blah

blah? And we'd grown up together, Bailey and me. Maybe we were meant to be together.

'Uh, come out to the balcony with me. I want to look at the view,' I said. Bailey shrugged and acquiesced.

It took a long time, though, to cross the room. Everyone wanted to stop and ask Bailey something or congratulate him on the speech. My heart was beating fast – what was going to happen? What was I going to do? Should I say something? Just lean over and snog him? Should I take his glasses off first? Should I take my high heels off? My stomach was incredibly nervous. Did I have some gum in my bag? Oh, no. Well, I'd only been drinking champagne – and all that caviar, gah, yuk. I'd have to get rid of that. I did find a mint, and my hands were shaking so much I almost couldn't get it out of the wrapper.

Bailey was speaking to someone near the French doors – but he kept glancing at me to check where I was, so he obviously knew something was up. His face looked a little concerned. He must be wondering what was going on. I was slightly wondering myself. I took another gulp of champagne, which didn't mix well with the mint at all. But maybe tonight was meant to be . . .

I smiled at him in what I hoped was a slightly encouraging, come-hither manner (though it might have looked freaky, or a bit frightening), and stepped out onto the balcony alone. The sun was setting over the mild-looking blue sea, and everything looked tinted with roses in the soft, warm evening air that seemed to caress my skin like a shawl. The breeze smelled of flowers and lemons, with an undercurrent of car fumes on hot road, from the busy route behind the hotel, and out in the harbour, white and blue boats bobbed up and down; some huge, some just pottering about, one whisking a water-skier behind it, the wake a paper-cut of white in the blue. It was beautiful. I sipped my drink and sighed. This was more like it.

My attention was drawn to the beautifully tended garden that led towards the cliffs. It was laid out with per-fectly straight flowerbeds, and topiary lined the immaculate sheets of lawn – but there was somebody down there. No, two people. No, make that one person and one dog. Oh, goodness. It was Tom, and a red setter. Heaven knows where he'd found the dog, but the huge beautiful creature was bouncing about gloriously, its russet hair streaming in the breeze – and that was just Tom. They were having a wonderful time, running about on the perfect lawns, wrestling with a stick and rolling about together before leaping up to tear across the green.

I couldn't help but smile; Tom looked about nine years old. There was a gracious lack of self-consciousness to his movements that had been entirely lacking in the slightly nervous, studious demeanour I'd noticed when we'd talked. He looked graceful too, even lolloping around with a dog; his legs and arms were long and sporty-looking.

It felt like I watched him for a long time. It's very rarely, especially if you live in a city, that you get to study somebody. Everyone is nervous, everyone is so ready to believe you're a mugger or a terrorist; and there's never any space, you're never so far away from everyone that you're not conscious of being watched, of the proximity of millions and millions of other people all around, cramming into every nook and cranny. But here, despite the roomful of people behind me, there was space, and calm, and peace and quiet. So this was what money bought. The money I saw every day on Harley Street was pushy, trashy and flashy, desperate to get itself noticed, but I saw now that it could be tranquillity, and beauty. I felt very happy, for some reason, and no longer nervous at all.

At that moment, Tom turned round. I thought he was about to see me and nearly ducked behind the stone balustrade, but he was looking up behind me, further up into the hotel. He seemed to wave and then, suddenly, caught my eye. He looked surprised – so did I, I imagine. Then, after a split second, he grinned, showing white healthy-looking teeth, and I grinned back. He came bounding up to the balcony, the dog a little way behind. His head was level with my feet, so I crouched down.

'Is this your girlfriend?' I said, reaching to pet the dog. Why did I say that? What a terrible thing to say. At worst, I'd just accused him of bestiality, ugly-looking girlfriends at best.

'Second cousin,' he said, smiling at me. 'What are you doing out here?'

'I came to give you this,' I found myself saying, and passed over the glass of champagne I'd originally picked up for Bailey. What was the matter with me? I felt like some kind of wild tramp.

'Thank you,' he said, giving me a direct look. There was a tiny bead of sweat just visible at the top of his hairless chest. I suddenly wanted to lick it.

That wasn't right. I mean, I was just about to see my oldest friend, the person who'd been with me through thick and thin . . . I couldn't possibly be thinking about licking other people's chests. That was just ridiculous. I mean . . .

'What are you thinking about?' said Tom. 'You look like you're trying to do quadratic equations in your head.'

'Are those the extra-tricky ones?' I asked.

'I'm good at them though,' he said. I looked at him. He had the same jokey-looking smile on his face, but it was impossible to read what was in his eyes.

'Did you bring this dog all the way to France?' I asked.

'No.' He smiled, 'He's . . .uh. I don't know, I just met him in the garden.'

Tom rubbed the creature's head with a hard but tender stroke. The dog closed its eyes in pleasure. I suddenly found myself jealous of the dog.

No! This wasn't right! This wasn't right at all! I must just be carried away with the champagne, and the sunset, and the beautiful surroundings and the romance of it all. But sod romance. You should settle down with your best friend, everyone said it. Courteney Cox said it, lots of my romance novels said it, bloody Dr Miriam Stoppard said it. You should end up with your best friend. That was the way to build something enduring, something wonderful.

'What about,' said Tom, 'if you scramble up on top of the banister and I lift you down and we can play in the garden?'

I eyed up the slightly crumbling balustrade, considering it. Considering what it would feel like to have a pair of strong arms around me, his long body . . . oh, God, was I drunk again?

'Hi, there,' said Bailey, arriving on the balcony in a flurry of papers. 'Sorry I took so long. Now, what was it you wanted to talk about?'

Chapter Seven

It wasn't Bailey's fault that he was caught at such an unfortunate angle. It wasn't his fault at all that I was crouched down by his feet – not a position he usually found me in. And it wasn't his fault that before I straightened up, I couldn't help noticing what he was wearing on his feet.

I never normally noticed what Bailey wore. He hadn't gone through a big teenage transformation, dying his hair one week and dressing entirely in black the other, like I had. In fact he'd pretty much gone from school uniform to tidy, button-down preppy-looking shirts without changing noticeably at all. He didn't wear a tie to work, which, for ages, I'd taken to mean that he was just a backroom boy but in fact, as I was discovering, just meant he was too big a cheese for anyone to have any say in what he wore at all. And dressing exactly the same your entire life has the huge advantage of never making you look any older.

Anyway, here I was, crouched on the stone floor of a balcony for the most ridiculous reason – i.e. I wanted to go play with another man, and his dog – when I noticed something. Bailey's shoes.

Well, I call them shoes. They were a bit more difficult to pin down than that. The sole was thick rubber, as, perhaps, in a climbing boot or snowboarding shoe. But the top was brown suede, like in a pair of Hush Puppies. But there were thick black laces like in – well, like I'd never seen. The entire effect was ghastly, a horrible mishmash that suggested someone trying to buy built-up shoes but who couldn't quite bring themselves to go the whole hog.

I glanced upwards. Bailey was glancing down at me, blinking through his thick glasses.

'What's going on? Did you find a glass slipper in the garden?'

'No,' I said, scrabbling up. I could feel my face go red hot. And I sensed Tom watching us closely from down below.

'Well, what is it then?'

He looked at me intensely. I stared at his shoes. Was it likely, really, that I was in love with someone who was just a friend? That I could make myself in love with someone that I really just liked, just because I was lonely?

Or was I just getting desperate and going for anything with a pulse, because people said we'd be 'good together'?

'I've forgotten,' I mumbled. 'I think I just wanted to say well done.'

'Out here?' He frowned. 'I should probably get back in. I don't like unprotected UV rays on my scalp.'

'No,' I said. 'You wouldn't.'

He turned to go then paused for just a moment and looked back at me. I didn't quite know what to make of that look. Had he guessed? Did he know? Was he really still into me after all these years (as I liked to think)?

He stopped. 'Are you having a good time?' he said.

'I . . . I think so,' I replied, finding my voice had gone a bit strange.

'Good,' he said. 'Well, I suppose I'm going to head on out to dinner with Lydia . . .'

Lydia! Oh for Christ's sake. OK, maybe I didn't want to snog – at this particular moment in time – someone who wore schizophrenic shoes, but the last thing I wanted was that evil princess getting her mitts on him.

'Oh, yeah,' I said. 'I'll call you . . . to catch up.'

This was a complete lie, I had no intention of calling anyone out here. I'd got the cheapest price plan at the available time, which meant to call overseas was effectively the same cost as the interplanetary conversation in the old hit song 'Clouds Across the Moon', when she can only afford to call her boyfriend for three minutes once a year.

Bailey nodded, turned round and headed back into the

room, where I could already see groups of people opening up to welcome him in.

Turning back I realised that, stupidly, by turning down dinner with Bailey and the rest I'd made it look completely like I was up for, well, something else. If I'd been doing what the books tell you, I should have immediately left with Bailey – arm in arm probably – thus rendering Tom mad with jealousy and willing to lay jewels at my feet until I capitulated etc. etc. (By the way, has anyone ever met any of these guys? Where are they? The ones I meet all just tend to be . . . well, drunk, I suppose, now I think about.) On the other hand, if I wanted to be with Bailey, I suppose I'd just done exactly the right thing. It was very confusing.

Sure enough, as I turned round I swear I could see a bit of a smirk in Tom's eyes. Bugger it! But then if I pretended I had other plans now he might believe me and I'd be all on my own without dinner with *anyone,* which really *would* be disappointing, and the waste of a beautiful evening, on my holiday.

'So . . .' said Tom casually, still rubbing the dog. God, I don't think I'd found a redhead so attractive since David Caruso. And the sunlight made his hair more gold than red anyway, I told myself. Disliking redheads was a ridiculous prejudice, like making preferences on the colour of skin and totally not based on fact at all. *And* I liked his freckles too.

I realised I was drooling a bit when he added, 'Do you have plans for the evening?'

'Well, I thought I might have a quiet night in, you know . . .'

I thought of what a quiet night in would be like in my tomb-like hotel room with no air conditioning and the tiny window completely covered to keep out the noise. Like being buried alive in a coffin, I supposed. Well, think positive.

Tom raised his eyebrows. 'Oh, that's a shame,' he said. 'Because I still have to walk this dog, and I wondered if you'd like to join me.'

I tried to look calm and collected.

'Well, I suppose it's on the way back,' I said. (Coolly, I thought.)

Tom looked confused. 'Actually, walks can go pretty much either way. Are you along the beach?'

'Well, kind of in a beach-hill type of direction, I suppose,' I muttered.

'Good idea,' said Tom. 'Come on.'

And we walked through the most lovely rose garden, which led down a secret flight of stone steps to a wrought-iron gate that opened directly out onto the sand. The dog bounced on joyously ahead.

'Seriously, whose dog is it?' I said, taking off my shoes as we hit the sand. 'We're not going to get done for dogknapping, are we?'

'No,' said Tom. 'I just ran into someone I knew and offered to borrow their dog. He's called Cachou.'

'I thought you didn't know anyone here,' I said. 'I thought that's why you had to follow me about.'

'I have to follow *you* about,' said Tom, 'otherwise you won't have a clue what's going on.'

'Yeah, yeah, yeah,' I said.

The cool water felt absolutely delicious on my bare feet and I stood in the lilac-coloured waves enjoying the calm in the air.

'Ta dah!' said Tom, as if out of nowhere producing a clearly pinched bottle of champagne from behind his back, and we swigged from it happily as we wandered up the beach that ran alongside the Croisette, looking at the fancy cars and hotels which seemed a long way away from the quiet peace of the water's edge. It was so easy to talk to Tom, he was so likeable and funny. For the first time since I'd got to France I felt unstressed and properly relaxed, like I was having a real holiday. Cachou bounded joyfully around as we tossed him the occasional stick, and sometimes our hands brushed together, but neither of us pulled away. I was trying to catch sight of Tom out of the corner of my eye as he told me a very funny story about old ladies falling over in Norwich (it was funnier than it sounds). Deep in my stomach, I couldn't quite believe it. Come to France, meet a handsome (if ginger, nothing wrong with that) young doctor, have romantic strolls along the beach . . . coupled with all the champagne I felt entirely lightheaded; daring and dramatic and not my normal moany self at all.

I mean, things like this just didn't usually happen to me. But why shouldn't they? Why should Paris Hilton get every bloody bit of romance on earth? How come Girls Aloud got all the lush blokes? Statistically, it had to happen to someone, didn't it? So why shouldn't it happen to me?

'You're miles away,' said Tom, and I realised he was looking at me. My hair whipped around my face – it felt heavy, and not too frizzy. Salt water was actually quite good for my hair, it made it look thicker. The champagne and the evening air made me feel heady and free. I looked at him.

'I'm not, actually,' I said, quite boldly for me. 'I'm right here.'

And, as we turned back to walking up the beach again, he tentatively took my hand, and I let him. I hoped my hand didn't feel clammy – his felt big and warm and reassuring. Oooh! Ooh! Holiday romance alert!

We were reaching the end of the beach, or rather, a big piece of land was in the way of the next beach. The beaches just go on and on and on, all the way to Spain and Italy. Cachou was having a splash around in the water. Since Tom had taken my hand conversation had slowed and now it stopped completely. He led me gently towards an overhang of rock, looking at me questioningly to make sure I knew what he meant. I looked back at him, making it clear that I did.

I love the moment before the first time you kiss someone, but after you know you're going to. It feels like everything slows down as you come into the orbit of someone else's body; it's like there are sparks that jump from your skin to his as you get closer and closer together. And it was like that with Tom. A delicious sense of anticipation followed by his putting his big hand on my face, which I liked very much. Then he leant closer and closer and I tipped my head up towards him and we kissed. And somehow I'd already known that he'd be a good kisser. As I gave myself up to him completely, I knew that this was the best holiday I'd ever had.

Minutes, hours later – it must have been hours, it was dark and there was even a chill in the air – we reluctantly pulled apart. Cachou had started to howl piteously and it was really getting late. The bottle of champagne was empty, but I was more drunk on lust; Tom's eyes were glazed too, and we clung to one another a little desperately.

'I have to go,' I said. Frankly that was the last thing I felt like doing, but lusty as I felt, I didn't want to go too far on our first date . . . oh, all right. Honestly, I just didn't want to get sand in my pants. I really liked this man, and I wanted it to be special and, frankly, the risk of having a jellyfish sting me on the bum made me feel it would be anything but.

'Really?' said Tom, looking wickedly at me.

'Really,' I said, trying to look like I was a modest picture of chastity, rather than someone frightened of getting bitten by a crab in a sensitive area. 'We could . . .'

I trailed off, hoping he'd immediately say, 'Hey, let's take the day off together tomorrow and run through the sand and eat ice cream and do all sorts of things that if you saw them in a film would make a bit of a montage,' but he didn't. He said, 'Well, *you* may not have to go to lots of boring lectures tomorrow, but I do.'

'Oh, who'd know?' I said. 'Just write down, "*Tighten skin with Sellotape*" and send it in. That's all they'll be saying anyway. "Chop into skin with great big knife."'

'They're doing a seminar on vaginal modification,' said Tom musingly, caressing my back.

'Anyone who lets a scalpel anywhere near there needs therapy, not bloody plastic surgery,' I grumbled, and suddenly, the moment was gone. Amazing how just one little mention of designer vaginas was enough to ruin the mood. Tom twitched his eyebrows.

'Well . . .' I said.

'We should get back,' he said. And I felt low. But then he added, 'Or maybe . . .' and pulled me back into his arms. Just a little while longer.

Chapter Eight

I opened my eyes, feeling a burst of unaccustomed happiness. What was it again? Oh, yes! I was on holiday in France with a gorgeous, if slightly freckly bloke after me! Joy, joy, joy! I bounced up. It was going to be a perfect day on the Côte d'Azure. I figured I'd go out for breakfast – I had some time off! There was some assessment thing, but I was free to go and finish up reading the briefing (or, in my case, start) and make sure everything was ready for the party tonight – which I'd already done! Well, I'd phoned the number of the party organisers, and they'd said, '*Oui*, madame, everything is ready,' so you couldn't do much more than that, could you?

The sky was clear with a few perky-looking clouds bouncing around in the ether, but it was early enough that there was still a cool breeze flowing through the streets as I bounced down in my new espadrilles, heading for the shore. The restaurants were sloshing out and getting ready for the day, and the little shops were busy.

Now this is how life should be, I thought, looking at the bustling street market as I approached the beach, clutching gigantic almond croissants in my hands. I had *meant* to go in and ask for '*un croissant aux amandes, s'il vous plait*,' and had been practising it under my breath until I actually got to the boulangerie. There was a huge queue and everyone was yelling and chatting at a ridiculous speed, all at once, and I lost my place in the queue about nine times and by the time I got to the front I was so flustered and nervous I just stabbed my finger in the direction of the biggest ones they had and grunted, like I was a helper monkey that had been trained to do the shopping. Still, I'd accidentally bought two.

I decided to forgo the umbrella option when I found out that to hire one for the day would cost fifteen euros, which, frankly, was my wine money. So I found a nice spot down by the water's edge, where the sand was deliciously cool, and took a sunbed. I dabbled my hand in the water as it lapped around my toes and let my mind drift to seeing Tom at the party tonight. I'd wear my new red dress – or would it clash with his hair? No, it would be fine. The dress was THAT good. So, I'd walk on to the yacht, and . . .

*

AARGH! Oh, God! Where was I? What time was it? Why couldn't I move? I felt pinned to the sunbed. Trying to move was agony. Checking my watch – which, I noticed, had an ominously white patch of skin underneath it – I saw it was afternoon. Oh, God, I'd fallen asleep on the beach! In the middle of the day! The sea had receded and I was stranded, spreadeagled on the sunbed in full view. Gingerly I tried to raise myself up. Ow ow ow ow. This was *not* in the holiday plan.

I trudged painfully up the beach. It had taken ten minutes to stand up. My back was on fire. So much for my morning off. The strap of my beach bag was agony across my shoulders, and I'd have to find a shop to buy some aftersun. I didn't know what that was in French. *Après soleil?* That would surely be too obvious. It was probably called something like *Oui, c'est moi, le complet idiot.* I sighed and traipsed on, feeling entirely sorry for myself, and a little sick.

Picking its way gingerly down the promenade steps was a bizarre-looking figure, even for here. I'd already been amazed by the women on the beach. I'd always thought that beachwear meant a bikini or swimsuit, flip-flops and a sarong for chubby moments. And I'd assumed that those articles in magazines that told you which jewellery to wear with which bikini and how to take your beach look into your evening look were just made up bollocks to sell suncream (and which therefore, in retrospect, I ought to have paid attention to).

But no, here, for the first time in my life I was witnessing women – gorgeous, tanned, young women, or scrawny, liver-spotted older women – actually wearing high heels. On the sand. High heels, on the sand. Really, it should be an Olympic sport, or a circus act. 'Come watch the amazing ladies – who can walk in stilettos *on the sand*!'

Not only this but they were indeed bedecked in jew-ellery – and not just any jewellery, or a couple of beaded necklaces picked up from the local market. Oh, no. This was full diamond earrings, gold necklaces and bracelets (the gold, I noticed, had the unfortunate effect of making old brown skin look even older than it was; the smooth surface of the precious metal only pointing out the crêpe-paper effect of the skin beside it.

And it didn't stop there. There were turbans, with jewels in the middle of them, like a maharajah, or Elizabeth Taylor in the seventies. There were ankle bracelets and toe rings. There were bikinis made of gold, or sequins, or what looked like two pieces of cheese wire. Having always thought of the beach as a place to relax, I now realised how wrong I had been. These women couldn't lie down or get wet. It was very very strange.

And the woman in front of me – unless I was becoming delirious, not entirely out of the question – was the strangest of all. Her hair was sprayed into a huge puff at the front which gave it the texture of candyfloss. She was wear-ing full make-up, including bright blue eyeshadow and pale pink lipstick, even though it was incredibly hot. Her bikini was entirely studded with what looked like Swarovski crystals, which glistened and caught the sun. The top half was simply two triangles which actually perched on top of the pointy breasts rather than supported them – the breasts were so solid they didn't look in the slightest need of support. And the bottoms were so narrowly cut you could tell exactly what explicit instructions she'd had to give her waxer.

'EVIE!' shouted the vision. Oh, God, now I really was hallucinating. Where were five hundred doctors when I needed them?

The figure tottered over on the ridiculously high shoes, and lifted up the humongous pair of sunglasses it was wearing.

'It's me! Kelly!'

Christ on a bike, so it was.

'I was just going to the beach!' she squealed.

'What – while dressed for church?'

Kelly lifted up her huge sunglasses (with some effort) and peered at me. 'Oh, ma Gawd, Evie, what happened to you?'

'What, this? Oh, nothing,' I said. 'I got attacked by a bear.'

'Getting too much sun on the first day is *very dangerous*,' she scolded. 'You should have been going to three sunbeds a week, like I do.'

'Well, I'm done now,' I said.

'Your back's done,' said Kelly.

'Thanks.'

She examined me closely. 'You know, I think that's going to come up nicely brown.'

'I've got second-degree burns, Kell. I'm on my way to hospital.'

'Yes, but it'll be worth it now, won't it?'

'No, it won't. I'm a div. Where's JJ?'

'John Jr . . . he said he had some business to do.' She looked a bit embarrassed. 'He was a bit . . . OTT last night.'

'I'm used to it.' I thought back, wincing at the memory, as well as my back.

'In front of that nice doc too. He was a bit of a hunk.'

'Dr Maitland? You are joking. He wears three-piece suits.'

She raised her eyebrows. 'Oh, Evie, you have to introduce me to your docs. I have to do something about these wrinkles.'

'You're saying this as you prepare to baste yourself in cooking oil and lie in the sun?'

'You're one to talk,' she said. 'I know. You've got to struggle to be beautiful.'

I laughed. It really wasn't Kelly's fault she'd promised herself to John Jr 'for fatter, for thinner'.

'OK,' I said. 'There's a yacht party tonight. Wall to wall docs. Fancy it?'

Her eyes went wide. 'Yeah!'

I gave her the details. 'OK. I'm just off to call an ambulance.'

'And I'm off to self-baste like a chicken. Mwah!'

*

I paused only to stumble into a pharmacy, where I simply showed them my back and got exceedingly worried at the look of terrified shock on the sales assistant's face (*Mon dieu!*). They piled me up with creams and ointments that took a ridiculously large chunk out of my holiday budget, but by now I was feeling a bit shaky so I just nodded. They offered me some pills too but I'd heard that in France you had to take all pills up the arse, so I shook my head.

At least my hotel room was dark. Very dark, in fact, and stuffy too, but I didn't care about that right now. I examined myself in the bathroom mirror. There wasn't even a proper bath there, just one of those crappy half-baths.

Oh, God. I looked . . . well, I looked like two halves of a person stuck together. My face was half milk-white, with a few unavoidable freckles popping up here and there, and half bright red. Plus some really obvious 'I was snogging for four hours down the beach on holiday' stubble rash all over my face and chin. From the back I looked like I'd been tied to a mast of a pirate ship and whipped solidly for six hours. I groaned, running my wrists under the cold water. I felt kind of fine just as long as no portion of my back touched anything.

My arms felt like big plump sausages that needed pricking, to let all the juice ooze out – wow, that was disgusting. For a second I thought I was going to be sick. Then I fell onto the bed face first and, thankfully, into a deep sleep.

*

If there's anything worse than waking up in the middle of the day when you don't know what time it is, sticky, sore and headachey in a hot airless little room, I don't know what it is. How could I have gone from cheerful to cross in such a short time? I felt sweaty and horrible.

I found my pharmacy bag, which I'd forgotten about, and took it in the shower, which made me feel a bit more human and a bit less like a dirty, old, stuffed toy full of gunk. In fact, I had just groaned – perhaps a little too graphically – when, after the briefest of knocks, the door was pushed open and Lydia stormed in. Why did I give her the address?

'Oh, *sorry*,' she announced, in a way that clearly meant she wasn't sorry in the slightest. 'I didn't realise you were . . .uh, busy. Oh, my God, look at you.'

I'd turned round to put on some clothes and of course she'd caught sight of me.

'Your neck . . . your back . . . it's *everywhere*.'

She sounded absolutely delighted.

'Yes, I know,' I said. 'Good, isn't it?'

'Is that what you think?' her voice took on a very fake concerned tone. 'But, Evie, you know, burning your skin can lead to all sorts of unpleasant consequences.'

'Oh, it's not burnt,' I said. 'It just goes that colour.' I finished putting my bra on, with difficulty. 'Doesn't hurt a bit.'

When she saw I plainly wasn't going to get in to it with her, she changed her tack.

'Well, anyway, I just came over to see where you've been all day. The reception is in twenty minutes.'

I couldn't believe I'd slept the entire day. No wonder I felt groggy and thick in the head.

'Oh, *God*,' I wailed. 'But I've got a date! Shit! Shit!'

Lydia's face took on a look of consternation. As it did so I realised a little something about our relationship – normally, I would go round to her office, complain about my shitty life and she'd smile superciliously and let me yabber on. I'd thought this was because she was nice and a good listener. In fact, I now realised, my moaning made her feel superior about herself. It did neither of us any good. She could sit and polish her nails whilst listening to a stream of consciousness from me that reassured her that although she was only working in reception and not yet the wife of a billionaire, she was nonetheless still winning in some hypothetical life competition. Meanwhile I just got whingier and whingier. Ugh.

'*You?*' she said now. 'Who with? Did you hook up with a waiter? You want to watch the waiters round here, Evie. They're infamous for loving and leaving . . .'

'With one of the doctors, actually,' I said. I hadn't really meant to say anything about it at all – for once, I was going to be a quietly dignified person who was reticent about her private life, damnit! – but I couldn't help myself. Anything to get that smug look off her face. 'The young one, you know.'

'The ginger?' she said, but I could tell I'd got to her. Tom was by far the youngest and best-looking doc there. Well, Dr Bennet was probably better looking, and Dr Maitland wasn't as old as he looked, but apart from that there wasn't much in it; most of the docs were over forty and either looked like stereotypical doctors on television – white hair, little round glasses, concerned expressions (trade secret: they do it on purpose to look reassuring) – or like they were using too much of their own product.

'Mmm,' I sniffed. 'Strawberry blonde, actually.'

'Ever heard you shouldn't crap on your own doorstep?' Lydia asked sweetly. 'It's so unprofessional.'

Well, that was rich coming from a woman who had already registered the website www.huntandtrapyourdoctorhusband.com.

'Aren't you supposed to be working?' Lydia asked suspiciously.

'Yes, well . . . Dr Maitland decided I should be in more of an advisory capacity after the whole profiterole incident.'

I turned to my suitcase. What the hell was I going to wear that wasn't going to cause me terrible agony? My lovely red dress would just make me look like a burns victim. Alas, I ended up in a black vest to go with my pretty, if outdated, orange skirt. The orange was about the same hue as my skin, and the vest felt painful already, but what else could I do?

I looked at myself properly in the mirror. Oh, God. Oh, God. Oh, God. I was a monster from the black lagoon.

'So Dr McCarrots loves the way you tan, does he?' said Lydia sweetly. 'Wow, you two sound really compatible.'

I must have been sleeping on the lounger with the right side of my face down, because the left side was completely red and the right completely white. I looked like Janus. The effect was startling; there was practically a line down the middle of my nose.

'Oh, Christ, I can't go,' I said, not even caring that Lydia was there. 'I'm not going. I'll stay in and play hard to get.'

'But you can't,' said Lydia. 'It's the yacht, remember?'

Oh, God. I couldn't miss it. And I had to tell my mum I'd been on a yacht.

'They can do it without me,' I moaned. 'Say I'm sick.'

Lydia sniffed. 'But what about your sister?' she said suddenly. 'I saw her at the beach. You couldn't miss her.'

'She's not my sister,' I said.

'She was really looking forward to meeting up tonight. Seemed really excited.'

She glanced out of the tiny window.

'And you don't want to play *too* hard to get. After all, the conference is only on another two days, and there's lots of models round here. Although of course I know what a great advocate you are of inner beauty. I'm sure thingy – whatever his name is – will see yours.'

Her mouth twitched.

'OK, OK, OK. All right, let's get this over with,' I said, and we headed for the door.

*

The lights of the harbour gleamed, bobbing up and down on the scented airy breeze, which felt good on my overheated body. Maybe with a couple of cocktails I'd feel all right. We passed by the little boats, the fishing boats and pleasure cruisers, which had names like *The Office* (ha ha! I'm just at 'the office' etc.) and *The Other Woman*. I reckoned they were owned by idiot accountants from Surrey – or the foreign equivalent – with more money than sense who frankly didn't deserve them.

Then we went past the slightly larger yachts, with tables and chairs placed out on the rear deck, and vases of flowers stuck on top of them. Slightly stiff middle-aged couples sat there, drinking gin and tonics and looking awkward, even though they were obviously there to be looked at by the promenaders strolling up and down having a sticky beak before their evening meal.

'They should wave,' I said. 'Like the queen.'

'They're all too drunk,' said Lydia in a haughty voice. 'If they stood up to wave they'd fall in the sea.'

'Know lots of yachting types, do you?' I asked her. I was horribly nervous. I hadn't heard from Tom all day, and he had my number. I mean, he could at least have texted me or something . . . maybe he'd woken up this morning and thought it had all been a terrible mistake? And let's face it, I was hardly going to change his mind looking like this now, was I?

'A few,' said Lydia, looking contemptuously at a boat emblazoned with gold curlicues everywhere and entitled *Paradise IV*.

'Well, you do get around a bit, don't you?' I said, betraying my nerves.

We passed on by the medium-sized boats and came up to a gated area manned by a man wearing very smart shiny boots and a cap. I felt a bit nervous; there wasn't anyone else around and it didn't entirely look like we were meant to be there. Lydia, however, flounced up to the bouncer and rattled something out in loud French. I was impressed despite myself.

'I do not understand you,' said the guard. 'Speek more slowly, pliz.'

Excellent! Looking furious Lydia held out her card.

'Invitation,' she hissed. 'Party. *Comprendez?*'

'Of course, madame,' said the guard, raising the barrier with a slightly supercilious smile.

Now we were in a completely different world.

'It's called the *Quai des Milliardaires*,' said Lydia, obviously anxious to maintain her French superiority. 'That means . . .'

'Millionaire's Quay?' I said.

'No, actually,' said Lydia, delighted. '"Milliardaire" actually means "billionaire".'

But I couldn't listen. I could hardly speak; I was just gazing at the sights before me. The yachts here . . . well, they weren't like boats at all. They looked, to me, like huge shimmering palaces. Strung with lights and gleaming; their hulls, white and blue, shone like they'd been polished with toothbrushes, which they probably had been. I could see helicopters sitting on top of the boats; huge salons stretching onto goodness knows where; what looked like jacuzzis on huge decks.

What must it be like, I wondered, to have one of these. One of these great, huge, luxurious toys to play with. What would you do? I supposed you would just pay someone to take it anywhere in the world you wanted to go. Or you could just go out into the middle of the sea, and stop, and dive into the clear water with no one around you for miles and miles and miles.

You could have parties and invite hundreds of friends. Mind you, I didn't have hundreds of friends. Maybe if you were rich enough to have a yacht you automatically got loads of friends thrown in as a job lot. It would have to work like that, because presumably to earn enough money to buy one of these things you wouldn't have time to make your own.

'Wow,' I said. 'I can't believe we're going on one of these.'

'Oh, they're all pretty much the same,' said Lydia, trying to look blasé. Oh, for goodness' sake. I know she desperately wanted to pass herself off as good rich-man fodder and every-thing but this was ridiculous.

'So you're a yacht-hopper, are you?' I said, using a term I'd picked up from *Hello!* magazine. 'You've been on loads of boats as big as this?' I indicated the boat in front of us, which was four storeys high and looked more like a luxury hotel than anything actually built for the high seas.

Lydia shrugged. 'I've been on boats.'

'Boats. Big boats. Just as big as this one?'

'Well, not quite *that* one.'

I pointed to another, slightly smaller sleek-looking white craft. 'OK, as big as that one then?'

'I wasn't measuring.'

'Come off it,' I said. 'You've never been on a yacht, have you? Your dad's fishing trip to the Isle of Wight? The car ferry? Have you been on a booze cruise? Did you get two hundred Regal King Size and stock up on bottles of Malibu?'

'Stop it,' said Lydia.

'Did you roll on, roll off?' I said.

Lydia stuck her nose in the air and tried to walk in front of me like she wasn't with me at all. But I was perking up.

She pulled up, finally, in front of one of the largest boats in the marina. It was a ship, really, and towered over us, level after level. It was lit up entirely with tiny lights illuminating its lines, with a huge ornate staircase at the back. People were everywhere and we could hear the tinkling of glasses and polite chit-chat in the air. I felt excited and nervous all at once; I'd never been anywhere like this before (though I'd seen *Titanic* a few times). It was so glamorous and elegant and . . . I swallowed hard. Well, they'd just have to deal with me too. I could be glamorous and elegant. When half my face wasn't hanging off, obviously. But I could manage it. I was going to shimmy onto this boat and wave to Tom like I came to parties on yachts every day of my life. We were going to drink champagne and dance the night away. I saw us, dreamily, in each other's arms as he whisked me about to romantic orchestral music. Of course, in my mind's eye I was wearing a big *Strictly Come Dancing* dress and could actually dance – as could he – but it perked me up nonetheless. I felt slightly better when I saw the name of the boat was *Let's Have a Party*. Something that naff couldn't be that scary, surely?

Lydia looked like she was making her mind up about something too.

'OK,' she said, looking around at me. With the lights reflected off the water behind us she looked wonderful: enchanting and mysterious. I'm about as mysterious as a chicken pie but hopefully the romance of the evening would do something for all of us.

'Let's go,' she said. 'That's a billionaire's yacht full of doctors and free champagne. Frankly, if we can't pull in that we don't deserve the title "doctor's receptionist".'

And she stalked off towards the gangplank.

After removing our shoes (de rigueur apparently) and flashing our invites at a young, terrifyingly hearty-looking young man in a pure white uniform, we scampered aboard. The deck was thronged with people, and waitresses carrying canapés and champagne were circulating amongst the crowd. I relaxed: obviously they'd been fine sorting things out without me. You'd think these folk having spent all their time together would be short of things to talk about, but no. I looked out for Bailey, which was quite difficult amongst the tall women and loud men. The noise levels were increasing. I noticed there was a band; a jazz band with men playing clarinets and trombones, and wearing interestingly patterned ties. Nobody was dancing yet, though, and it made things very cramped and incredibly noisy. Heavy perfume fell on the air and without my high heels on I felt squat and invisible, especially next to all the glamorous women in their peacock dresses; turquoise, green and yellow, shimmering over taut, nut-brown bodies.

'Hello!' came a familiar voice at my elbow. Then, as I turned round to greet him, 'Christ on a bike, what happened to you?'

Suddenly, I noticed lots of people looking at me and making murmuring remarks to one another. There was almost a gap in the crowd opening up for us. I felt extremely red and hot all of a sudden.

'Nothing,' I replied sulkily.

'Did you fall asleep in the sun?' asked Bailey, with his PhD in stating the bloody obvious. 'Don't you realise it's dangerous?'

'Really?' I said. I guessed I was going to have to answer these kinds of questions all night. I'd hoped the soft lighting and heavy make-up would have covered me up sufficiently, but obviously not. 'I had no idea. You'd think they'd give out some kind of warning about a fiery ball of molten gas.'

'OK, OK,' said Bailey. 'You're being very sensitive about it.'

'That's because it's very sensitive, but there's absolutely nothing I can do about it now.'

'Oh,' said a large doctor from Ghana. 'Look at this. You should have kept your skin out of the sun.'

Another doctor leant in to have a look. 'Yes, you should protect your skin in the sun . . . there are these things called UVA, you know, they're like rays.'

'All right, all right,' I said, grabbing a glass of wine off a passing waitress. 'Wow, what amazing geniuses you've gathered here.'

'Oh, come back, Evie,' said Bailey, turning round to the doctors apologetically. 'She's always so moody.'

But I was pushing my way through the throng to a narrow set of stairs set in the side of the ship. I could see through the window a completely over-the-top salon, filled with gold antiques and an indoor waterfall. It looked dreadful and quite good fun, but the lighting was even brighter, and I didn't really feel like being a medical specimen.

Upstairs there was a formal dining room, with a huge buffet table being set out with seafood and fruit and fresh bread. But I kept on climbing the stairs. Finally, I was on the top deck – the entire top of the ship. There was a large jacuzzi, covered over with an awning, though I wouldn't take bets on that remaining on for long.

I crept along the side of the boat, holding the railings. I could hear the murmur of voices. One, French-accented, was saying, 'But how much then?'

The other, to my surprise, was Dr Bennet.

'Look, it doesn't matter, OK? Once we're at sea, the sky is the limit.'

'The limit. That is not the exact figure I'm looking for from my British partners, *n'est-ce pas*? It's sloppy.'

I didn't have a clue what they were talking about, but cleared my throat loudly so I wasn't sneaking up on them.

'Uh, hello,' said Dr Bennet, looking startled. The other man made a quick farewell and vanished into the shadows on the other side of the boat. 'What are you doing here?'

'I just came to get some fresh air.'

'Well, I hope . . . yes. Have a good party. I must go.'

And he turned on his heel and walked off. It wasn't like him to be so abrupt. Had I done something wrong?

Worried, I headed to the very front of the boat (I know there's a name for it but I don't know what it is) where there was a cluster of seating; moulded plastic benches with plump blue- and yellow-striped cushions over them. They were, thankfully, completely deserted, which, after the cluster and clamour of downstairs, was a huge relief. I padded over to them and sank down in the deep plush cushions with a sigh of relief. I'd wait here, remarshal my forces and . . .

'Owww! Get off!' came a voice.

Shocked, I stumbled and found myself rolling right off the cushions and onto the deck of the boat with a thud.

'Who the hell's that?' I said.

'Well, I could ask the same question, seeing as an elephant

just dropped out of the sky,' came a cross, familiar voice. I sat up.

'Tom?'

'Uh . . .'

He sat bolt upright in the cushions with an almost comical look of disbelief on his face.

'Evie?'

I saw myself through his eyes. Sprawled, dishevelled and completely red in the face. I compared myself to all the elegant girls flitting about downstairs like they were born to yachts and inwardly cursed.

'Hi,' I said.

Tom looked just as discombobulated as I felt.

'Uh . . . uh . . . sorry I called you an elephant.'

'Yeah,' I said, 'you should be.'

'But it felt like you fell from the sky.'

'I gracefully jetéd from over *here*.'

'Oh.' He looked down.

'What are you doing?'

'Uh, nothing,' he said guiltily. I saw his hand grab his mobile phone.

'Who are you calling?'

He still looked unsettled. 'Uh . . . you?'

I grinned at him and he smiled shyly back at me.

'You look . . .'

Then his eyes must have adjusted to the light. 'Well . . . Christ, were you out in the sun?'

'Yes, yes, yes, blah blah blah,' I said. 'Do you kiss burns victims?'

'I don't know . . . are you crispy?' He looked anxious suddenly. 'But shouldn't we also be getting down to the party?'

'You looked like you were up here hiding from the party.'

'I was, but I was only . . . waiting for you.'

Well, obviously he wasn't, but I figured I'd take it anyway.

'Well, lucky I threw myself on you then.'

'Yes, I was thinking that.'

And then he drew me close and gave me a kiss.

Magazines say that you should just be confident then you'll give off an inner beauty that will make you shine far more than some boring model or something. I have never for even a millisecond thought that that might be true. Most men will take a brain-dead slug who looks like Cameron Diaz over a pig-faced personality a hundred times out of a hundred. Nonetheless I definitely felt a little taller and a little better as we headed back into the crowd, me with good-looking Tom at my side.

'Hey!' I said cheerily to Lydia, who was in intense conversation with a dark-haired chap. She waved to me wearily as if I was someone she'd met six years ago and couldn't remember the name of. Bailey, as usual, was surrounded by people wanting to talk to him. He was like a mini-celebrity. Personally, I'd rather have stayed upstairs with Tom, a bit of peace and quiet, a bottle of champagne and those very deep and comfortable-looking cushions, but here we were, doing our bit.

'Can you introduce me to your friend Bailey?' said Tom.

'I thought you didn't know who anybody was,' I said, slightly miffed.

'I heard him speak though. He's very interesting.'

'He's not really,' I assured him. 'He's a geek.'

But we made our way across anyway.

'Hey, Freddy Krueger,' said Bailey, handing me a glass.

'Ha ha. That is just so funny,' I said, taking it. 'This is . . . Tom.'

Tom shook Bailey's hand. 'I really enjoyed your speech. I was wondering if I could ask you a few things about it.'

This was good. Maybe he was trying to impress me by taking an interest in my friends.

I couldn't help comparing Bailey with Tom when I saw them standing side by side. A ridiculous thing to do, I knew. Tom was a sandy hunk, frankly. Bailey was not. But Tom was bent over, listening intently to Bailey like a little boy, and asking him esoteric questions I didn't even understand, about supply chains and scarcity values. Ooh, my boyfriend was so smart, I mooned.

After a while, Tom went to find us both a drink, and I tried to keep the smug smile off of my face. After all, Bailey must be feeling a bit usurped.

'You know,' I said, 'I think I could just about get used to this.'

I looked out over the dark water, as the lights reflected in it shimmered. It was so beautiful I wanted to hug myself. I looked up at the candles dancing in the light breeze.

'You'd think the candles would blow out,' I said to Bailey.

'They're windproof candles,' he said absent-mindedly. 'You get them for boats.'

'*Do* you?' How did that work then? Why didn't they make all candles like that.

Bailey looked a little nervous suddenly. 'So, Tom is . . .'

Oh, Bailey. This must be hard for him.

'So you two are . . .' Bailey took off his glasses.

' What?' I said nervously.

Ah, poor Bailey, he couldn't help being a bit jealous I supposed.

Dr Maitland sidled past our group, suddenly, in his normal dour way. He shrugged, though, looking as if he wanted to talk to us but not quite knowing how normal conversation was actually started.

'Hello,' I said, thinking I'd better be the one to take responsibility for the social niceties. 'Yes, ha ha, half my face is peeling off in a terrible radiation accident. Yes, I'm an idiot that doesn't understand even the rudimentaries of skincare. Yes, that makes me a terrible liability at a plastic surgery conference.'

Dr Maitland held up his hands. 'It's all right,' he said quietly. 'I saw you and I just wanted to give you this. I had it in my sample case.' And he handed me a small tub of cream. 'Stick this on tonight, you'll feel fine in the morning.'

And he nodded awkwardly then moved away towards Bailey, as I looked at him, speechless.

'Uh, Dr Arnold, can I have a word?'

'Sure,' said Bailey, and they wandered off into a huddle.

Tom sidled back up to me. He took the cream out of my hand and stuck out his bottom lip, impressed.

'Wow, this is the stuff . . . costs a fortune.'

'Does it?' I said. 'Will I wake up with the skin of a new-born baby?'

'Maybe one with severe colic,' he said. 'Shall we . . . go and explore a little?' And he shook the cream at me in a suggestive fashion.

The party was getting increasingly loud and excitable – champagne and noise was flowing. The lights of Cannes were glistening all the way up into the hills, and I could see the smart villas that perched over the bay. The water lapped at the bow of the boat and the band were playing something romantic and dreamy. I let myself almost casually sink into Tom's arms. Or rather, I kept leaning in his general direction until he took the hint. To his credit, he didn't say 'oof'.

'Come on,' he whispered.

He led me downstairs to the lower decks. Sporadic giggles and expostulations could be heard but it was much quieter than elsewhere. There was a lower salon where a vast plasma screen was showing what looked like fashion catwalk shows. Couples were dotted around the place, smoking and drinking and generally looking pretty relaxed as they reclined on huge squashy sofas.

'And that's me at Milan,' I heard someone say. I rolled my eyes – model alert! – and we beat a hasty retreat.

Pushing back into the ship I marvelled at the sheer wanton weirdness of the whole thing. The doorknobs were gold, inlaid with what looked like real jewels. The wood was panelled in intricate shapes. There were mosaics on the floor. It was as if someone had said, 'This isn't quite expensive enough in one piece. I want it all broken up into tiny pieces because I think that will probably be more expensive.'

Logos were everywhere – Versace, Gucci. I'd always thought logos were for people who couldn't actually afford to buy designer items, so you'd wear a cheap T-shirt that said Chanel on it, or buy some knock-off Louis Vuitton bag. But apparently if you could afford to buy every last piece of nasty designer tat on earth, down to the Chanel skis (which I could see parked in a corner), you still wanted the brand. Kelly would love it. Personally I'd have thought having the fuck-off boat would be evidence enough that you had all the money in the world, but maybe not.

'Who owns this place?' I said, breathless.

'A schizophrenic with a platinum Amex?' said Tom, looking at the carpet, which appeared to be a priceless Persian rug trimmed with Burberry.

'With *class*,' I said, nodding to a huge oil painting of a grotesque nude women painted entirely in different shades of burnt orange. Hung next to it were large blown-up photos from magazines from around the globe, showing what had to be the same woman, but it was the naked painting that truly drew the eye.

Tom smiled at me. 'You know, I was in the mood, but somehow, now . . .' he trailed off, and I grinned back, but started to feel really nervous. This obviously wasn't just a nosy about, this was, well. Tom meant business. Yikes!

And I thought about it. After all, here I was. And I wanted him, didn't I? I mean, guys like Tom . . . they just didn't pop by every day. I mean, I did really fancy him and everything. But at a party? It felt a little . . . teenage.

On the other hand, this wasn't every party, was it? I suddenly pictured us, in ten years' time, telling people, why, yes, we got it together on a party on a yacht and everyone laughing at how hilarious and cute we were.

And what alternative did I have? I didn't fancy my hotel room much . . . and the conference would be over in a couple of days and he'd be gone, and then I'd be miserable and regret it horribly for the rest of my life and end up having to take the veil and enter a convent.

Gah, it was all so difficult.

Tom slung an arm casually around my shoulders.

'Your heart,' he said. 'It's beating really fast.'

He looked at me, his lovely strong face open and sexy looking.

'Is it because of me?' he said softly.

I nodded. 'Yes.'

*

He was gorgeous. Oh, it was lovely. I felt like a rusty old bike, unused for years but suddenly getting oiled up, getting a paint job; setting off to ride again . . . I couldn't not enjoy it. Even the satin sheets we'd found in the surprisingly small but eminently luxurious room. (The carpet went right up the walls! Why going up walls was a feature particularly to be treasured in a carpet I had absolutely no idea but obviously it was just all part of the mega-luxury – 'Get the carpet up the walls, goddamnit, the floor alone is not enough for a jillionaire like me!') Anyway, even the satin sheets felt oddly romantic and wonderful and I forgot all about my silly sunburn and my crappy job and low-level simmering feuds and practically everything apart from my young, muscular, radiant redhead.

Afterwards I crept into the bathroom. They had a huge triangular bath there with jacuzzi jets poking out of it. Oh, goodness.

Well, I'd already done a few unpredictable things this evening, and I wasn't going to pass up on this one.

'Mmm, lover boy,' I purred seductively, tilting the paler side of my face round the bedroom door.

'Mmhmm,' said Tom sleepily.

'There's a jacuzzi in here . . .' I said.

'Wow,' he said. 'Maybe you should use it to try and seduce me . . . oh no, hang on, we already managed that . . .'

'Don't you think it would be fun?'

'We've just had fun,' he said, but heaved himself off the bed nonetheless.

The jacuzzi filled in two seconds flat and I poured some of the expensively packaged potions indiscriminately from the side of the bath.

'I hope none of these react with each other,' said Tom, but leant over to kiss my shoulder to show he didn't really mean it.

I slithered into the water. Oh, it was absolutely blissful on my poor ravaged back.

'Ahh,' I said.

'Better than sex?' asked Tom with a twinkle in his eye.

'*No.* But nearly as good at making me forget my sunburn. Are you coming in?'

'I thought I'd stay here and rub your back.'

'Well, don't. I don't want any of it to come off in your hand.'

It was blissful in there in the soft lights of the bathroom. Tom found something which brought up an iPod – a full iPod, in the bathroom! – and he'd managed to find Prince on it. He was gently playing with the hair at the back of my neck and I was idly wondering how long we could stay there without getting into trouble – personally I liked the idea of about nine or ten years – and whether anyone had ever died from falling asleep in the bath and then drowning when he leaned over next to my ear.

'So,' he breathed. 'Your friend Bailey?'

I felt my brow furrow. What did he mean? He couldn't think Bailey was my boyfriend, could he?

'What about him?'

'You're close, aren't you?'

I smiled. 'Oh, darling, not like that. I mean, once, years ago, but really, we're just friends.'

'Oh, not *that*,' he said, a bit insultingly I thought. 'I mean, do you know lots about his plans and stuff?'

'Why?' I said. 'I mean, he yabbers on, but I don't really listen or anything. But why are you asking?'

'Oh, I just wondered,' said Tom, nuzzling my neck in the most amazing way. 'I'm just interested in what he's doing. And Dr Bennett. Just to show I've been paying attention.'

'You want me to be your spy?' I said, giggling.

'Yes,' he said, tickling me. 'That's what I want. I need you to be a super spy.'

'So you can get extra kudos?'

'That kind of thing. And rapid advancement and international fame and glory.'

'I thought you were just a humble med student.'

'A humble med student with big dreams.'

'How big?'

'*Very* big,' said Tom and he jumped into the jacuzzi with me, splashing the water everywhere.

'The roof-to-roof carpeting!' I gasped.

'I think whoever owns this behemoth can probably afford to get the carpets cleaned, don't you?' he said. And then he started kissing me again.

Just as I was getting into it he surfaced and winked at me.

'So,' he said. 'Bailey and Yuri's ship is ready . . .'

I drew back. 'What on *earth* are you talking about? What ship? Why do you keep asking me this stuff?'

Tom looked a bit confused then, as if he knew he'd gone too far. He backed up onto the side of the bath.

'Why? I mean it, Tom.'

I was a bit peeved now; he looked really guilty, like a boy who'd been caught out doing something naughty.

'Eh, just, you know . . . making conversation . . .'

'We were *snogging*! You can't chat and snog. Spit gets everywhere, it just doesn't work!'

I was getting a little upset now and looked around for a towel so I could get out of the bath.

Suddenly, from the other room, Tom's mobile telephone went off. He froze. I stared at him. He looked . . . well, he absolutely did *not* look like a man making love to his new girl-friend for the first time who'd suddenly been mildly irritated to hear the phone ring. He looked shocked.

Tom grabbed the first towel that came to hand – it was huge, hot pink and had the Versace logo emblazoned on it nine thousand times – and backed out of the bathroom.

'I'm just . . . I'll just go see who that is . . .'

'Why?' I asked, quite sharply, but he'd already retreated into the other room.

'You just stay in the bath and I'll be through in a minute!'

'OK,' I said cheerily, making some splashing noises. Then using my very best Nancy Drew girl detective skills, I turned on the tap then crept to the door where he was crouching – actually crouching – right at the other side of the room behind the bed, whispering into the phone.

I held my breath and took the little water glass off the sink. Did this actually work? I couldn't remember. The boys used to use it on my door if I ever had a friend round, but they always gave themselves away by grunting and snorting by accident. Still, I leaned in closely to the crack, placing the glass against the door.

'Yeah,' he was saying. My heart was now beating dangerously fast but for very different reasons than before. Was it his wife? Girlfriend? Gay lover?

'Yeah. I know. But she doesn't . . . she doesn't really seem to know much.'

Who was he talking about? Me? Know much about what? What did he mean?

'No, I know she's friends with B but I don't think she's got much info.'

B? Did he mean Bailey? What was he talking about? Was he some kind of *spy*?

'I know, she's pretty useless.' Then, there was a smirk in his voice that I hadn't heard before. 'Well . . . not *completely* . . .'

I took a sharp intake of breath. A red mist descended. A fury grew behind my eyes and I felt like I was going to burst. What was going on? Was Tom . . .? What was he doing? Was he doing something bad and had pumped me – literally – for information. I couldn't believe it. I couldn't . . . what the FUCK was this shit doing?

'What the FUCK are you doing, you shit?' I howled, throwing myself out of the bathroom, only another hot pink Versace towel protecting me. Tom jumped up, a vicious flush spreading over his freckled face. 'Are you talking about me?'

'Uh, no, of course not . . .'

'Give me the phone then! Who are you talking to?'

'Nobody . . .'

'GIVE ME THE PHONE!'

'NO!'

He snapped the phone shut and held it above his head, just like John Jr used to do with my Tiny Tears. Nothing was more guaranteed to send me into a rage. I tore at him.

'GIVE IT!'

I caught a flash of panic cross his face just before he turned on his heel and bombed through the door, with nothing more than the towel round his waist. I was half crazy with fury, but not so crazy that I didn't quickly grab up the nearest thing that came to hand – his boxer shorts, in fact, and his grey T-shirt. I threw them on as quickly as I could and charged towards the door, howling in rage.

He had obviously gone upstairs; there were wet footprints on the wooden decking. Also, as I ascended at full speed I could hear people starting to mutter and giggle, which meant there was obviously a six-foot, freckly, practically naked man ploughing through them. But I HAD to catch up with him – if

157

he ran off and escaped, well, I just didn't know. What was he doing? What was he after? Had I just . . . I mean, was he like a spy? Had I just been Mata Haried? The idea made me absolutely crazy. Pretty useless? *Pretty useless??*

'Stop that naked man!' I screeched as I reached the top of the stairs. This didn't have quite the desired effect, however, as all the beautifully dressed party guests immediately turned to look at me rather than trying to catch Tom's skinny arse, which I now saw was trying to push its way through the throng to the exit.

'Oh, look, he's stolen her honour,' said one supercilious voice.

'Do you think she's one of those lady boys and he got a shock?' said another.

'With those hips? Don't think so.'

'Catch him for God's sake!' I screamed. 'He's a SPY!'

'Where's he hiding his gun, then?' shouted someone else, to general merriment. Tom was nearly at the gangplank now, having given me a cursory backward glance. There was no way I was going to reach him across the crowd of people and even if I did, what was I going to do? Wrestle him to the ground?

He must have been thinking the same thing because he made it to the gangway and – the bastard – gave me a quick, but obvious wink. Then he turned back, only, suddenly, to find his way blocked.

I gasped in amazement. Standing right there, all eight-foot

square of him, looking pink and fat and out of place, was none other than John Junior. Truly, I had never been so pleased to see him in all my life. He was implacably huge, hanging onto the ropes on either side of the gangway. There was no way for Tom to get past him.

John Jr grunted with satisfaction. I could tell that even though he didn't know what was going on, it looked like there was whomping to be done, and whomping was what John Jr liked to do best. Behind him I could see Kelly, teetering in her spiky high heels going, 'Leave it, John, he just isn't worth it.' But John was oblivious to all that now. I waved hard at JJ and made a punching motion with my hand.

'What you doing with my little sister?' he growled menacingly, in his best *EastEnders* voice.

'Nothing,' said Tom, sounding offended. 'Can I get past here?'

'You can,' said John Jr, 'if you give me that towel.'

The entire deck had gone silent. Even the jazz band had stopped playing.

'He, um, snogged me under false pretences,' I squealed. 'He's a spy! He tried to get information out of me.'

There was a rustle among the crowd now. Obviously having a big fat bloke on my side made my word much more reliable.

'Is that true?' said John Jr.

'Get out of my way,' said Tom, sounding a lot less sure of

himself. 'If you do anything to me there's lots of witnesses.'

'Neh, we're on the sea,' said John Jr (dubiously, I thought). 'Law of the briny deep, innit? Now, were you spying on my sister?'

'I'm not *spying*,' said Tom, suddenly looking extremely exasperated. He looked around realising the game was up. He turned to face the crowd.

'I'm information gathering, that's all.'

There was a shocked intake of breath from everyone there, including me. He *was* a spy. Some kind of industrial spy. Which meant that all the romance . . . all the kissing . . . even the bloody stubble rash . . . was, oh, God, nothing at all. I'd been taking in by a tall good-looking idiot. Not for the first time, admittedly, but this was even worse than normal. This was completely awful.

I noticed Bailey stepping up to face him.

'Why? What for?'

'Let me explain . . .' said Tom, looking slightly wild-eyed. Thank goodness he was naked, at least he couldn't possibly be concealing a bomb, unless it was a really tiny one, and even then, I think I'd have probably come across it earlier.

Tom, however, did not get his chance to explain. To widespread cheering from the assembled throng, John Jr hoisted him up over his shoulder in a fireman's lift, marched to the side of the yacht and threw him into the dark oily water below.

There was a gasp from everyone as we all dashed to the side to see what had happened. I hoped he could swim – oh,

God, what if he drowned. There weren't sharks round here, were there? John Jr came up to me.

'What did you do that for?' I yelled. 'What if you've killed him.'

John Jr grunted. 'Then you could thank me,' he said. 'Hanging's too good for 'em.'

John Jr says this about anyone who commits any crime of any sort at all.

'OK,' I said. Then before I could think about it, I gave him a huge hug. 'Thank you. You're not all bad.'

'Family, innit?' said JJ, but he seemed pleased.

I pored over the side. I could just make out the sandy head above the water, splashing and choking, but striking out towards the quay.

'What on *earth*?' Bailey said.

I sighed. 'It's a long story,' I said.

'Oh, well done,' said Lydia. 'It looks like the party's over. And you ruined it.'

On the contrary, actually, it looked like somebody being thrown into the water might have been exactly what the party needed. The excited chatter was reaching fever pitch. Four burly bodyguards wearing dark glasses, at eleven at night, with wires coming out of their ears were humming and hawing around looking grumpy. Lots of people were staring at me – again. Bailey and John Jr were heading for the gang-plank, along with Dr Bennet and a few other people. I followed them as Tom clambered up the metal bars that served as a rough staircase out of the docks. Several fisher-men and crowds of passers-by watched him in amazement. As he stood up you could see by the lights of the nearest boat – all the crew was leaning over the top – that he was absolutely filthy, covered in black patches of oil and seaweed and goodness knows what. And – oh, joy, oh, joy, it became clear as he turned around – the towel had got lost some-where in transit.

Bailey and John Jr, looking like Little and Large, had reached him. The whole party followed, heading down the gangplank carefully. I was still in Tom's T-shirt and boxers which, I noticed, smelled just like him.

'Well?' John Jr was shouting. 'What were you doing to my little sister?'

Tom's face was a picture of consternation. Hurrah for JJ!

'No . . . nothing,' he said, both hands still covering his crotch. I could have gone back and got his clothes, but I didn't want to miss anything.

'Who do you work for?' said Bailey. 'Are you even a doctor?'

The four big bodyguards had come out. I'd forgotten there were various rich people from around the globe here – investors and so on – who actually needed, or at least had, people like bodyguards. Wow. How annoying must that be? Did they stand outside the loo when you needed to go for a poo? Did they time you? Did they bitch you up between themselves? They must do. Anyway, the bodyguards were standing behind Bailey and you could see Tom looking really frightened.

'Not exactly,' said Tom. My skin bristled. Oh, God, I'd been taken in completely and utterly. Any old idiot could fool me. Completely fooled. Stupid self-obsessed Evie. Half my face was peeling off and I was such a pointless conversationalist that I didn't even know about Bailey's big plastic surgery plans. Tom wasn't even looking up, he couldn't even look at me. Although to be fair he was also trying to keep his goolies out of the way of some rather burly men who looked like they might want to kick them.

'I'm a vet.'

Oh, God.

'But that's not important.'

Well, it was quite important to me. Given that I'd inadvertently slept with someone who stuck his hand up dog's arses.

'I'm part of Earth Friends,' he said. 'We don't like what you're doing.'

'Well, you don't know what we're doing,' said Bailey. 'Presumably that's why you're here.'

'You want to use untested material.'

'We want to give people options.'

'What about giving animals options?'

'Didn't I see you eating the caviar?' said Dr Bennet.

Hang on, hang on, what on earth where they talking about?

'You have to stop,' said Tom. 'It has to be stopped.'

'By a naked ginger man trying to shag my sister?' said John Jr. 'I don't think so.'

'I was *information gathering*,' said Tom. Then he caught sight of me, hiding behind the bodyguards. 'Sorry,' he said.

'SORRY?' I yelled. I'd thought my anger had dissipated when he'd fallen into the sea, but it turned out I was wrong. Everyone turned to face me. 'I'll give you SORRY.'

And I raced towards him. He saw his chance, with everyone looking at me he turned round and legged it back to the bright lights of Cannes.

'Oh, let him go,' I heard Bailey say to the bouncers. 'He didn't get anything.'

I stopped running after I lost sight of his body, fleeing in and out of the excited crowds. On the pier all I could catch was the occasional glimpse of pale white buttocks, like the bobbing lights of the boats on the bay.

'The gendarmes will probably pick him up,' said Bailey, coming up behind me. 'God, a spy. Wow, I had no idea.'

I turned round, all my anger gone and just a huge sadness and embarrassment settling on me.

'Neither did I,' I said, and burst into tears.

Everyone was very solicitous, bringing me drinks, and Bailey wrapped me up in a blanket (I don't know why, it was still about twenty-five degrees outside) whilst listing all the hideous and deadly diseases Tom had certainly caught from swimming in the harbour. I said that I hadn't slept with him, but I don't think anyone believed me.

'I don't even understand *why*,' I said to Bailey, choking through my sobs.

'Because you're an irresistible creature,' he said encouragingly, but his face was distracted. 'You're sure you didn't tell him anything?'

'Anything what?'

Bailey shook his head. 'Well, from your private briefing paper.'

'But I'm on *holiday*. I haven't . . . exactly . . .' I noticed Dr Bennet hovering awkwardly and stopped.

'Evie, you seem, by virtue of your ignorance . . . to have helped us out.'

'Is that good?' I said. 'What's going on?'

Bailey and Dr Bennet glanced at each other.

'Tell me, then.'

'Well,' Dr Bennet started. 'You know Bailey designs hospital facilities?'

I nodded. Someone had handed me an Irish coffee, and I was suddenly very grateful to have something to hang on to.

'Well, we're launching a new one. And launching is the operative word . . .'

'It's on a yacht,' said Bailey. 'Not this one. A really big one. Brand new. It's coming into port tomorrow for the first time. Yuri is finding investors, and we're showing it off here so that doctors will tell their clients, and money men will want to invest. Selected surgeons will be able to operate on board.'

I must have looked confused.

'So,' went on Bailey. 'To hide people from the paparazzi . . . to ensure complete and utter confidentiality—'

'Very important for celebrities,' said Dr Bennet.

'And to give an all-round surgery experience which is—'

'A cut above,' said Dr Bennet. Bailey winced slightly.

'A slightly different experience. Anyway,' Bailey's eyes lit up excitedly, 'it's like a cruise, or chartering a yacht – but with surgery. Hundreds of miles out at sea away from prying eyes. First-class care and a luxury cruise to boot.'

'Are you joking? That sounds like the set-up for the new *Die Hard* film.'

'Not at all,' bristled Bailey. 'Our security procedures are excellent.'

'Yes, I could tell that by the way nobody's managed to infiltrate your defences or anything,' I said.

'And we'll be in international waters,' said Dr Bennet dreamily. 'So we can use the most up-to-date and cutting-edge procedures. Tax free.'

I took a long sip of my coffee.

'I don't understand. Why would some Earth Friends vet be against that?'

Bailey shrugged. 'Craziness?'

'They don't like the cutting-edge procedures,' said Dr Bennet. 'They're against science and progress.'

'Oh,' I said, not really understanding.

'You've had a very tiring day,' said Bailey, looking concerned.

'No, I haven't! I slept all day! Now tell me about these cutting-edge procedures.'

'That's more your department,' said Bailey, looking at Dr Bennet. 'I'm off to bed.'

Bailey was right, though. I was tired. It had been a long night, and really I wanted to get back to my hotel room, throw myself on my pillow and have a good bawl. It wasn't too bad talking to the guys but I knew as soon as I was on my own and the memories of what I'd done started to hit, I wouldn't be able to control myself.

'So, we're not calling the police?' said Bailey.

'I think he'll probably have to call us when he needs bail,' sniffed Dr Bennet. 'Useless cretin.'

Suddenly there was a knock at the cabin door and Dr Maitland put his head round.

'How's our little Mata Hari?' he said stiffly.

'Mata Hari was the other one,' I said sulkily. 'I'm the rube.'

Dr Maitland patted me gently on the shoulder. 'Well, it sounds like you didn't let him get away with anything.'

'Mmm,' I said.

'Opposition, though,' said Dr Maitland, looking at Dr Bennet. 'Interesting. I can't believe he stole your name. That's quite ballsy.'

'It's unacceptable,' said Dr Bennet, turning on his heel and walking out.

I remembered the conversation I'd overheard earlier that evening and wondered now who Dr Bennet had been talking to. I felt a faint chill in the air.

Chapter Nine

The next morning I woke up feeling horribly alone on the lumpy bed. At first I felt kind of all right, before I was properly awake, then suddenly I remembered everything and let out a heartfelt groan. I had cried myself to sleep, which had worked, but now it was a new day, the sun was trying to push against the grimy window and I, God help me, was supposed to spend all day working at the conference. What did they do with the bits they chopped off on a hospital boat? I wondered. Maybe there were sharks following all the way from shore. Why had everything good turned so bad?

Still, maybe everything would look better after breakfast. I couldn't be feeling that suicidal if I still felt hungry. The worst of it was, after everything, I still found Tom residually attractive. How stupid was that? But it had been so romantic and lovely. I wondered if James Bond's abandoned ladies felt like this. Betrayed . . . yet seduced. And a little bit hungry. I should take this as a positive sign. Then I remembered the conference.

I couldn't believe I'd forgotten. Oh, God, why had I thought this was a holiday masquerading as a couple of minor annoyances? Today, they were having a team-building day. Team-building day? The schedule was 'fun' exercises in the morning followed by a golf game in the afternoon, which of course I was going to be able to do seeing as I knew as much about golf as I did mitochondrial enhancement. But that morning I'd been instructed to turn up, hand out briefings and generally look helpful.

It took two coffees, two croissants and a croque-monsieur before I managed to pluck up the courage to walk into the room. Today the venue was a large marquee parked next to the beach. Dress code was 'smart but casual', which meant that every single male was wearing chinos, loafers and a blue chambray shirt. They looked like a line of prison inmates from a particularly swanky jail.

Dr Bennet grabbed me by the entrance.

'You read French, don't you?'

Uh-oh. I'd been dreading this moment.

'Well, according to my CV . . .' I said timidly. He ignored

this and thrust a *Cannes Matin* into my hands. Right on the front page was a picture of Tom's rather foxy – no, no, evil – behind.

Étranger mystérieux, said the headline. Well, you didn't need to be a translating genius to figure that one out. 'Mysterious stranger,' I said confidently.

'Yes, yes, I'd got that far,' said Dr Bennet impatiently. I forget all the time that he is already perfectly fluent in a second language: English.

'Well,' I said. 'Well, that's it, isn't it? They obviously have no further information, otherwise they'd be calling him the "we've found out everything stranger".'

Dr Bennet sniffed. 'You seem to be bringing a certain notoriety to our launch.'

'I'm just efficient,' I said, and immediately grabbed a handful of folders to give out to people as they came in.

Lydia drifted up, wearing very red lipstick, which made her face look pointy.

'Ah, it's the talk of the town,' she said, and not in a nice way, if there is a nice way to say that. 'You're such a dark horse! Who else have you been sleeping with, huh? We need to know if any other secrets are being bandied about.' Then she laughed as if she was actually just joking.

'Here, take these,' I said, handing over a pile of the brochures. She picked them up and wrinkled her very small nose.

'Love in medicine?' she read aloud, then gave me a very sharp look. 'Is this a joke?'

'What?' I said, and glanced down. Yet again my lack of preparedness in everything except bikini choice was showing through; I'd scarcely glanced at what this team building would contain (though this time I had an excuse). But sure enough, there it was: 'The Healing Hand – bringing love and spirituality to medicine.'

'Oh, for goodness' sake,' I exclaimed loudly. 'What the hell is this bollocks? I don't think there should be love in medicine. I think love and medicine should be as far apart as possible. You don't want some surgeon all shaky with love and his heart pounding every time he chops into some old girl's carcass.'

I realised suddenly, with that horrible sixth sense, that there was someone standing right behind me. Lydia's face took on its favourite mocking expression. I turned around as slowly as I could. It was Dr Maitland, and his mouth was twitching.

'Actually,' he said. 'I couldn't agree more. In fact I'm only here because you terrified me so much with your skin damage yesterday that I didn't want to go out in the sun.'

I smiled at him. 'Brochure?'

He took it. 'Is this going to be what they call "touchy feely"?'

'You can bet on that with Evie around, sir,' said Lydia unctuously.

A commotion at the entrance hall caught our attention. As we turned round, I saw it was a tiny woman, tight as a drum from head to toe, wearing a hot-cerise suit over her small rump.

'Is this it? Is this the space?' She had a huge voice for such a little person. It came howling forth like an annoyed cheese grater, harsh American tones bouncing off the walls like hailstones.

'I'm not feeling it, Judy,' she said warningly. Next to her was a woman about the same height but twice the weight; much older-looking and slightly depressed. I guessed this must be Judy. I know you're not meant to judge by first impressions, but my heart went out to her in about ten seconds flat.

'If it's not a heart space I'm not sure I can work it . . . I specifically said a *heart space*.'

'It's a marquee,' said Judy.

'I can *see* it's a marquee, Judy. I can *smell* it's a marquee. But is it a *heart* marquee?'

Dr Maitland and I looked at one another in some bewilderment. Maybe I could see the wisdom of his constant customer avoidance.

The little woman stalked into the room. Huge arrays of flowers had been placed on plinths around the outskirts of the chairs. They must have cost tons of money. The lady sniffed.

'Pink roses. Not carmine. For goodness' sake, I thought we were dealing with professionals. *Wrongly*, obviously.'

Judy wrote something down on a clipboard which doubtless meant bad news for somebody. As she did so, Dr Bennet came bustling over from the coffee machine where he'd been fussing.

'And you must be Jal-Vita?'

Jal-Vita? 'What is that, a name or a snack?' I whispered to Lydia.

The woman's demeanour immediately changed, and she actually started to simper.

'Why, hello,' she said, putting out her hand. 'I am indeed. Of course, Jal-Vita is just my spiritual name. My real name is Janey.'

'And which do you prefer?' said Dr Bennet in full smooth-ness mode, as he picked up her hand and kissed it. Yuk! He had no idea where it'd been!

'Whatever you like!' she tinkled as if it was hilarious that she had a real name and a completely made-up bullshit name.

'And you're our star attraction,' went on Dr Bennet, purring like a vintage car, which was rubbish, as even I'd picked up by now that unveiling the boat was going to be the star attraction, and everyone knew it. Dr Bennet seemed to have his mojo back, though.

'I don't think of it like that,' said *Janey*, although she obviously totally did. 'I think of it as a spiritual journey for everyone . . . as they career down the heady highway of sur-gical success, to stop for a while and smell the roses. That's me.'

'You're indeed a rose,' said Dr Bennet pukily.

Janey smiled, equally pukily. 'Oh, no, I wouldn't say that.'

Well, she just did say that, I thought mutinously. I leafed through the brochure. An airbrushed picture of Janey, looking like she'd been entirely moulded out of Barbie doll material, complete with a coat-hanger smile, beamed out from the page.

'Welcome,' it said, 'to a safe space to leave all your worries and cares behind.'

Great, a carefree non-worrier with a scalpel in his hands; just what the world needed.

Lydia had put her super-positive face on and gone bounding up to meet the new girl. This should be interesting, I thought. Two evil witches in a smiling competition.

'Jal-Vita, I'm a great fan of your work,' said Lydia, holding out her hand, which was graciously shaken. 'I really enjoyed *Spirituality in the Workplace – why love is there for everyone 9–5*.'

She had? I turned over a page in the brochure. The book had a full-page advertisement. The cunning fink! All she'd read was the blurb!

'Why, *thank you*,' gushed Janey. 'Which bit did you feel spoke to you the most?'

Ha ha. Take that, you gobshite.

'Well, I found it really spoke to my inner soul?' said Lydia, in an upturned inflection that matched Janey's. 'Or does that sound stupid?'

175

'Yes,' I said quietly, forgetting once again that Dr Maitland was right behind me.

'Not at all,' said Janey. 'Releasing your inner soul-ness is very much a part of what I'm trying to share with the world. Thank you for sharing your insight with me. What's your name?'

'Lydia.'

'And what's your heritage, Lydia?'

Lydia is *not* one of those people who likes discussing her heritage. I think she would just like everyone to assume she's an exotic Eastern princess of some kind, who descended to earth on a gold-tinted cloud.

'My parents are from Malaysia,' she said, almost grudgingly.

'Wow,' said Janey, taking Lydia's hands in hers. 'That's an amazing thing. An amazing heritage to have.'

'Yeah, whatever,' said Lydia. (For once, rightly, in my opinion. Why congratulate someone on their random genetics? You might as well say, 'God, you're left-handed; that's *amazing*.' Which is the kind of thing Janey probably did say.)

'Now, I know this is just going to be the most wonderful day,' said Janey. 'When do they all arrive?'

Dr Bennet looked slightly worried, but as he turned to face the entrance of the marquee – which was huge, with row after row of those gilt-edged, red-seated chairs lined up around it – the docs, looking a bit hungover and slightly sheepish, started to sidle in.

Janey prepared her razor-toothed American grin in welcome, but to her – and my – surprise, they all headed towards me.

'Hey, what happened to you last night? Are you all right?' asked one.

'You were really brave, chasing a spy like that,' said another. 'Amazing really. You probably saved the whole project. Under torture, too.'

Out of the corner of my eye I caught sight of Bailey grinning. Oh, bless him! He must have spun some story about me where I didn't look like a hapless slut after all!

Another one was nodding. 'Yeah,' they said. Then they turned to Dr Maitland. 'You must be really proud of her.'

And Dr Maitland said the most surprising thing; he replied, 'Yes. Yes I am.'

I was so taken aback, I nearly started crying again. Fortunately there must be some kind of term limit on tears, or I'd just dried up, I didn't know. Tom had knocked my confidence so hard I was just amazed they didn't all want me to lie on the floor so they could take turns kicking me.

'*Hello*,' said Janey very loudly. The doctors slowly turned round to face her. She looked annoyed that her attempt to get all the attention had failed. Near me, her little runt Judy looked a bit shaky.

'If I can just ask for your attention for two minutes . . .'

The docs smiled at me, and chuntered their way towards the chairs. I stayed standing at the back.

'My name is Jal-Vita and I am lucky enough to have been blessed in my life enough to now pass on the secrets of love and spirituality in business that I have learned along the way.'

There was a little bit of noise from the audience at this, and the latecomers looked somewhat wistfully towards the coffee machine.

'Today, through some *fun* games and exercises I hope we're going to find a way to take forward a little bit of the love and spirituality that we can carry around with us all the time – even when faced with that difficult patient or tricky operation. But first, a little bit about me . . .'

'Oh, Christ,' said Dr Maitland. I realised he hadn't gone and sat down but was still standing beside me. 'I knew this would suck. You know she negotiated it with Yuri in return for some free filler.'

'She did not!' I said. 'That's . . . corrupt.'

'Well, she is a professional . . .'

'Professional what?'

'. . . and then that's when I started what I call my *whole life journey*,' emphasised Janey.

'Will you help me out with the "exercises"?' said Dr Maitland. 'I don't think I can bear it. And if she says the word "diversity" I'm out of here.'

'. . . that brings a whole new paradigm of love and diversity into the workplace,' said Janey. I looked at Dr Maitland pointedly.

'Oh, I can't leave,' he said, fumbling with his bow tie. 'I promised Yuri.'

'Wimp!' I whispered back and, amazingly, he smiled. He had a rather lovely smile, I couldn't help noticing. Like the sun coming out from behind a cloud.

After about another forty minutes of Janey wittering on about how being a nurse in a casualty unit had taught her more than she'd ever dreamed of about love in the workplace, which was news to me, because one of Patrick's girlfriends had been a nurse in a casualty unit and she said it had taught her more than she'd ever dreamed of about drunks, Janey finally stepped forward off the podium, her beady eyes sweeping the room.

'OK, guys and gals,' she said, in a horrible attempt to appear playful – pointless anyway, there was only one gal there, Miss Hodgkiss, who specialised in bum implants and herself had a massive one (which I guess was reassuring to her clientele).

'Now, the first thing we're going to do is find a partner so we can all relax with a trust game.'

I swear you could almost here a groan go through the room. Was this worth getting up early for? The shiny new career on the ocean blue?

'We can't expect to *spread* love if we don't at first *love ourselves*,' said Janey severely. 'And we do that by finding trust in others.'

'I think I've got to go outside and check the ticket

179

stand,' I lied suddenly, getting up. Let's face it, I was probably the least trustworthy person in this entire room. I'd probably get dropped if we had to do that 'fall back into somebody's arms' thing. From the corner of my eye I saw Lydia immediately grab Bailey's elbow. Well, but of course she would. I stood up.

'No!' said Dr Maitland suddenly.

I turned round.

'I mean . . .' His face looked stricken. 'I mean, I thought you were going to stay and be my partner.'

Janey was now chivvying people into position and hollering, 'Now, don't worry! This is going to be lots of fun! JUDY!'

Judy instantly stepped forward with a huge box full of blindfolds.

'Now, cover up your partner's eyes.'

Dr Maitland and I looked at each other. This was bizarrely uncomfortable. Judy waddled up to us awkwardly and handed the blindfold to Dr Maitland. He took it, looking at it as if it was a big black eel he'd just accidentally pulled out of the water.

'Um,' he said.

'There's still time to set the tent on fire and make a run for it under cover of all the smoke,' I said.

'Come on, you two at the back!' came a wild American screech. 'Get with the PROG-ramme.'

'*So* much love and spirituality,' I murmured, as Dr

Maitland tentatively approached me. I stopped talking as he draped the blindfold over my eyes. Suddenly I was so conscious of his body very close to mine. Perhaps because I'd had sex so recently, my senses and pheromones were up. I could feel my skin prickle.

Dr Maitland was quiet, but I could hear him breathing as he carefully, but with a steady hand, tied the blindfold at the back, not too loosely or tightly. I nearly asked him if he'd done it before, but already felt awkward enough.

'Now, you're going to guide your partner around the room using just your fingers and your voice . . . gently touch them from behind . . .'

It is to several medical professionals' complete credit that they didn't immediately start sniggering when they heard this, which I would certainly have done had I not been sad and very close to my boss. Instead, I felt a finger quite gently but firmly poking me in the back and a voice saying, 'I'm terribly sorry about all this.'

'Don't give it a second thought,' I said, stepping forwards in the pitch black and immediately falling over a chair.

'Whoops!' I shouted, as Dr Maitland made a grab for me and fetched me up with my bra strap, which he dropped as if it had bitten him.

'I'm sorry,' he said again.

'Now you two,' came the loud voice, sounding right next to my ear. 'You're not trusting each other.'

'She marched off!' said Dr Maitland.

'I thought you were pushing me in that direction.'

'Why would I push you over a chair?'

'So that I'd hurt myself and require expensive reconstructive surgery?'

There was a silence and I really wanted to pull up my blindfold and see what was going on, but a tiny claw came down on my arm and gripped it in a steely embrace.

'You,' said Janey, without as much love in her voice as I could have done with at this particular instant. 'Come here.' And she yanked me back round the chair.

'Stand here.'

And she shoved me into a large pair of tweedy arms.

'OK, *you*,' she said, and I knew it wasn't me she meant this time. 'Guide her.'

'Where?' said Dr Maitland.

'It doesn't matter where. It just matters that she trusts you.'

We were both silent then. And I realised, suddenly, with a flashing instant of clarity, that after last night I wasn't actually sure if I did trust him.

'Do you trust me?' said Dr Maitland suddenly, as if he was thinking the same thing. It seemed a very odd thing for a boss to ask his receptionist.

'Don't ask like that!' said Janey, trust expert extraordinaire. 'Just get moving!'

'Left,' murmured Dr Maitland in my ear then, and I took a little step that way. His finger moved down my back a little bit as he whispered, 'Forwards. Slowly.' And we gradually tiptoed out of Janey's orbit. Being in the dark in the huge marquee – I could barely hear the other pairs rustling about in the distance – was a very odd experience. I felt we could walk for ever, or straight into the sea.

'The project . . .' began Dr Maitland, but it was like he didn't know how to go on. 'The ship . . . I mean.'

He nudged me to the right. It felt a little like we were dancing. I was incredibly aware of him behind me. Oh, God, what was the matter with me? One whiff of testosterone and I was all over the place. This was my boss we were talking about.

'Uh, yes?'

He paused then as if sensing something. Oh, God, I was probably giving off some weird hormonal thing. I couldn't help it, though; as I felt his sure, strong fingers gently guiding me, it was hard to concentrate.

'You know, not all of us are as gung-ho as Yuri and Bailey . . . I mean, we're not all so determined.'

'What *is* it?' I said, as he prodded me again, lightly in the small of my back and I nearly shivered. 'What's getting everyone so riled up? So bad that someone sent a *spy*?'

He sighed. 'Well, in law, once you're out of sight of land . . . well, once you're in international waters, you can do . . . you can do pretty much anything.'

I spun round to face him. 'What do you mean, *anything*?'

'Well, new techniques. Face transplants. Anonymous work. Some women, you know . . . they'll stop at nothing to look better. And some doctors don't feel the pace of ratification by drugs bodies is quite fast enough. And then there's Radoflux 9000.'

I screwed up my eyes trying to remember where I'd heard that name.

'The drug that keeps failing its FDA?' I said.

'Yes,' said Dr Maitland. 'Side-effect issues.'

'Isn't it made out of something really dodgy?'

'Seal foetuses.'

'Urgh.'

'Everything's made out of something.'

'So what's the problem with that? You can't use it, end of story.'

'Well, some people aren't so sure about that . . .'

I didn't say anything and waited for him to continue. I wasn't sure but I thought we were near the corner of the marquee by now. I pulled up my blindfold and looked at him in disbelief. 'You want to use an unratified drug.'

Dr Maitland looked at the floor. 'Well, maybe. Yes.'

I couldn't believe it.

'So Tom was right! This *is* a bad idea.'

'Shh,' said Dr Maitland. He looked around. Various twosomes were hopping along or running into each other. They all looked very innocent.

'And these guys . . . they could use the boat to do, basically, anything they wanted?'

'And SWITCH!' yelled Janey.

'Look normal,' said Dr Maitland. 'I shouldn't really be talking to you about this.'

'So why are you?'

'Maybe I'm having doubts, I said that already,' he growled.

I had to get right up on my tiptoes to tie the blindfold around him. He had very clean ears, I noticed. Probably doctors knew quite a lot about terrible ear diseases.

'Is that too tight?' I said.

'It doesn't matter,' he said. 'We're having a conversation, not actually playing this stupid game.'

He sounded completely different; much less tentative than normal. He'd obviously crossed a line; he wanted to talk to me and talk about this. I prodded at his back reluctantly.

'It would be easier,' he said, 'if you just held onto my braces.'

It was.

He heaved a sigh. 'Well, you've proven you can keep a secret – even under the *deadliest* torture.'

'Could we not mention that, please?' I said. 'Just from, like, a basic standard of human dignity? And I think maybe Bailey slightly embroidered the torture thing anyway.'

He nodded his head. His back, as I studied it, was much more muscular than I'd have divined from those ridiculous tweed jackets.

'Sorry,' he said. 'The thing is. That holiday boyfriend of yours . . .'

I rolled my eyes, but he couldn't tell.

185

'He made me think. Or think more. What do you think, Evie?'

I thought about it as we negotiated a couple of the gilt chairs someone else had knocked over earlier.

'Why should I care what a couple of really rich cows do to themselves?' I said, considering it. 'If they want to shoot themselves full of monkey bollocks so that their face is rendered completely immoveable even in tornadoes, why should I care? Why should I care if they get swept overboard? You know, hypothetically.'

'Thanks for adding "hypothetically" on at the end there,' said Dr Maitland. 'Otherwise it might have sounded, you know, a bit twisted and bitter.'

'I'm just saying,' I said, realising I was getting quite het up, 'for most people in this world what some stupid rich person wants to get up to in her own spare time is miles away from anything even vaguely useful, like how you're going to pay your council tax or getting your landlord to fix that ridiculous drip that's been coming in from the roof for years. It's all bollocks. And I can't imagine why a good doctor would waste his training and his life on it, quite frankly. It's immoral. I mean, it's OK for idiots like me, but to go to medical school, learn how to help people, learn how to fix people, get trained up by the NHS and then piss it all down the drain for a six-figure salary . . . it's pathetic, really.'

'And stop!' shouted Janey. 'Now, is that all better? Do you really feel you're starting to trust one another now?'

Dr Maitland looked at me, blinking his big eyes in the light.

'Well, just as well you know everything,' he said.

'What did we learn?' shouted Janey at the group.

'I know, because I'm only a receptionist,' I said. My blood was up now. I was probably – no, make that definitely – going to lose my job, but I didn't care. Who were these people who thought they could take people out into the middle of the ocean and gut baby seals for money? Maybe I just didn't want to be anywhere near them any more.

'I'm not rich, I'm not willing to throw thousands of pounds at you so you can hack me open and make me look like I've been caught in a wind tunnel. Amazing, I know. If I made any money – which I *don't*, by the way, you lot all act like I should feel unbelievably privileged to be working for you and should be doing it for the love of it – I'd spend it . . . well, I'd spend it on a home, and on beautiful things around me and hopefully, one day, someone I loved and who loved me, and it wouldn't be about how small a nose I had or how tight my bottom was. It would be because it was fun, and warm, and happy and we liked spending time together and spending our lives together. And do you know how many of those stupid people you think are so great have that? Hardly any. Hardly any of them at all. They're all bloody miserable. That's why they come and see you. And with all your bloody money and qualifications – you're bloody miserable too. And that's moral, is it?

187

Along with all the other bullshit, this boat is literally a drop in the ocean.'

'God, you don't stop when you get going, do you?' said Dr Maitland. He just stood there.

'I've stopped now,' I said. And I had. It was like all the anger drained out of my feet and I changed from red to white. I knew what I'd done. I'd buggered up my job – a job, as Bailey would point out, that I was lucky to get – and wouldn't get a look in at another one once word got round about the crazy girl at the Cannes conference, as I'd be known for evermore. I hoped they'd let me keep my ticket stub to get home.

'Good,' he said.

'You, girl! With the frizzy hair.'

To my horror, I realised that Janey was pointing at me.

'Were you volunteering to tell us what you've learned?'

I shook my head mutely but it was too late. She was advancing down on me, her red talons outstretched.

'Come on! It's a safe space here! Share what you're feeling about love and spirituality in the workplace!'

I opened my mouth. I'd already pissed on my chips, it wasn't going to hurt telling a few more people and I quite liked the idea of Lydia getting the smile wiped off her face.

'Well,' I said, 'I've learned that . . .'

Suddenly I felt a pressure on my arm. Dr Maitland had grabbed me, quite hard.

'She's overcome,' he said loudly. 'She's been so

overwhelmed by all the, uh, love and spirituality in the room that . . . that I have to take her outside for a sit down.'

'You do no—' I started, but his hand only clamped down even harder.

'So, we're just popping out,' he announced, pushing me backwards firmly towards the exit.

'Now, I do find it amazing when the power of love and trust just *fills* the room,' said Janey loudly. 'Look at that! And next, it's going to get even *more* intense.'

A quiet groan went up from the group as Dr Maitland manhandled me backwards. I caught sight of Lydia looking at me with narrowed eyes.

'What are you doing?' I yelled, as Dr Maitland got me out and took me to sit on the sea wall. 'What? I've learned too much about your evil plans and now you're going to have me killed? That's it, isn't it? I've stumbled on your evil secrets and now you're going to make me pay.'

'Are you getting hysterical?'

A small group of teenagers rollerbladed past under the palm trees. It is difficult to feel hysterical when there are teenagers and palm trees about.

'No,' I said sullenly.

'OK. Well, I wanted to think for a bit.'

'About whether to strangle me or just push me off the sea wall?'

'You are very, very annoying, you know?'

'Only when faced with certain death.'

Dr Maitland sighed and looked out to sea. 'Look, every-thing you said . . . calm down. I've been having doubts about this the whole time. Not unlike your friend.'

'He's not my . . . never mind.'

'Dr Bennet, you know. He's very keen. To push the boundaries. Try new things. He likes the money, yes, but you know, he's a very committed doctor too.'

'He's a very committed schmoozer, you mean.'

'That's part of it.'

I looked over the sea wall. Someone had carved a great sand sculpture of a mermaid. It was absolutely beautiful, I couldn't imagine how it was done. It must have taken some-one ages. All that work to make something beautiful that would be washed out by the tide. It reminded me of some-thing but I couldn't think what. Oh, yeah. Life. I pointed it out to Dr Maitland.

'Well, just because time and the tide wash everything away eventually . . . is that a good reason not to at least try to create something beautiful?' he said.

'Beauty is one thing,' I said. 'Health is quite another. And better, in my opinion.'

'Science is beautiful,' he said, looking mournful. I looked around in case I should be planning my escape but I reckoned the worst of the danger had passed.

'Where's the beauty in tearing a baby seal from its mother?'

'I don't know,' said Dr Bennet, his eyes on the far horizon. 'I just don't know.'

We sat there, side by side, for about ten minutes. It was oddly restful. Then, finally, Dr Maitland turned to face me. His eyes had a spark to them I'd never seen before.

'OK,' he said. 'Well . . . if you were serious about what you said . . . if we want to stop this ship, we'll need a plan.'

Chapter Ten

Lunch was a buffet sponsored by a wrinkle-plumping company. I was staying away from the cold chicken. Actually I was staying away from anything that looked like it might have been injected to plump it up before hitting the table.

'Does this food look *smooth* to you?' I asked Bailey. I'd timed it properly, so we were hitting the table at the same time.

'How are you getting on, Captain Catastrophe?'

I smiled at him. 'I've had worse holidays.'

Bailey looked around. We were in a dim room that seemed to be attached to a car park. 'You're joking.'

'No, I'm not. Remember that year we went to the Borders and I couldn't talk about it?'

'Oh, yeah. The trauma trip.'

'John Jr buried me in the sand.'

'That doesn't sound so bad.'

'The wet sand. Actually, it was clay. In the rain. Vertically. It was like *Merry Christmas Mr Lawrence*. But with more rain.'

'So you went on a holiday that was actually worse than a Japanese internment camp?'

I nodded vehemently.

'Oh, Evie.'

He put his hand on my arm affectionately. 'Have you heard of the calamity theory?'

'No.'

He bit his lip.

'You'd better tell me. Not everyone gets *Supergeek Monthly*.'

Actually, I was meant to be pumping him for information – step one of the plan – before turning him over to our side – step two.

'Oh, it's nothing. Silly really. There are some studies that show that certain circumstances will almost always attract adverse conditions. So, for example, if you have an earthquake then you'll probably get a flood, then cholera then . . . you know, just bad things attracting other bad things.'

'That's what you think about me?' When someone says something to your face that you've always secretly thought about yourself, it can take your breath away.

'No, of course not,' said Bailey.

'Oh, right. You were talking about parallel universe Evie.' I poked my crackers, feeling sorry for myself and cross with him and not quite sure what to say.

'It was meant to be a humorous analogy,' said Bailey.

'That turned out deeply hurtful,' I pointed out.

'Sorry,' he said. 'You can call me short if you want to.'

'It's OK.'

Bailey played with his three-bean salad. 'I'm sorry,' he said, again. 'Sometimes I'm not sure that this "mixing friends and work" thing is going as well as I'd hoped . . .'

I figured this was my chance – whilst it was quiet and he was feeling on the back foot – to get him on side.

'Bailey,' I said. 'This project.'

He arched an eyebrow at me. 'Yes.'

'Well . . . can you fill me in?'

'The project you said you didn't care about as long as you got to go somewhere sunny for a week?'

'Yes.'

'The project that I tried to explain and you said, "Be quiet, I can't listen and eat pancakes with maple syrup at the same time?" The secret briefing you never read . . .'

'All right, all right.'

'OK,' said Bailey. He sat back. 'Well, yes. Technically. The boat can go into international waters and do anything. It's not the one we were on last night – it's not here yet. They're just finishing her up in the shipyard. She arrives tomorrow. The hospital is a totally new design – it's beautiful. Do you know, however much the boat moves, the operating theatre remains totally stable. It's got four pivoting stabilisers, and is suspended from above . . .'

'OK, forget the technical details,' I said.

'Pancakes?' said Bailey.

'OK, OK. Who commissioned it? I mean, I know Dr Bennet's running the show. But it's not his money, is it? I mean, he's always complaining that he can't afford his own private island and stuff.'

Bailey looked uncomfortable.

'Well, we just work through Dr Bennet, on behalf of a holding company.'

'What? You mean, you don't know?'

Bailey shook his head.

'You don't know who the holding company is? So it could be anyone. It could be, like, Mafia Associates plc.'

'I don't think the Mafia is a publicly listed company.'

'Bad Guys inc? Drug Runners International. Don't you see, though? That this whole place . . . I mean, it could be really, really wrong.'

'Look, Evie, people build prisons and things. They design guns. I mean, bad things happen out of design, and I'm just a designer. And we don't even know it's going to happen here. Don't you think your imagination is running away with you?'

'I would have done, if I hadn't been caught in a SPY SET-UP HONEY TRAP.'

We both looked around, then, nervously, in case we were overheard.

'OK,' said Bailey, leaning forward with an intense look on his face. 'That guy was a nut job, OK?'

'But if he was right?' I said, persistently. 'If it is bad. Don't you think we should stop it?'

Bailey's eyebrows crept together. 'Oh, Evie,' he said. 'When would things be that simple?'

'*Hello!*' Lydia pushed herself between us. Her entire buffet lunch consisted of three strips of peppers and two prawns. 'Mmm, prawn and pepper salad, delicious,' she said. 'What are you having, Evie? Are those deep-fried cheese balls again?' Without waiting for an answer she beamed her full attention towards Bailey. 'How are you doing today, Dr Millionaire Smartie Pants?' she asked perkily.

'Actually, we were having a conversation,' I said. I'd rather Bailey had said it, but needs must.

'Ooh, gossip?' she said. 'Dish, dish, dish! It's Evie again, isn't it? I saw her throwing herself over Dr Maitland at the love and spirituality workshop this morning.'

At that point, I decided. I was going to have to get Lydia out of the way. I didn't want to do it, but I was going to have to bring out my big guns – I needed a secret weapon.

Oh, crap. Lydia was now laying into Bailey with a whole bunch of bollocks she'd obviously picked up by scanning Janey's book.

'Don't you feel, when it comes to exciting new ventures

like yours that the most important thing to get right is the soul-space?'

'The what now?'

Maybe Bailey had already started to get tired of her. Well, that would help.

I excused myself and went outside.

I took a walk along the beach to try and clear my head. This was all happening so fast. I looked out to sea, at the big boats bobbing up and down in the harbour. Who knew what was happening out there? Could be anything. I felt my head had turned round 360 degrees. First, meeting Tom. Then, finding out he was using me. Then, finding out he may have a point . . . argh. My head hurt, and for once it wasn't just from too much champagne.

And Dr Maitland being against it too . . . it was too weird.

Along the beach I spied a stocky figure rubbing sun-cream on a skinny one. Not exactly an unusual sight round here.

'Hello, Evie!' Kelly shouted cheerfully, as if nothing had happened the night before. 'Great yacht.'

I half smiled. John Jr looked uncomfortable. His belly was going pink. Family skin.

'Hi, JJ,' I said. I felt shy too. 'Thanks again for everything last night.'

It just felt so odd to be saying something nice.

'No probs, sis,' said JJ. Kelly kicked him with a French-manicured toe. 'Oh ... and ... sorry. For ruining things at dinner with that doc.'

'You didn't,' I said. 'Don't worry about it.'

And we half smiled at each other.

'Great,' said John Jr. 'Because Patrick's coming out.'

'WHAT?'

'He heard the chicks here are amazing. He's on his way.'

'No chance! I can cope with one of you, but ...'

'Maybe we'll find him a nice girl,' said Kelly, who honestly thinks Patrick is just misunderstood, rather than an indiscriminate shag beast.

'No way.'

'Gets here tonight, just in time for your casino night.'

I'd forgotten all about casino time. God, there wasn't a second off.

'Boys on the town,' said JJ.

Although it had given me an idea. Usually I let Patrick's glands do their own thing ... but this might just work ... was he really as irresistible as he liked to think? I steeled myself for the wildly expensive mobile call.

'Yeah?'

The voice was surly, like I'd just got him out of bed. Except I knew I hadn't, because he still worked nine-to-five, however much he liked to pretend he was a good-looking bad boy who obeyed nobody's rules but his own.

'Patrick?'

'Who is this?'

I sighed. 'It's your one and only sister, Evie.'

'Oh. What do you want?'

'When are you coming to Cannes? All the booze is free, the sun is shining and it's absolutely crawling with . . .'

I hated to say it, but I was going to have to.

'What?'

'Muff.'

'Yeah. Today. Right. Didn't think you'd be so happy about it. JJ says you've been right slapping it up.'

'JJ says a lot of things. Anyway . . . I've got a really pretty friend here who'll be happy to show you around.'

Patrick snorted. 'Is she as pretty as Jilly?'

It was true; pre-Cassandro, Jilly had mooned around Patrick endlessly when we were growing up, eating cheese strings whilst conspiring to be constantly in the corridor outside his bedroom. His bedroom was next to the bathroom; he must have thought she had a terrible bladder problem.

'Miles better looking. In fact, are you in front of your computer?'

This was unfair. I know Patrick would have preferred me to imagine he was out on the open road somewhere on a Harley, chatting up a waitress in a truck-stop café on Route 66.

'Hnn,' he said grudgingly.

'OK, go to www.yourperfectface.co.uk.'

I knew they used Lydia on the home page of the surgery she worked for. It was a pouty, Posh Spice-style photograph, which I had always thought gave off the message, 'Piss off, you could never look like me, you fat losers.' But this hadn't seemed to deter people.

'Is that her?' he said admiringly.

'Uh-huh!'

'For real?'

'And John Jr has a huge suite and would be delighted to see you' – I crossed my fingers – 'and, tonight we're all going to the casino and you get free money to play with.'

'And you can get me in?'

'Sure, the security's rubbish.'

Well, it was.

'Yeah. I'm on my way.'

That was Lydia taken care of. He may be an arse, but I haven't met a woman yet with the power to resist Patrick, at least on first glance till they find out what a tit he is – and not always then.

But I still had to get Bailey on our side. I headed back to the marquee, but he was *still* deep in conversation with Lydia, who was on full power, so that would have to wait. At least I'd sown the seeds. The next plan on my list, whilst Dr Maitland went off to spy on the docs, was the one I was least looking forward to. But it had to be done.

I found a quiet Internet café, took out Dr Maitland's mobile phone (mine is pay as you go and lasts for about one second overseas, as I'd just discovered phoning Patrick), and sat down with Google.

I had to find Tom. He presumably had access to all sorts of documentation about the project, hence his motivation for why it was wrong. He could help us stop this thing. Even if he was a horrible, sexy, nasty, sexy man.

I couldn't help it – suddenly, even though I was nervous about finding Tom, I was a little bit excited. This was like a proper adventure! And we were the good guys! Fighting for seals and against bad people getting new faces! Yeah!

OK. Obviously the mobile phone number he'd originally given me no longer worked. I'd taken that as a given; it wasn't even the first time in my life that that had happened to me, so ha ha ha, meanie pants.

But he had said he came from Cumbria. I think I'd have to assume from the slightly posh Northern accent that he was telling the truth. Cumbria wasn't a large place, was it? OK, lots of sheep maybe, but how many vets?

I didn't know how to divide sheep by vets, so I searched for Cumbrian vets and got a website listing all UK vets. (Wow, I mean, really, have you ever met someone who designs vet websites for a living? Is it for pigs that can use the phone?)

I started dialling, then stopped. Was Tom his real name? Bennet certainly wasn't. Well, you know, I think I'd just have to assume it was because he'd turned round when people were shouting it as he was running naked across a pier, when presumably your mind would be on other things apart from remembering your fake name. Plus James Bond always called himself James. It was all I had to go on.

I'd just have to try and be casual.

'Hi, is Tom there?'

'Tom who?'

'Oh, you know, just Tom.'

'Tom the carthorse Tom?'

'Uh, no.'

'The cat? Or I think we have a python . . . no, that's Tomasina . . .'

OK, maybe another approach.

'I'm trying to track down a vet called Tom. He's got bright ginger hair and his ears stick out.'

Responses varied from, 'We've got a ferret that fits that description' to 'Are you *sure*, luv?'

But finally, on the twenty-fourth call, I hit it.

'Tom Livingstone? Yes, he's not in today. He's away at a veterinary conference.'

Oh, was he now?

'Oh well . . . it's quite urgent I get in touch with him. He was advising me about . . . a hamster.'

'Was he indeed?' the voice sounded amused. Maybe they were used to getting phone calls from desperate girls with imaginary hamsters.

'Is it anything someone else could help you with? Tom's not really a . . . hamster specialist.'

'No,' I said hotly. 'Gingerbread is very important to me and he's happy with Tom.'

'OK,' said the receptionist. I'm usually quite good at getting round receptionists, being one and everything.

'Is there any way I could get in touch with him . . . ?' I tried to make my voice sound pathetic. 'It's just . . . Gingerbread's got the most persistent cough. I couldn't bear to lose him. Maybe Tom could reassure me over the phone.'

'Mobiles are really just for emergencies,' said the voice.

'I understand,' I said in my smallest voice. 'I hope he lasts the night . . . when's he coming back?'

'Not till the end of the week.'

I sniffed loudly and didn't say anything.

'OK,' said the receptionist finally. 'Here's his mobile number. Just to set your mind at rest. I'm sure it's nothing.'

'Or TB,' I said. I was getting quite worked up about Gingerbread my imaginary hamster. But as she gave me the number and I hung up, I punched the air. I could be good at this!

My euphoria was short-lived, as I realised I was now actually going to have to make the call. Call the man who, just the night before, had humiliated me in front of everyone. Who I had had sex with. Not just with a man I hardly knew but with a man I knew all the wrong things about. Ugh. Oh well. Spies have to be very brave. I would just have to pretend that I was undercover too.

A thought struck me. What if he thought I was only calling him to get back together? Like he'd just been so absolutely amazing in bed that I didn't care that he was using me, I was just desperate for it? Oh, God, that would be awful. I should have got Dr Maitland to do this bit. But I wanted to show him I could handle it, that I was cool. Who was I kidding? I wasn't cool. Not even a tiny bit. With shaking fingers I dialled the number. At least he wouldn't recognise this phone number.

'Hello?' The voice sounded gruff and business-like, not the easy-going charmer I'd met. I steeled myself and hoped my voice wasn't about to wobble too much.

'Tom?'

'Who is this?'

I rolled my eyes. Torture me, why don't you?

'It's Evie.'

I could hear his brain gears tick over – he obviously wasn't expecting this. I prayed he wouldn't hang up.

'Uh,' he said. 'Look, I have to go . . .'

'No!' I said desperately. 'Don't hang up. It's nothing to do with last night.'

'How did you track me down?'

'You're helping me with my sick hamster.'

'Well, that's a new way of putting it.'

'Look, this is nothing to do with last night,' I repeated.

'Nothing at all? Are you sure?'

'Did you get arrested?'

He sucked in his breath. 'Not for want of you lot trying, no.'

'Uh, tell me you're not trying to *blame me* for last night. Please tell me that, before I have you arrested for indecent exposure.'

'You nicked my boxers and chased me like a loon!'

'Well, then . . . sex under false pretences.'

'It's hardly my fault if you refuse to see what's right under your nose, is it?' he said suddenly. 'I mean, I know you work in beauty so you hardly give a damn, but they're extracting live foetuses from seals to make some stupid fucking face juice and you think it's OK? They're going to completely ignore international protocol and do anything they like out on the high seas, but you don't mind?'

'I mind being taken advantage of,' I said softly.

He paused for a long time. Then his voice lowered. 'Actually,' he said. 'I'd already realised you didn't know anything. The day before, really, when we were walking along the beach. I mean, it was obvious.'

That winded me a bit. 'What do you mean?'

'I mean . . . you know, I still liked you.'

'That's not what you mean,' I said. 'I mean, you were sent to do a job and saw an opportunity. What was I, just another piece of meat like your dead bloody seals? Just something to take advantage of, even though I wasn't any *use* to you?'

'No . . . it wasn't like that,' he said.

'It sounds exactly the fuck like that,' I said. I was getting wound up again. Then I tried my best, my absolute best to get a grip on myself. I took in a huge breath and tried to blow it out through my nose, like yoga teachers tell you to do.

'Are you being sick?' asked Tom.

'No!' I said. But oddly, his remark made it a bit easier to get a hold of myself.

'Look,' I said. 'Forget all this. Me and Dr Maitland have been talking.'

'Uh-huh?'

'And . . . well, he has doubts . . . we have doubts about the project.'

'Do you now? What gave it away, the amount of businessmen around wearing sunglasses indoors and surrounded by goons carrying walkie-talkies?'

'They aren't . . . Oh,' I said, thinking about some of the larger men at the conference. 'I thought those were just really old-fashioned mobile phones.'

'We got some really bad intelligence, picking on you,' said Tom, but he said it with a smile in his voice.

'Shut up,' I said. 'You're not allowed to mention that ever again.'

'I won't,' he said, immediately sounding chastened. 'And . . . I'm sorry. I'm really sorry.'

'So you should be,' I said.

'Um, could you stop punishing me? Remember, you did make me run through Cannes in the nuddie.'

'What did you do?' I said. 'We thought you'd get arrested.'

'Lucky I didn't. I found a wine cellar and hid down there.'

'Don't tell me – you put a cork in it.'

'*No*. I improvised with a couple of aprons and made it back.'

I half smiled at the thought. 'Can we meet?' I asked. 'Dr Maitland and I have some questions.'

'OK, Nancy Drew,' said Tom. 'Do you know the Metropole hotel?'

'Yes,' I said.

'OK. There's a little ice-cream shop next to it. I'll see you in there.'

I couldn't help feeling a little excited as I pushed my way through the crowds on the Croisette. After all, they were just silly sheep on holiday. *I* on the other hand was on an exciting secret mission. With ice cream. So it was like a bonus holiday.

When I found the place, though, I didn't see Tom. I was slightly curious to see him again, just in case I wanted to accidentally kick him in the face, but he didn't appear to be there. Perhaps I'd just sit down, order a Knickerbocker Glory and wait for . . .

'Psst,' came a voice. I looked behind me. 'Psst,' again.

It was coming from the corner of the restaurant. Sitting there was a man with dark hair and a baseball cap, behind a Russian newspaper. I moved closer.

'*Tom?*'

'Shhh!'

He pulled me down by the arm to sit next to him. I could hardly contain myself.

'I am Rudi. Russian engineer,' he announced loudly.

'You *are* joking.'

'Shh.'

'You're in disguise.'

'Well, seeing as my face and arse are all over *Cannes Matin* and everyone that was at that bash knows it was infiltrated, it seemed wise, don't you think?'

'To cover your head in boot polish and jam your ears together? I'm not sure.'

'Did anyone follow you?'

'*What?*'

'I should have told them NEVER to hand out my number . . . my phone's probably been tapped.'

'Aren't you taking this a little too seriously?'

'Well, we're trying to derail a fifty-million-euro project – what do you think?'

I hadn't really thought of it like that. 'You mean, we could be in danger?'

'Sometimes it's hard to do the right thing,' said Tom pompously.

'You know, that would sound a lot more manly and impressive if you didn't have a smudge of raspberry sauce on your cheek. Where's my ice cream?'

'I wasn't sure you were coming.'

'What, you thought I'd get kidnapped on the way? Or double-cross you?'

He looked at me strangely then.

'What do you mean, double-cross me?'

'I don't mean anything. I mean, can I have some choco-late ice cream, please?'

'It would be a very quick change of tune for you,' he mused. 'From know-nothing receptionist to suddenly being interested in finding out everything I know.'

'Yes,' I said. 'Plus, they said if I screwed you over they'd throw in a free boob job made from starving baby elephants. Stop being an idiot.'

He lowered the paper.

'OK,' he said. 'It's hard to trust sometimes.'

'It certainly is when your job is screwing people over,' I said. '*Une glace, s'il vous plaît? Chocolat, oui.*' At times, my French is fine. 'Now. Who do you work for again?'

'Earth Friends,' he mumbled. 'It's a loose collective that tries to argues against the more . . . evil extremes of capitalism.'

'What, like those people who throw stones at Starbucks? I hate those people.'

'*No*, we're a bit more subtle than that. Why do you hate those people?'

'Because a cup of coffee is not that evil. Compared to . . . I don't know. Men that set women on fire if they've been raped. Or send people to fight in pointless wars. Or, you know, commit genocide.'

'Do you protest against those things?'

'Not *as such*. But I disapprove of them. A lot more than some stupid cup of coffee.'

'Well, I'm glad you're managing to provide such a vital stance against things you disapprove of in society by doing absolutely nothing at all.'

'Right, I'd be much better off taking a brick and throwing it through a shop window of a business someone's actually spent time building up and . . .'

'Can we get off the whole coffee thing for a minute? That's not my point. Earth Friends is more . . . think of a charity you do approve of.'

'Uh.' I couldn't think. 'The RSPB?'

'The *RSPB*?'

'Yes?'

He sighed. 'OK. Well, we're more like the RSPB. We campaign against grossly dangerous environmental projects and things we feel mark a really bad direction for society. And we make examples of specific things. Like, for example, a practically completely illegal boat where they're going to carry out dangerous medical procedures whilst getting through, incidentally, twenty thousand litres of fuel a week, whilst they experiment with God knows what.'

'So what did you want out of me?'

'Where it was headed . . . itinerary . . . whether Bailey knew, or whether you controlled Dr Bennet's diary... celebrity clients...'

'What, after you'd shagged me so spectacularly that the names of show business clients had come out of my mouth?'

Tom shrugged a little uncomfortably.

'Well. Maybe if you'd had dark hair and a Russian accent,' I said.

'It was just an idea,' said Tom sulkily.

'Has it ever worked before in the history of mankind?'

'Yes, all the time,' he said. 'Admittedly, mostly the other way around. Girls seducing boys, that kind of thing. Or boys seducing boys.'

'Well, at least it kept you off the letter writing campaign.'

I picked up a large spoonful of chocolate ice cream and devoured it. 'What I don't understand is why you didn't just ask me? Look, I'm here now, ready to come over on your side and fight the good fight.'

'How could I ask you? What would you think if some lunatic came up to you and suggested that you went against your friends and your employers and everyone you know on some crazed scheme?'

'I'm very open-minded,' I said.

'True,' said Tom, getting a faraway look in his eyes.

I ignored him and kept eating my ice cream. 'So,' I said. 'What's the plan?'

'Well, the original plan was to go to the papers with all the blueprints and celebrities and things,' said Tom. 'Can I have some of your ice cream?'

'NO! Dr Maitland and I think we should have a better plan. One that involves talking to Dr Bennet.'

'*Talking* to him? Talking him out of ten million euros? How are you going to do that?'

'*Ten million euros?*' This was ridiculous. It couldn't be true, could it? Who had that much money?

'Or, well, you know. Something like that. Lots and lots of money from his boat, all offshore.'

'Oh,' I said. 'So you don't know how much money he stands to make. You meant –' and I did the Dr Evil pinky lip – 'ten *meelion* euros.'

Tom didn't answer. He was too busy stealing a bit of my ice cream.

'So even if you could talk him out of it, they'll just get somebody else,' said Tom.

'OK, well, if we talk *everyone* out of it.'

'Everyone on earth? I still think getting agitation in the press is a better idea. Get them to stake out the place with paparazzi. Get some of our youth members along to demonstrate.'

'*Youth* members?'

'Yes. You know, some politically switched-on types have even heard of us.'

'Stop stealing my ice cream, you communist.'

We discussed lots of things. To me, it seemed crucial to get to Dr Bennet and get him on side. If Bailey couldn't give us valuable information about who exactly had commissioned the ship and was behind the job, Dr Bennet ought to be able to. Then the next stage was to threaten them with exposure or . . . well, we weren't sure about the 'or'.

'Couldn't they take all the money and build a children's hospital or something?' I said.

'What, for baby nose jobs? Anyway, look around you: you're in France. They're up to their eyeballs in totally perfect children's hospitals. Mind you, it's one up on what I thought you'd say.'

'What's that?'

'That you thought they should donate all the money to the RSPB . . .'

'Ha ha ha. Birds are very important, you know.'

'I know. Look, Earth Friends has the contacts, the press – we can lobby against this kind of thing once we know who's doing it.'

He looked up at me. 'So we're in this together, right? You can get me a pass to this casino shindig tonight?'

'I guess so,' I said.

Tom sat back on the banquette, looking pleased with himself.

'But don't smirk.'

'I'm not smirking! It's the drawn-on moustache.'

'You look like you're smirking to yourself. You look like you're thinking, Ah, my shagging plan worked. But I'm telling you it didn't.'

'OK.'

'Dr Maitland convinced me.'

'OK.'

'It was nothing to do with you.'

'Not at all.'

'And you're paying for the ice cream.'

I called Dr Maitland on his other phone. He'd gone to find Dr Bennet but hadn't managed to locate him.

'That's unusual, isn't it?' I asked. 'He's usually schmoozing up all over the place.'

'That's what I thought,' he said. 'Maybe he's headed up to the casino to sort things out for tonight. Or maybe he's back in his hotel room?'

We decided his room might be a good place to tackle him. Just a chat – a staff meeting between the three of us. Just to get a bit more clarity on the direction the practice was going (out to sea by the looks of things) and so on . . . nothing heavy.

The afternoon sun beamed down strongly on the beach and I stopped off and bought a large floppy hat. My redness was retreating somewhat, but I didn't want to risk round two; I already had freckles popping up over every available surface. Plus it might come in handy for a disguise.

Dr Maitland almost smiled at me as I met him in the cool marble lobby of the Metropole.

'Is that you in disguise?' he said. 'The big hat and sunglasses?'

'No! This is totally normal!'

'OK,' he said. 'You know, there's a new laser pen for freckles that . . .'

I shushed him. 'You know, some people *like* freckles.'

He frowned. 'Do they?'

'Yes. They think they're cute.'

He came closer and gave my face that penetrating clinical doctory stare thing straight at my face.

'Oh,' he said eventually, straightening up. 'You know they're marks of skin damage?'

I rolled my eyes.

'But yes,' he said. 'They are quite cute. OK, shall we tell the desk to call Yuri?'

Ugh, it was the same snotty pretty man on the desk as before. Did he ever go off duty? Was this whole place staffed by robots? He looked at me, quite convincingly managing to indicate that he had X-ray eyes that could look into my soul and see if I was wanting in the 'being served in a posh hotel' department. Obviously I was as he actually looked around to see if there was anyone else he could help before us.

'Let's not bother,' I said. 'Do you know the room number? We can just go up.'

'OK,' shrugged Dr Maitland.

I've always felt slightly odd in a lift with a man, I don't

know why. Probably just so many silly films and dumb Black Lace books, but there's something about being in that enclosed space . . . I suppose that's why everyone just ignores each other and stares straight ahead. Because there's always that ridiculous idea that creeps into your head along the lines of, Wouldn't it be *awful* if I suddenly just leapt cougar-like onto this near-stranger and gave them a big . . .

'I think we're here,' said Dr Maitland.

The door pinged open to reveal, waiting for the lift to go back down, a somewhat dishevelled-looking Janey reapplying her lipstick!

'Hello!' I said cheerfully. I didn't move to get out of the lift; this was (or could be) too good to be true! 'Are you staying here too?'

Janey looked at me with absolutely no recognition in her eyes, but perked up when she saw Dr Maitland.

'Hello, Doctor . . . I mean, well, what a coincidence seeing you here.'

'Is it?' said Dr Maitland gruffly.

'I was just . . .' She gave a self-conscious giggle. 'Uh, going over some paperwork with Dr Bennet.'

'Is that what they're calling it these days?' I wondered aloud. After all, she was already ignoring me. Dr Maitland trod heavily on my foot to shut me up.

'Of *course*,' he said. 'There's so much to go through, isn't there? Health and safety, disclaimers . . . it ties us all up in knots, red tape.'

He gently but firmly started manoeuvring us out of the lift so Janey could step in.

Janey had regained her composure fully now.

'Oh, abso*lutely*,' she said. 'As I was just saying to Dr Bennet . . . so ridiculous. Plus what *must* I look like coming out of his room in the middle of the day! People will talk. Mind you –' she regarded us frankly – 'you could say that about you two! Ha ha!'

My eyebrows shot up in surprise. Turning it round! Boy, she was good!

'Didn't mean to make you blush,' she said to me merrily, convinced now she had the upper hand. 'Well, buh bye!'

And the lift door pinged, and she was gone.

Dr Maitland and I looked at each other speechlessly.

'Well, it could have been innocent,' he said.

'She was putting lipstick on!' I yelled. 'How did her lipstick come off?'

'But . . . you know, women like her wear a lot of lipstick.'

This is indubitably true. They slather it on like they're about to be filmed for high-definition IMAX.

We headed up the corridor.

'Well, if Dr Bennet's naked from the waist up,' I suggested, 'this could be a useful bargaining tool. Where is Mrs Bennet again?'

'Shopping for teeth sharpeners,' said Dr Maitland, preparing to knock on the door.

'What?' he said as I stopped short.

'That is the first time I've ever heard you make a joke,' I said. 'I thought it just wasn't possible for you. That humour had been surgically removed or something, like an appendix.'

Dr Maitland sighed. 'Well, we all know what a good judge of character you are, Evie,' he said. Then he knocked the door, and we entered.

Alas, Dr Bennet was not, as I had hoped (and partly feared), picking up a pair of stockings with his teeth whilst singing, 'Hurray, hurray, it's adultery today,' to himself and sipping the last of the champagne from a glass stiletto.

He did, however, look quite surprised to see us, given that we were his right-hand men. Or so I thought.

'Wilf . . . Evie. Hello, my dears. Um . . .'

Was that a sneaky checking round the room in case of tell-tale signs? Mind you, I would have had to check around my hotel room too if someone turned up unexpectedly, just in case I'd left any of my *own* knickers draped over the chair or whatnot.

'To what do I owe the honour . . . Janey was just here dropping off some paperwork, so it's like Piccadilly Circus round here today!'

Curses! Still he didn't get away so easily – he must have guessed we'd have run into her by the lift.

'What papers?' I said. 'Why don't I take them away with me so I can file them promptly.'

Dr Bennet looked at me, then fumbled on the table for his reading glasses.

'Well, aren't *you* efficient? Here you are then – the course recommendations, the assessment forms . . . here, you can take all these ones from the other seminars too.'

He started loading down my arms with folders.

'And the extra-curricular sign-ups – actually, if you could input those on the database and cross-reference to the original attendance that would be extremely helpful to us . . . start sorting out the wheat from the chaff.'

'Yuri,' said Dr Maitland. 'Can we talk?'

'Of course, of course.'

Dr Bennet looked at us, beaming.

'So nice to have the team together, yes? How do you think it's going? I think it's going very well, very well indeed. Well, apart from a couple of minor . . .' He came over to me and patted my arm. 'How *are* you, my dear? Did you file charges?'

This wasn't like him. He must be worried I had come here to sue the firm.

'No, it's all right,' I said. 'I don't want to get prosecuted for being an idiot.'

'That's the spirit,' said Dr Bennet, as if that actually was the spirit. 'Janey says that you have to be bigger than the set-backs in your life.'

'Does she?' I said. 'But she's three-foot six.'

'Don't be personal,' said Dr Bennet.

'Yuri,' said Dr Maitland heavily. 'We need to talk. We've got some concerns about Operation Sunshine.'

Dr Bennet stopped moving about. 'What. Both of you?' he said, all business suddenly. He poured us all glasses of water. 'Together?'

We both nodded.

'Go on then. Out with it.'

Dr Bennet listened while we explained everything that didn't add up about the project; the lax laws, open access to goodness knows who; the environmental impact. He didn't say anything, just looked at us as we talked – it felt like presenting something to your form teacher, who listened to you indulgently as you told him, wide-eyed, that God didn't exist.

After we'd finished we kind of tailed off with a few 'So's . . .' and 'So that's whys . . .' and then sat back. Dr Bennet still didn't say anything, he just sat there, cradling his fingers in that way they teach them at Being a Doctor college. His brow nearly furrowed.

'Wilf,' he said. 'Wilf. Didn't we discuss this?'

Dr Maitland looked uneasy. He took off his glasses.

'I didn't realise it was such a big deal, Yuri. I thought it was a side project, an offshoot that would bring us in some extra income and provide an interesting diversion . . .'

'A diversion, eh?' Dr Bennet looked a little nasty. 'So the research opportunities were of absolutely no interest to you?'

'Well, yes, obviously, but now I'm feeling . . . conflicted.'

'Conflicted?'

Suddenly the smooth calmness of Dr Bennet – the only mode I'd ever seen him in, Mr Charming – vanished, and he stood to his feet.

'*Conflicted?*' We have a fifty-million-euro boat out there that's just been refitted and you're saying you're *conflicted?*'

Dr Maitland shuffled uncomfortably. Suddenly this felt horribly serious.

'Don't tell me you don't have a vested interest in this.'

I looked at him. He looked haunted.

'So maybe I'd go against my own interests.'

'Would you?' said Dr Bennet. 'Look, you two. Obviously *you* –' and he pointed to me – 'have been completely compromised by that lanky ginger idiot.'

'Lanky ginger idiot . . . with a point,' I said.

But he'd already turned his attention back to Dr Maitland. Now his voice went back to its normal, encouraging, wheedling tone.

'Come on, Wilf. Don't be daft, it's just progress. If we don't do it somebody else will.'

'So let's not do it,' said Wilf. 'That's not a good argument for anything. Plus if you get wrapped up in anything illegal it might be dangerous.'

Dr Bennet harrumphed at this. 'Science is not legal or illegal, Wilf. You know this.'

'I don't,' said Wilf. 'In fact, I think the practice should pull out.'

Dr Bennet set his glass down with a thump.

'Pull out! After all this money spent and the engineers employed and the doctors and the bankers lined up begging to get let in? Are you *crazy*?'

'No,' said Wilf. He stood up suddenly and took a deep breath. 'But I'm out.'

'You're what . . . you're resigning?'

Dr Bennet was trying to keep his cool, but I could see he was furious.

'I don't have to resign,' said Dr Maitland. 'You're not my boss. I'm your partner. I'm dissolving our partnership.'

Dr Bennet's mouth was open. So was mine. Oh my God! This wasn't a little holiday flirtation with activism! This was really serious! I knew, you see. Dr Maitland was miles better than Dr Bennet. Dr Maitland was what kept us on Harley Street, and in the celebrities' secret notebooks, and on the recommended lists. Dr Bennet could do the schmooze and the charm, but Dr Maitland was the one who wielded the knife; who could give nose jobs that don't even look like nose jobs (and believe me, when you've seen as many as I have you realise how rare that is).

'Wilf,' said Dr Bennet. 'You don't mean that.'

'I've been sleepwalking,' said Dr Maitland. He sat down, and didn't look at either of us. 'All this time, thinking chopping open stupid dumb blondes was fine, it was just training till I could take my skills somewhere else, some-where useful. Go work in a war zone, or with burns victims in India. That was my plan. But then what happened? I got used to the easy money, coming in at ten every morning, not having to talk to anyone if I didn't want to, living a nice life.'

I didn't think it sounded that nice, apart from the money part, but I didn't want to interrupt.

'So I never did any of that . . . all the big plans I had at medical school. The good life I'd mapped out for myself. I didn't want to go to Africa and get bitten by bugs and have to sleep in tents. I didn't want to go and work in dirty hopeless conditions in the Third World. I *liked* being comfortable.'

He stood up and walked over to Dr Bennet.

'But this *is* dirty. This is dirtier than . . . one of those countries where dogs eat dead dogs in the street. This smells worse than somewhere I'd have to wipe my scalpel on the long grass. Because this is what happens when you get complacent, when you get comfortable. Bad things happen. And bad things are going to happen here. And I'm not doing it.'

'Fine,' said Dr Bennet. 'Then we'll do it without you.'

And *then* he punched Wilf on the nose.

I knelt next to Dr Maitland, whose nose was discharging thick gouts of blood, while Dr Bennet, whistling slightly, washed his hands and picked up his briefcase. I was shocked, and breathing hard. I mean, obviously I'd seen plenty of blood, but usually people were anaesthetised.

'So I guess this is goodbye, Evie,' he said chirpily. 'I won't be paying you compensation . . . I'm sure you'll understand.'

'What, after you let me be assaulted at your conference? We'll see about that,' I said, white-hot with fury. 'You'll be hearing from my lawyers.'

'Who are your lawyers again?' he asked, looking amused. 'Ambulance chasers dot com? Well, I wish you good luck with that – there are very few extradition treaties between the UK and . . . the middle of the sea.'

He stood, looking impatient.

'Could you move now, please . . . I have an important session to run. And a new staff to recruit.'

I looked at Dr Maitland, but he still seemed too stunned to say anything. Dr Bennet didn't even look a tiny bit perturbed; simply ushering us out in his usual charming manner as if on his way to a hairdresser's appointment.

I drew myself up to my full height (five foot five) and tried to look him straight in the eye.

'You won't get away with this,' I said, voice trembling.

'What is this, *Scooby Doo*?' he said. 'What's to get away with? I'm pursuing a legitimate business interest without my partner. Big deal.'

'So why did you just punch him on the nose?'

'Are you joking? Six years without so much as a "good morning"? Do you know what it's like working with someone like that? I wish I'd done it years ago, the rude bastard.'

Hmm. He almost had a point there.

Chapter Eleven

'It's true,' Wilf – as he'd now suggested I called him – was saying, as we sat in the lobby drinking a restorative *citron* as he held a tissue to his nose. 'But I'm just shy, that's all. Shy and . . . I was slightly ashamed of my job.'

'I've always wondered,' I said, figuring it was now or never, 'why you wouldn't take your obvious skills somewhere more useful.'

He looked defensive, as if he wanted to avoid the question.

'Plenty of good doctors just work for the cash.'

'Yes, well, there's a difference between a good doctor and a good person.'

'Hmm,' said Wilf, looking uncomfortable. He dabbed at his nose some more. Then he turned to face me.

'You always tell the truth, don't you, Evie?' he said. 'It's an unusual habit.'

I looked into his grey-blue eyes. '*Good* unusual?' I found myself asking, a little short of breath.

Suddenly there was a huge commotion in the lobby.

'Hey, look, it's my half-naked slutbag sister,' came the cheery voice booming across the lobby. The concierge raised his eyebrows nastily. Obviously JJ had got over our touching family reunion.

'Hello, John Jr,' I said, trying to insinuate that I had much better things to be going on with. 'Is Patrick here yet?'

'I'm just going to get him, in I?'

He stared rudely at Wilf. 'Ooh, the doc again. You don't mess around, do you?'

'Hello, again,' said Wilf, a little stiffly. Oh, crap. Just when Wilf and I were getting along he'd be reminded that, technically, I was related to an orang-utan. Bugger. Though what was I being so snotty about – my GCSE in general studies?

'You know they've got brandies here for two 'undred euro a glass?' said John Jr. He paused to allow us to take in the impressiveness of his statement. 'I didn't like mine much. Only 'ad four. Ah well, all goes on the company credit card, eh, Doc? Eh? Eh?'

Wilf smiled nicely, which I liked.

'Gawd, if I had to add up the time I've spent waiting for

the missus to get her slap on . . . Stupid cow. 'Ere she is now.'

Kelly tottered towards us, her face in the widest smile I'd ever seen.

''Ello!' she said. 'Feeling better?'

'I'm totally over it now actually,' I said.

'And you with that awful skin peel too. You know, you want to get some Crème de la Mer – it is expensive, but it's *so* worth it. Anyway,' she said, 'you won't *believe* what's happened!'

'What?' I asked. I wasn't quite up to telling her my news: sacked, in trouble, penniless, etc.

'Well, I ran into your gorgeous Dr Bennet at lunch . . . and he asked me to be his *inaugural* client when he launches his new venture!'

Wilf and I looked at each other in consternation.

'Bloody hell,' I said. 'What did they say they're going to do to you?'

She smiled. 'Oh, this is the exciting part. It's completely new. They've never done it before. Roxy – something. They inject it under my entire face, and it apparently looks like I have completely new skin! Like a baby's! I'll look twenty!'

'You're only thirty-one,' I said.

She pouted. 'Exactly. Nothing like twenty.'

'Why do you even care? You're married, you've got a big house . . . I mean, what's it to you?'

'Well,' said Kelly, 'it's just a matter of personal pride and self-esteem, that's all.' Then she realised she might have insulted me and looked apologetic.

Wilf was looking anxious.

'Mrs Kennedy . . . this treatment they described to you . . . is it called Radoflux 9000?'

Kelly's face lit up. 'Yeah, that's it!'

I looked at Wilf. 'It's those bloody seals again, isn't it?'

He nodded.

'Do you think it's dangerous?' I said.

'We don't know if it's dangerous yet,' said Wilf. 'Possibly. And the use of animal stem cells in plastic surgery – or at all – well, it's very controversial.'

'There you go,' I said to Kelly. 'It's dangerous. Possibly. You'd be mad to do it, it's not even legal.'

'Well, why would a doctor have recommended it if it wasn't legal?' said Kelly, pouting a bit.

'And there, in a nutshell, is the problem with this fucking boat,' said the odd-looking person waltzing through the circular door.

'Who are you?' said Kelly. 'Why is everyone ganging up on me?'

'Don't listen to them, sweetheart,' said John Jr. 'They're just jealous.'

'I'm not jealous,' I said. 'We're just trying to stop her from having a procedure that might harm her!'

'But it's just a minor procedure, Evie,' said Kelly. 'It'll be fine.'

'Yeah,' said John Jr. 'You're just jealous she's getting something for free that you really bloody need. Look at you lot.'

Sure enough, with me, Tom arriving with boot polish under his nose and Wilf with dried blood trickling on his face we did make quite a sight.

Kelly appeared to think about it.

'I'll see you lot later,' she said finally. 'I'll be the twenty-year-old in the corner.'

And they swept out, or rather Kelly swept; John Jr waddled after her.

Wilf let out a heavy sigh. 'This is not good,' he said. 'This is not good at all. And who the hell have you come as?'

Tom looked a little insulted.

'Uh, sorry,' I said. 'This is our mystery man in heavy disguise.'

'A mystery man, eh?' said Wilf, looking puzzled. Pretty much every eye in the foyer was on Tom. A bit of his hair dye had run down onto his ear, making it look smudged. His sunglasses were a little wonky. And he had salt stains on his shorts. Out of the corner of my eye I felt the evil concierge send a little death ray in our direction. I clutched at my drink to show I had the right to be there.

'Oh, wow,' said Tom. 'Did you get in a big ruckus with Dr Bennet?'

'Not so much a *big* ruckus,' said Wilf.

'He got biffed on the nose,' I added helpfully.

229

'Oh, good,' said Tom. 'Did you discover all his backers? When is the boat coming in? What other evil plans he has up his sleeve?'

'Not exactly,' I said.

Tom thought about this. 'You know, we really need to know when the boat is coming in, so we can intercept it.'

'Maybe it's a surprise,' I said.

'It's a fucking liberty,' snapped Tom.

'He doesn't seem to think he's being evil,' said Wilf.

'Well, he *is*,' said Tom. 'And that injection thing is completely out of the question.'

'It didn't . . . it didn't go quite as well as we'd hoped,' I said.

'You mean, you guys messed it up?'

'He didn't seem to want to talk to us much,' mumbled Wilf. He checked out his reflection in one of the big gilt mirrors hanging overhead.

'It's all right,' I said. 'I don't think you need stitches.'

'Thank you, doctor,' he muttered.

Tom threw his hands up. 'Well, this is great. Did he sack you?'

'Well, he can't sack me, I'm his partner,' said Wilf. 'I resigned.'

Tom put his hands over his eyes.

'He sacked me though,' I added helpfully.

'I have to make a phone call,' said Tom.

*

'But I thought you guys had a *plan*,' Tom was saying as the three of us walked down to the seafront.

'We did!' I said. 'We thought we'd explain the error of his ways and then everything would be all right. Now I think about it, not such a brilliant plan.'

'So . . . all your contacts and hope of getting on that boat . . . it's all gone.'

'And I lost my job,' I said. 'And I'll never get another one in the same field now they've all seen me in your boxers.'

'You can come work for me,' said Wilf.

'I thought you told Dr Bennet you were going to work in darkest Africa,' I said.

'Oh, yeah,' he said, looking a tad disconsolate. 'So I am.'

'No!' said Tom. 'What do you mean! We're not giving up!'

'Well, we kind of have to,' I explained. 'Because, you know. We're not a part of this any more. Dr Bennet is just going to run the boat and it's our tough luck, and, I don't know, Kelly will probably end up taking liquids through a straw for the rest of her life.'

'I can't believe you're taking it like that,' said Tom.

I turned to him seriously. 'What do you expect me to do? I'm sorry, Tom. The boat is horrible. So are lots of things. It's going to happen with or without us, that's perfectly clear. But we did try. We all did. Why don't we just go out and have a few glasses of wine and try and forget all about it . . .'

'That's a shit attitude and you know it,' said Tom.

He left our group and looked at the road.

'You say you want to help and then you do fuck all.'

'I got a bloody nose,' said Wilf, but this only seemed to enrage Tom all the more.

'Fucking dilettantes. Don't you care what happens to this planet?'

'Yes,' I said. 'Let's discuss it over a glass of rosé. Maybe Wilf could help your charity.'

'Yes,' said Wilf, brightening slightly. 'With, you know. A UK-based helping job. Where I could still use my skills . . . maybe in the London area . . . research perhaps.'

'Forget it,' said Tom. He backed away from us, and onto the open road, stepping off the narrow pavement. He obviously didn't want to be anywhere near us. 'Forget it. This whole thing . . . You guys were a complete waste of time. I should have known it from the start.'

'I'm sorry,' I said, and I was. But what else could we do?

'You're not,' said Tom. Scooters and cyclists were having to swerve to avoid him. 'You don't give a . . .'

Suddenly a car, which should have gone straight past us, screeched to a halt. It was a huge, heavy-looking silver thing – a big steely Mercedes. It had blacked-out windows, which gave it a sinister appearance. Completely without warning the back door opened and two sets of arms came out. They hauled Tom backwards into the car's dark maw.

Taken completely by surprise from behind, Tom didn't even make a sound as he disappeared. His big gangling feet were the last to go, kicking in the air. Even before they were fully in, the car sped off. It couldn't have stopped for more than four seconds; it had barely inconvenienced the cars behind it. But suddenly, Tom was gone.

'TOM!' I screamed into the air. I threw myself forward, but the car had already taken a left turn and disappeared into the swiftly moving traffic before speeding away on the four-lane raised motorway that cut through the heart of Cannes like a knife. 'TOM!'

Unbelievably, under the shady palm trees, it seemed like no one else had even noticed.

Chapter Twelve

We went to the only place I was sure nobody would find us – my horrible guest house. The landlady hadn't looked me in the face once since I'd arrived so I could be reasonably confident she wouldn't be able to pick me out in a line-up or betray me to mysterious goons.

We sat there awkwardly, on my bed.

'Oh, God,' I kept saying, although it didn't really help matters much. 'Oh, God.'

'We must go to the police,' said Wilf. 'We must.'

'But they're already looking for him! They want to arrest him for being naked! Plus, what on earth would we tell them?'

'That a man was pushed into a car!'

'What kind of car?'

'A big silver car.'

'And where was it going?'

Wilf looked really concerned. 'This is serious, isn't it? This is serious stuff with bad guys and everything. This isn't like a holiday adventure at all.'

'What if they kill him?'

'They can't kill him,' I said, realising I was shaking. 'They won't.'

'Who, though?' said Wilf. 'Who are we even talking about? *Bloody* Yuri. We need to get to him.'

He tried his phone again. Dr Bennet wasn't picking up.

I glanced at my watch. 'He'll be at the casino. That thing will be starting.'

'Well, we'd better get there, then. Once we finally find out who's responsible and where he is we can call the *gendarmes*.'

We were going to rush off to the casino straight away, but this was a posh night and presumably Dr Bennet had already taken us off the guest list. We didn't want to stand out more than we already did. I sent Wilf onwards and, finally, slipped into the bloody red dress. In my head I'd imagined myself taking a long time getting ready in my large marble bathroom before slipping it over my sun-drenched skin. Not shoving it on over my blistered shoulders before running out to try and find our friend who'd been *kidnapped*. My holiday dreams seemed long ago and far away. And what had seemed like a bit of excitement was suddenly careering out of control.

I looked at the high-heeled shoes I'd bought to go with

the dress. Well, they weren't going to work because I had to run all the way to the casino as it was. Which meant I had a choice between my boots that I'd worn from London, a pair of red Converse – which were the right colour but made me look as if I was trying to make a ridiculous Lily Allen style statement – or a pair of flip-flops. Flip-flops it would have to be. At least my skin seemed to be settling down a bit. Though I hardly had the chance to do more than glance at myself in the mirror and bung on some red lipstick before throwing myself out of the hotel and tearing down towards the seafront. My heart was pounding. OK, Tom was an idiot, but he didn't deserve this. I had a sudden horrible mental image of him cowering in a room somewhere, or being thrown into the sea. And I was *furious* with Dr Bennet. He was going to tell us where Tom was if I had to . . . bloody pluck out his bloody eyebrows.

Holding my skirt with both hands – and tripping over every two minutes in those bloody flip-flops – I finally made it. Completely breathless and with sweat dripping off my forehead, I pelted up to the front of the casino, chest heaving.

The casino was white and palatial with steps leading up to it. Outside was a cashpoint machine. This put me off somewhat. I mean, obviously, it's useful for people to be able to pick up cash, but I didn't like the idea of people desperately pushing cards into the machine in the middle of the night just to feed their gambling addiction.

Expensive cars were disgorging expensive-looking

occupants as tourists walked past rubbernecking. I looked for the silver car but couldn't see it. Stealthily dangerous-looking bouncers hovered round the entrances. And there, looking tall and smart and slightly concerned, his bow tie untied around his neck, out of breath like I was, was Wilf.

He didn't see me at first so I waved furiously. Then, when he did, his face changed. The anxiety drained out of it – not completely, but enough to soften up his features and give a spark to his eye. And for a second I forgot that our friend had disappeared; that I'd lost my job; that this was a really weird holiday; that we'd failed in our mission to stop the project; that, in fact, my life had gone from mundane to disastrous in the space of about three days (and I was probably going to die of skin cancer too). Just for a second.

'Hello,' he said, coming down the steps towards me.

'Hello,' I said. We looked round. There was nobody there that we knew. He grinned that lopsided smile at me.

'You look . . . you look nice.'

'That's impossible,' I said. 'I just threw it on in two seconds. Literally. I'm not wearing any make-up or anything.'

Wilf shrugged. 'I don't like overdone women.'

I stared at him.

'You are joking. That's what you do.'

'Haven't we already established that I'm not *exactly* over the moon about what I do?' said Wilf. Then, shyly, he leaned over and planted a kiss on my cheek.

I stepped back, feeling my heart beat.

'Uh,' I said. 'Uh . . . we'd better go and do this thing.'

'Absolutely,' said Wilf. 'Fortune favours the brave. Let's go find Yuri and, I don't know, *tickle* the answers out of him.'

'Er, yeah,' I said.

'Um,' said Wilf. 'Could you do up my bow tie first?'

Bow tie looking like a badly wrapped party gift (hey, it's not like I sent my brothers out to black tie dos very often), we vaulted up the steps, planning our strategy. If Dr Bennet didn't come clean we were going straight to the police – well, as strategies went it wasn't a bad one. As long as we were on time. But I also thought, I mean, they'd probably just take Tom somewhere and make him walk home naked again to get him back for ruining their yacht party, wouldn't they?

First we had to get past the bouncers. I hoped against hope that Dr Bennet would have been too busy or annoyed to waste time getting our names taken off the list. And the person he'd usually have ordered to do so was, of course, me. He couldn't really find his way around a sheet of A4 without me.

Clattering up the steps we were conscious that there was an aura of low-key elegance about the place. Beautiful waitresses glided about with cocktails on trays. Smart music was tinkling. Expensive-looking paintings lined the walls. Everything about the place seemed designed to make you completely forget that its sole purpose was to send you down the road to rack and ruin and end up owning your house and, ideally, wife.

'Just look like we fit in,' I whispered as we mounted the red-carpeted steps.

'You're the one in flip-flops,' Wilf whispered back, then he took my hand and squeezed it. I squeezed it back, then let it stay there. It felt comfortable. I felt – even though we'd been thoroughly bested so far – that if I was with him, then maybe we were going to be all right.

'Aha,' came the familiar voice, and the face peered quizzically down on us from the top of the stairs.

'*Quelle surprise!*'

Lydia.

'I wondered if you two would have the cheek to turn up,' she sneered. 'But here you are – waif man and the deep-fried tomato. Holding hands. How touching.'

Lydia was clutching a large clipboard with names on it. Witch with a clipboard – ominous.

'You know, you don't have to be nasty all the time,' I said. 'It's not in your job description. *Is* it?'

'*Me* being nasty?' said Lydia. 'I'm not the ones that tried to embarrass Dr Bennet and the entire bloody Harley Street community, am I? I'm not the ones who are having a cheap and tacky affair and had a big strop when it was discovered and then quit their jobs leaving poor Dr Bennet in the lurch.'

'Is *that* what he said?' I yelled, furious. 'He's lying.'

'So I can see by the fact that you're holding hands.'

239

'We really need to get in there, er, Lydia,' said Wilf. 'Do you mind?'

'Yes, I do actually,' said Lydia. 'Because your names aren't here on my clipboard. Which means you've been disinvested. Which means if you do try and get in I'll have to shout to the nearest two gigantic bouncers who, and I haven't seen it myself, but *apparently*, can kick your arse from here to doomsday.'

I looked at the stealthy bouncers again. Yup. It certainly looked possible, if not probable. As I was looking at them, one of them turned round to give me stink eye. Lydia made a little motion with her manicured hand which looked like it meant 'Come over here I think I'm about to have some trouble.' Sure enough, the goon touched his partner and the pair started to lumber towards us. Wilf and I looked at each other. Oh, God. This wasn't going well.

'Please, Lydia,' I said, resorting to begging. She liked this and looked at me regally.

'Well, the problem is . . .' she started officiously, traffic warden-style.

Oh, God, she was about to explain why she'd really, really *like* to help us out but couldn't because of her obsessive rule-following and unpleasant personality.

'The problem is . . .' But then she stopped talking altogether, and just stood there with her mouth hanging open. I stared at her, then turned around, following her gaze.

Striding up the hall in motorcycle leathers, five o'clock

stubble on his manly chin, a touch of engine oil on his cheekbone, which he must surely have contrived to do himself with something he found in an easyJet toilet, was Patrick.

I hadn't seen the Patrick effect in quite a while – I tended to avoid places he went as it got very tedious watching him fend off the women – but it was undeniably impressive. I knew my brother was a bit of a dick – partly, I suspected, because women had acted like complete idiots in front of him since he was eleven years old – but it absolutely didn't show. He looked fantastic; everyone else faded into the background as he stalked up, as usual looking like he was pretending to be in his own movie and that he was indubitably centre stage. I turned to face him.

'Hi, Patrick,' I said casually. Kelly and JJ must be behind him somewhere.

'Hi, sis,' he said, and even stooped to give me a kind of hug. 'You look shit. Did you steal that dress off a pig in a farmyard?'

'Pigs don't even wear dresses, though,' I said. 'So your comment makes no sense.' Mum told me that the boys and I wouldn't bicker like children for ever. I was still waiting. Wilf was watching closely, but not with a fraction as much concentration as Lydia was.

'Er. so, Evie, ha ha ha,' said Lydia. 'Aren't you going to introduce us?'

Patrick stood back to take a look at her.

'Is that her?' he whispered to me in his Neanderthal fashion. I nodded. 'Not bad, for once,' he said.

'Lydia, this is my brother Patrick. He was really looking forward to coming to the casino evening with us . . .'

Patrick roughly pushed past me and picked up Lydia's taloned hand.

'Who the hell are you?' he said. He always went for this crude approach, and his hit rate was extraordinary. 'You're fucking gorgeous.'

Lydia giggled. This was a new sound for her and she nearly choked on it before it came out, but she got there in the end.

'I'm Evie's friend Lydia.'

Patrick made it very clear that he was sizing her up.

'Normally Evie's friends are all dogs,' he said. 'But you . . . I mean, you're byoo-tee-full.'

'We're not that close,' said Lydia.

'You can say that again,' I said.

'Shh,' said Wilf, as we started sidling towards the door.

'Are you a doctor?' asked Lydia. She was trying to put up her favourite final line of defence, but I knew it wasn't going to get her anywhere. I think Patrick had that smell men are meant to secrete that makes women go into labour and things.

'Neah, fuck 'em,' said Patrick. 'Anywhere round here we can get a drink?'

And that was the last thing we heard as we slipped unnoticed inside the casino ballroom.

*

The private room was ridiculously over the top. Carved cherubs peered down from pink and eau-de-nil ceilings which were inlaid with gold, as if to suggest that angels were blessing you as you spunked the housekeeping on a puggy machine. Huge mirrors reflected back images of smartly dressed men and inappropriately dressed women, and overhead vast, multifaceted chandeliers glittered. The whole thing would have been lovely and classy-looking if it wasn't for the banks and banks of slot machines lining the walls, all beeping and flashing, looking as if they'd be much more at home in a pub with a sticky brown swirly carpet. In the middle of the room were roulette wheels and pontoon tables (I suppose it was vingt-et-un here), and a craps table which everybody was eyeing but nobody was playing at, presumably because nobody understood the rules except that you have to shout 'snake eyes' at various points. I couldn't see Dr Bennet, or Bailey.

'Good work,' said Wilf. 'Is that really your brother? We should get him to do some modelling for the clinic . . . Oh.'

'Oh, yes,' I said. 'We don't work there any more.'

'Yes.' He looked round. 'He should be here somewhere.'

Everywhere there were excited-looking men making squeaks of delight as they placed their 'money'. (There was free betting for an hour – a mean trick, I thought, getting everyone carried away with champagne and Monopoly money until they got into the habit of wagering huge sums and moved directly on to the whole rack and ruin thing.)

'Hang on,' I said. I thought I'd spotted Bailey. 'Stay here. Or look for Dr Bennet, but don't go far.'

Wilf squeezed me briefly on the hand and disappeared into the flurry.

'Bailey!' I hissed. He was hiding behind a curtain and making a pretty good job of it – if I hadn't spotted the laces of those horrible shoes poking out from under the thick red velvet I might have missed him altogether.

He poked his head out briefly. He looked haunted.

'Oh,' he said. 'It's you.'

'Who were you expecting, the cat's mother?' I said. I decided the curtain was actually a very good place to hide myself, before I got thrown out or kidnapped by goons, so shuffled myself into its luxuriant, smoky folds.

'I'm hiding,' said Bailey, unnecessarily I thought.

'Really? I thought you'd moved in here.'

'From Lydia.'

'From Lydia? You two have practically been smoochy smoochy icky poo since the second we arrived.'

'No, we haven't,' said Bailey, looking truly appalled. 'She's followed me around everywhere! I can't believe you didn't notice.'

'You're right, I've had very little on. Anyway, I've taken care of Lydia,' I said.

'What do you mean?'

'I've got rid of her. So I could get to you.'

'How?'

'I've Patricked her.'

'No way.'

'Way. He was coming here anyway, so it made perfect sense.'

'You're a marvel. You haven't Patricked anyone for years.'

'No. Because I try to be more moral than that. But thank you. Now. Listen. Things have got really serious.'

'What do you mean?'

'I mean, shit-hitting-the-fan serious. This boat – it *really* has to stop.'

'What do you mean?'

And I told him everything: about the threats and the resignation/sacking and the kidnapping of Tom.

'Oh, God,' he said when I'd finished. 'I heard you'd just quit because of a sex scandal.'

'Don't tell me you believed that.'

Bailey shrugged.

'Oh, for God's sake! It was a completely malicious rumour.'

'Yeah, uh, that's what I thought.'

'It *was*! Anyway, that doesn't matter. We need to find Tom. It's dangerous. Genuinely, seriously dangerous. We need to find out who's in charge here, when the boat's arriving, and then go straight to the police. I saw someone up on top of the party boat the other night, Bailey. Who was it? Who?'

Bailey looked unhappy. 'Oh, God. Well, it's a consortium, you know.'

'I don't know. What is that?'

'It's a holding company. Lots of middle men and so on, you know.'

'Well, are they here?'

Bailey poked his head out.

'No one I recognise . . . I suppose we could ask Yuri.'

'You know where he is?'

''Well, he's here somewhere.'

Bailey emerged from the curtain still looking a bit nervous.

'It's all right,' I whispered. 'Patrick'll be giving her tops by now.'

'Do you have to be so crude?' said Bailey.

'Well, seeing as Tom is being tortured to death *right now* then *yes*,' I said.

People bustled around us, moving between tables.

'That's a nice dress,' said Bailey. 'Shame about the flip-flops.'

'Shut up!'

The noise levels were rising and the cocktail waitresses were busy. I noticed that all the windows were covered in the same heavy drapes as the one we'd been hiding behind. I remembered how casinos liked to block out all natural light in the hopes of keeping you in there for forty-eight hours or something without you figuring it out. I liked the fact that the human brain was so easily fooled. 'Oooh . . . dark . . . must eat peanuts and stay out late . . .'

Bailey nodded and grunted to the people who were, as

usual, trying to get his attention. Most of them were asking when the boat was getting in and when they were going to get a look at it. He brushed off the questions.

'Don't you know?' I said.

'Yes,' he said, insulted. 'I mean, roughly. I mean, we've got a display on it tomorrow so it will have to be here by then.'

'But you don't know where it is now?'

'Not exactly.'

'So Tom could be on it, or at the bottom of the sea having been thrown off it?'

'Don't you think you're being a bit melodramatic?'

'He got pulled into a *car*! How is that being melodramatic?'

Finally we arrived at the far corner of the casino room. There, tucked well away behind the blackjack table, was Dr Bennet. He was concentrating hard, surrounded by a group of men. And, to my shock, just behind his left shoulder, was Janey. She was standing there, preening, like she was his lucky charm. I glared at her, but she merely smiled and looked back, waving her little fingers delicately.

There was nothing delicate about Dr Bennet, however, when he saw me again. 'You,' he said. 'You're like cranial fungus. You just won't go away.'

'Thank you,' I said. 'But . . .'

'But what?'

Bailey stepped forward. 'Yuri, look.'

'Oh, God, not you too. First Wilf, now you. What, does she give unbelievable head?'

247

Janey whispered something in his ear that made him grimace. I couldn't believe that the doc I'd always thought so smooth was actually as coarse as a sailor's armpit.

'No,' said Bailey. 'The young guy's gone missing.'

'What do you mean, "gone missing"? Who cares? He could fall off Brighton bloody pier for all I care.'

'He was bundled into a car,' I said. That got his attention. 'I saw it happen.'

'Don't be ridiculous.'

'I was right there. So was Wilf. Ask him if you don't believe me.'

Yuri was looking definitely flustered now. 'Well, he was asking for it.'

'What the hell do you mean by that? Asking for it? He could be dead for all you know.'

I was starting to make a scene. Again. Bailey touched my arm gently.

'Look,' he said. 'I know there's a lot of guys here who've been involved with the project and so on. I've met some of them, you know most of them, we've all been working together, right? But I really need to meet the top guy. The guy who signs the cheques, the guy no one meets. Because he's got to know what's going on.'

'Or she,' I added, out of habit.

Dr Bennet shook his head. 'Well, I don't know where he is. He's not here. Now if you'll excuse me, I want to get back to my card game.'

I looked around. Nobody was watching me. Janey, however, had both her hands round Dr Bennet's shoulders and
was leaning in to give him a good-luck kiss on the hair. Quickly,
I took my camera-phone out of my bag and snapped a
shot. I hardly ever used the camera facility – I'd been
talked into it by some spotty chap in the shop – but I was
incredibly grateful for it now.

'What? What was that?' said Dr Bennet hearing the
click.

'It's great I don't work for you now,' I said. 'I must delete
your wife's telephone number off my phone. Just as soon as
I've sent her this pic, of course.'

I held it up. It was incredibly compromising; I think Janey
was licking something. Of course, I didn't have his wife's
mobile number, but he didn't know that.

'Give me that!' said Dr Bennet.

'Tell us how to find Tom. Where's the guy in charge?'

'Give me that phone!'

'I'll give you the phone when you give us the information.'

'No!'

We glared at each other. It was a stand-off. Dr Bennett
looked around. I wondered if he had henchmen too.

'You are nothing,' he hissed suddenly. 'The girl who can't
even take a holiday on her own. I've seen you cowering about
the place.'

I took a step backwards. As a full-on assault his comment

249

felt just as vicious as if he'd punched me (which, as I'd already seen, he was entirely capable of doing too).

'"Oh, poor me, my brothers are horrible, poor me, my life sucks, I can't get a boyfriend, boo hoo hoo, pass me a magazine and let me empathise with Kerry Katona."'

'My life is *not* like that.'

'"I don't even have the decisiveness to go travelling. I'm so pathetic I need to go on holiday with the people I work with."'

'Shut up! Just shut up!'

'Give me the phone, little girl. And stop messing about in things you don't understand.'

His hand was nearly at mine and I couldn't think of a thing to do. I felt blinded with the pain of his words, I wanted to curl up in a ball and lick my wounds. Almost hypnotised, I felt my hand moving out . . .

Suddenly, the phone was snatched away and disappeared . . . into Wilf's pocket. I felt shaken out of my reverie.

'Where have you been?'

Wilf raised one eyebrow mysteriously. It looked strange, what with him in his dinner jacket and everything.

'Yuri,' he said. 'No hard feelings.'

Yuri rolled his eyes.

'What about a couple of rounds of vingt-et-un, for old times' sake.'

'What do you mean, "for old times' sake"?' he growled.

Wilf sat up at the table and ordered a martini. Really.

'Well, forget old times.' He leant forward across the table and opened his hands in a reasonable fashion. 'How about, if you win, you get the phone, and if I win, you tell us where Philippe is.'

I stared at Wilf. Philippe must be the big boss. And Wilf knew his name!

'Philippe, that was it,' said Bailey behind me. Ha, so, I wasn't the only person who forgot important things.

Yuri sat back in his chair, eyeing Wilf's pocket. The other men clustered round the table, muttering to themselves. A challenge! Yuri had to take a challenge!

It was true: he was looking at the male faces around the table. Wilf looked calm and unbothered, but he'd sent out a true threat to Dr Bennet's honour. I hung on closely. Janey did too. Wilf had brought a pile of chips to the table, and it was roughly the same size as Dr Bennet's. Dr Bennet raised his hands as Wilf threw a couple onto the table. Then he threw his own on too.

The dealer flicked out the cards in lightning-flash time. He put one of his own cards face up on the table. One was a ten. I looked at Wilf's hand. He had sixteen.

'Hit,' he said. The dealer gave him an eight.

'Hmm,' said Wilf.

After that, the game moved incredibly fast. Sometimes they'd double up the cards, and there'd be a flurry of cards on the table. Sometimes the dealer would fold without even looking at the other card. I was slightly bamboozled by everything that was going on, but one thing was certain: Wilf's pile of chips was getting smaller and smaller. Dr Bennet's expresssion was beginning to return to its normal self-satisfied look, and I felt my hand tightening its grip on the phone – Wilf had given it to me for safe keeping. Maybe I should make a dash for it – but so many people had come over to watch the game, and were now pressing up against me, I didn't know if I could fight my way out.

Finally Wilf was left with only a few red chips. He'd managed to make the wrong decision on practically every hand he'd had. He'd folded too early, he'd bust too high. He obviously had no clue what he was doing. I was wildly disappointed.

He looked at his hand, sighing, then threw them all into the centre of the table, as the dealer threw out a hand of cards, face down except for one of his own.

'All or nothing,' said Wilf. Dr Bennet smirked and took a long sip of his drink. The dealer was holding a four. 'All or nothing,' said Dr Bennet, pushing all his chips into the centre of the table. He'd had a run of winning on fifteens; he looked like he could afford to be generous. His eyes flicked to where I was holding the mobile phone. The dealer rapidly counted the chips and added an equal number from the bank.

Dr Bennet flipped over his hand. A ten and a queen. A gasp went up from the assembled crowd. The dealer turned his other card over. A ten. He had to hit. He did so, and got a jack – busted.

Then it was Wilf's turn. He flipped the first – yet *another* ten. The room, which had been so noisy for so long, now went completely silent. I realised I was holding my breath. Dr Bennet still looked quite nonchalant; what was going to beat his twenty? Then Wilf turned over his other card. It was the ace of spades.

The room erupted. I yelled out loud. Dr Bennet swore loudly and looked about to storm off as the dealer pushed the huge mountain of chips towards our seat. I couldn't believe Wilf had got this lucky. I looked at him, he hadn't even broken a sweat.

'Well done!' I whispered.

'Yuri?' Wilf was saying, getting down from his seat. 'Don't you have something to tell us? About the whereabouts of Philippe?'

There was a rustle of agreement from the crowd as Dr Bennet got up heavily from the table.

'Of course, you'll keep your side of the bargain?'

Dr Bennet muttered something, and Bailey, Wilf and I pushed our way through the crowd to get to him; Janey had already taken his arm.

'OK, OK, OK,' he said furiously as we surrounded him. 'Come with me. You don't want to make Philippe unhappy, though, you really don't.'

'Well, he's making us very unhappy,' I said. 'With *kidnapping.*'

Dr Bennet led us out of the main casino area and into a dark-panelled room off the main foyer. Out of the corner of my eye I could see Lydia and Patrick. He appeared to be unhooking her bra. I looked around for John Jr but I couldn't see him. It would have been very handy to have had some muscular back-up at this point.

I didn't see what he did, but suddenly Dr Bennet had opened a panel on the wall and was pressing in a key code. In front of us, a door slid open. Oh my God!

A short, dark corridor, lit with an illuminated cherub lamp, ended at another wooden door. Dr Bennet knocked gently. Someone grunted on the other side of the door, and Yuri said, 'Lysander.' A hand felt for mine and squeezed it. I didn't know whose it was.

Inside was a room so softly lit it looked like it was illuminated by gas lighting. It took a few moments for my eyes to adjust. Then I noticed that along one wall was a bank of monitors, showing every room in the casino, and the cars outside. This must be for security. Some of the monitors showed overhead views of the tables in the casino, I supposed to see if the dealers were cheating.

But then my attention moved to the shadowy figures in the room. There were three or four big men, who I supposed must be goons. Then, sitting down, with his head bent, was a figure I recognised, even though it was no longer sporting the moustache of the day before.

'Tom,' I shouted. He raised his head and peered through

a very black eye. Oh my God. He'd been beaten up. And what he said next shocked me to the core.

'Janey?' he said.

What? My eyes shot round to where Janey had inconspicuously followed us in.

'Darling,' she said, running forwards. 'What have they done to you?'

My brain couldn't take it in as she knelt down next to him.

'Are you all right?' She smothered him in kisses. 'Cachou misses you.'

'WHAT?'

I stepped forward, shaking off Wilf's restraining hand on my arm.

'What kind of a slut *are* you? Are both of you?'

'Evie,' said Tom, focusing on me suddenly. 'You found me.' He indicated his face. 'I told you it was serious.'

But I was looking at Janey. 'You were just in there trying to play suck face with Dr Bennet. Do you sleep with the dog too?'

'Information, darling,' she said to me, her American accent grating in my ears. 'And don't talk to the US head of Earth Friends like that, OK, sweetie?'

I stared at Tom. Oh, God, I felt I'd been betrayed twice. This was who he'd been calling; this was the person who owned the dog. My heart was pounding as a small man got up out of the swivel chair in front of the screens. I hadn't noticed him at all.

'Very interesting,' he said. 'But, Yuri, would you mind telling me what the *fuck* is going on?'

We all stared at Dr Bennet as he tried to explain he'd been blackmailed (which made me feel pretty good, I have to say; I didn't know I had it in me).

'But what do you want?' said Philippe – the little man – turning round to face us. His English was perfect, as was his suit. He didn't look threatening at all, he looked nice. If he was your doctor you'd feel reassured that he would never lose his cool or make a mistake. As soon as I heard his voice I knew it was the man I'd heard on top of the boat, talking to Dr Bennet.

We all began talking at once. He raised his hand for calm.

'You are activists, yes? I've heard as much from Tom.'

'Did you stand up under torture?' said Janey fondly, stroking his head.

'No,' said Tom, looking ashamed of himself. 'One of the goons elbowed me in the eye, and that was it. I pretty much told him everything. I hadn't realised torture would be quite so unpleasant.'

I rolled my eyes at this, which was cheeky because if anyone were to even so much as mention the word torture to me I'm sure I'd immediately start crying and betray everyone I'd ever met. But I was so furious that this pair had used us so ruthlessly. Earth Friends indeed. They could start by being actual normal human friends.

'Now, look,' said Philippe. 'The boat is going ahead, I'm afraid. There is really nothing wrong with it. There are millions of boats and millions of hospital procedures, and the two things are going to merge.'

'But Radoflux 9000 . . .' said Wilf.

'Radoflux 9000 will be *fine*,' snarled Philippe, suddenly cross. 'One or two minor flaws in the trials, that's all.'

'And stupid women who inject that stuff deserve all they get,' said Janey. 'Using animal products for their own vanity. It's disgusting.'

'You really are the queen of love and spirituality, aren't you?' I said.

She looked me straight in the eye. 'I think the time has come to get over Tom,' she said sincerely. 'I know some books that might help. *How to Stop Loving a Man That's Too Good for You*, that kind of thing.'

If I hadn't been wearing flip-flops, I'd have kicked her.

'Now I know what's up,' said Philippe, 'I think we have a solution. I'm sorry my men were a little heavy-handed, Tom – we're very afraid of terrorism, as you can imagine, and they had your picture on the CCTV from the other evening . . . we thought you were going to blow up the boat.'

'S'OK,' said Tom. That was the annoying thing about Philippe, I suddenly realised: he sounded so incredibly reasonable and spoke so gently it was hard not to believe what he was saying. He reached towards the desk and picked up a piece of paper.

'Here we are,' he said. When he held it up to the light we saw he was brandishing a cheque. A cheque for a huge amount, made out to Earth Friends. When they peered through the gloom to read the noughts on the end, Tom and Janey's faces both contorted.

'This is the precise sum of money that will carbon zero the ship,' said Philippe. 'It's for you. I want you to take it, plant trees, form a seal sanctuary. After all, it is the first rule of medicine, is it not: "Do no harm"?'

Tom and Janey were looking at each other. Janey had her stupid over-painted mouth open.

'Of course, this is annual,' said Philippe. 'We would hate to leave our footprint on the beautiful oceans of the world, even as we wish to render a service to make our world more beautiful through making its women more beautiful.'

They couldn't be swallowing this, could they?

Janey gulped and stepped forwards. 'Well, that's incredibly generous.'

Philippe shrugged. 'I am sorry we had such a misunderstanding. I agree; we should have thought more about saving the planet before we started our work. A little oversight, perhaps, Dr Bailey?'

Bailey stuttered, but didn't say anything.

'Well, then,' said Tom. He reached out and took the cheque. 'We can do a lot of good with this.'

'No, you can't!' I burst out suddenly. 'They're just buying you off! It's corrupt.'

Tom looked at Philippe as if they were both men of the world.

'No, they're balancing things out. We can do so much good with this money, Evie. Invest in saving millions of animals' lives.'

'Whilst they just sail around using illegal drugs and giving new faces to serial killers?' I yelled. Philippe and his henchmen laughed, and I felt really stupid and awkward.

'Don't be ridiculous,' said Philippe. 'This is a holiday cruise ship, that's all. Nothing for you to worry your . . . "average" little head about.'

Silence fell. Tom and Janey looked at each other and clearly passed a private message between them – to scarper.

'Well, thanks, Philippe . . . sorry for the trouble we caused,' said Tom. Oh, God, what a pathetic specimen.

'Not at all,' said Philippe. 'We'll all just keep quiet about it, *n'est-ce pas?*'

'And, *bye*, Yuri,' said Janey seductively. 'Give my love to your wife.' And she got up and prepared to sashay out. Tom got up to follow her. As she turned away, he turned to me. His face looked just a little regretful.

'Evie,' he said, 'I . . . I . . .'

I wanted to say something dramatic; a proper exit line. But all I could think of was 'you're a crap shag', and that wasn't even true, plus I didn't want to say it in a roomful of men. I didn't want to look pathetic.

'Bye,' I said. 'And stop pestering me with all those phone calls and flowers and things, please.'

259

He looked a bit confused for a second then shook his head. 'Right. OK. I'll stop.'

Dr Bennet was looking profoundly uncomfortable and staring at his feet as Tom and Janey left the room.

Chapter Thirteen

'Are you still here?' said Philippe, who'd turned back to look at the monitors. You could see Tom and Janey running across the foyer. I couldn't tell, but I thought they might be grinning like Cheshire cats. And Lydia's shoe seemed to be peering out from under a curtain. Well well well.

'Yes,' I said. 'You can't buy us off that easily.'

'Oh, can't I?'

Philippe looked at his watch and yawned.

'This is getting very boring,' he said. 'OK, here's the deal. If you' – he pointed at Wilf – 'want to work in plastic surgery again, keep your head down and shut up like a good boy. And if *you* –' this time it was Bailey – 'want to work in hospital design, do likewise.'

'What about me?' I said. He ignored me.

'You go to the papers, they won't be interested. You go to the police – we haven't done anything wrong, and the boat will be in at five in the morning and back in international waters this time tomorrow night. You have nothing on us, nothing at all. We, on the other hand – and it is regrettable, in international business – have absolutely no compunction at all about giving you a smack for wasting so much of our bloody time and making Dr Bennet look an idiot.'

One of the huge goons grunted in agreement, and Dr Bennet looked like he was going to say something about whether or not he was an idiot, then thought better of it.

'So. Fuck off now – no smack. Do you understand me?'

Both Wilf and Bailey looked really constipated. I suppose this is what it comes down to in boy world – whether or not you can handle a whupping. All the school bitching they avoid; all the body facism they get to skip; all the daft girlie hair removal stuff they don't have to spend money on, but it still comes down to this. Can they handle a whupping? Suddenly I wished John Jr were here.

Bailey looked at Wilf. 'The thing is,' he said. 'I was brutalised as a child, and I'm a terrible physical coward.'

Wilf nodded, looking relieved. Come on, wimps! My blood was up. Fight! Wilf held up his hands. 'I would, but . . . my hands are insured for half a million . . .'

'Yeah,' said Bailey.

'Come *on*, you cowards!' I yelled. 'Are you just going to let him get away with it?'

Philippe was already on the phone. 'Hi, yes . . . I'd like the saddle of lamb, with braised cabbage . . .'

The goons were moving towards us. God, they really were big. Big and fierce-looking.

Wilf and Bailey looked at one another. 'OK, RUN!' they shouted, and, pushing me ahead of them, we all tumbled forward through the secret passageway and into the bright lights of the chandeliered foyer.

'I'm not sure I'm cut out for this crime-fighting lark,' said Bailey, as we'd paced our weary way home along the seafront. The bars and restaurants were open and lively, and it was still warm as we found an empty beach-side table and took a seat. Wilf ordered '*trois grand* . . .' then looked at us expectantly. Whisky would have felt appropriate, but I hate the stuff, so I had a large Bacardi and Coke, which wasn't quite as world weary. The tie I'd tied on so badly for Wilf had undone itself and was lying open round his neck. The effect was quite sexy actually.

'No,' said Wilf. 'I'm much better at the job I've given up with no hope of getting another one.'

'You'll get another one,' said Bailey. 'Philippe can't know everyone who wants plastic surgery on earth.'

'Can't he?' said Wilf. 'Surely that's why he started this project.'

'Oh, yeah,' said Bailey, taking a large sip of his double advocaat (he's even worse at spirits than me).

Wilf sighed. 'Well, I suppose we should chalk it up to experience and adventure . . .'

'What are you talking about?' I said, spluttering through my drink. 'My sister-in-law is still getting on that boat tomorrow for a free shot of Radoflux 9000!'

Wilf's face fell and he took another sip of his whisky (at least he was drinking a man's drink).

'Oh, crap, I'd forgotten about that.'

'Well, I haven't.'

'At least your friend's safe,' offered Bailey. I harrumphed.

'I wish they'd thrown him off something just one more time for luck,' I said.

'Ah, a woman scorned,' said Bailey, and got up to go to the bathroom. I was about to take up my cause again on Kelly's behalf when Wilf leaned forward.

'Uh, can I ask you something?' he said.

'Sure.'

'Is that your . . . is Bailey your boyfriend?'

I blinked in disbelief. 'My *what*?' I said stupidly.

'Your other half . . . uh, partner . . . I mean . . .'

'Wilf, didn't you realise I, em, made out with Tom?'

'Well, yes,' said Wilf. 'I thought maybe that had caused a few problems.'

'Well, it would, wouldn't it?'

I sipped my drink again.

'Look. Bailey is . . . he's my friend. We grew up together. And, sometimes, I think, maybe we should be together, you know? Neither of us is getting any younger, and I really like him, and well, I could do a lot worse, and it's not like there's anyone else on the horizon, so maybe I should just settle down with him.'

'Wow,' said Wilf, obviously a little surprised by how much I'd told him. 'Nothing like aiming high in life.'

'Well, I aimed high for a holiday and ended up embroiled in some death boat, so maybe the time has come to stop trying.'

'And what does Bailey think of all this?'

'Oh, he's always had a thing for me. I know my face isn't a hundred per cent symmetrical but some men do, you know, think I'm all right looking.'

Wilf's face softened. 'Do they?'

'Do they?' echoed another voice, right by the table. Bailey pointed up above our heads.

'Toilet window. Right there. Er, Evie, do you mind if we have a word?'

We walked a little way along the beach, to where the sounds of the bars and the music of Cannes faded behind us and the noise of the sea was louder than anything else. Bailey seemed to be struggling with something. I couldn't believe myself. What had I said? If I hadn't been so keyed up and hysterical, I wouldn't have said nearly so much. There was just something about bloody Wilf being so quiet that made me talk too much. And I didn't know how to explain this to

Bailey. Or how great I thought he was, or how impressive – and not just because all the docs thought he was amazing, or Lydia was desperately trying to pull him, before I'd Patricked her.

'So,' said Bailey finally, as if he were pulling the words out. 'I'm your safety, am I? Your back-up plan?'

I couldn't possibly have let him see on my face how accurate those words were so I picked up a stone and threw it out to sea.

'Don't be stupid,' I said. 'I was a bit het up. I just told Wilf what I thought he wanted to hear.'

'That I'm your back-up plan that you don't really fancy but think would be better than nothing?'

I could hear the fury in his voice now.

'I mean, where the fuck do you get off? Who do you think you are, Scarlett fucking Johansson?'

I shook my head. I was mortified. It must be a horrible thing to hear about yourself; that someone thinks you're a lapdog, ready at your bidding to devote their life to you.

'Has it escaped your notice that my life is going completely fine without having you on my arm?'

'Yes, I *know* that,' I said.

'Do you really think I'm so pathetic that if I fancied you I wouldn't ask you out?'

'OK, OK,' I said. 'I'm sorry. I got it wrong. Obviously.'

'Obviously,' said Bailey. 'Look, Evie. I'm sorry you're single and that all your boyfriends have been dicks.'

'Not all of them,' I protested, then thought about it. 'Oh, yes. All of them.'

'But I'm not your knight in shining bloody armour, OK? I'm not your "make do". I'm not anybody's "make do".'

'I know,' I said.

'I know you still think of me as a six-year-old who's just wet his trousers, but it's just not like that any more. So get over it.'

'OK,' I said, feeling thoroughly chastised.

'Can we forget about this?'

I nodded.

'And you won't . . . I don't know, be expecting a ring on your thirtieth birthday or something equally cretinous?'

I shook my head.

'OK. Come here.'

And he gave me a hug. We didn't hug very often. As we did so I realised something; that some people have a smell. A smell you click with. Tom, alas, had it. It's something to do with pheromones, something below consciousness.

Bailey didn't have it. The chemistry wasn't there. Not because we were working too hard, or waiting for the right moment, or sowing our wild oats before we headed into the sunset together. But because it would never have worked out.

I squeezed him hard for helping me realise this.

'Oof,' he said.

I grinned. 'Come on. Admit it. I was your safety too.'

'You were not!'

'Was too!'

'Were not! Your mate Jilly was my safety and she went and married your bloody brother Cassandro.'

'Whereupon, you switched to me.'

We drew apart.

'Well, maybe a little,' he said.

'I knew it,' I said.

He gave me a half smile. The moonlight glinted off his glasses.

'Goodnight,' he said. And he turned and marched on up the beach.

I headed back to the café table. Wilf was still there, holding out a large gin and tonic.

'Everything OK?' he said, looking alarmed and standing up. 'Have you broken his heart?'

'No,' I said. 'I don't think so. Definitely not.'

'Has he broken yours?'

I smiled weakly at him. 'No. My heart is pretty used to being punched around.'

Wilf smiled at me. 'That's a shame.'

'Yeah, well, what can you do? Us lonely crime fighters, too busy saving the world . . .'

Suddenly, Wilf took my hand. An electric shock ran up my arm. What was this – friendly advice or something more?

'You don't need to make a joke out of everything, you know,' he said gently.

I swallowed hard, thinking over my many humiliations.

'Yes, I do,' I said. 'Anyway. What are we going to do about Kelly? I don't give a shit about what Tom and Janey are doing: this isn't over.'

Wilf removed his hand and sighed.

'Evie. You've met Philippe. He's a serious thug. What can we do?'

'I don't know,' I said. 'Something. To show we're not cowards and we're not giving up. We even know when the boat's coming in.'

'You're not a coward, Evie,' said Wilf. 'Not like me. But I think the time has come to give it up.'

We sipped our drinks quietly as we stared out to sea.

'It is beautiful, isn't it?' said Wilf.

The lights of the yachts on the far quay were still twinkling in the water. I thought of a cold, harsh operating theatre, out there on the water somewhere, all ready to perform God knows what kinds of things.

'Sort of,' I said. 'What's that famous quote about the Riviera?'

'A sunny place for shady people,' said Wilf.

'Yes,' I said. 'Like that.'

I headed back alone, bidding a quiet goodnight to Wilf. I didn't want him to walk me back to the hotel. I didn't think there was anything left to say.

After the evening's events I doubted I'd be able to fall asleep. By the side of my bed were some postcards I'd bought to send Mum and Dad but I couldn't think what to write on them.

Dear Mum and Dad. Wish you were here. Slept with a yellow-bellied eco-terrorist. Got burnt. Lost chance of marrying that nice bloke who lived down the road. JJ not quite as bad as we always thought. Sorry about the disfigured daughter-in-law, having a lovely time, E.

Instead, and to my surprise, I pitched forwards onto the bed, still fully dressed, then didn't wake up for five hours. I wouldn't even have woken up then if it hadn't been for my phone going off. Utterly confused as to where I was, I blearily stretched out a hand to the night table. It was still dark outside.

'Uh-huh?'

'Sis?'

'Who is this?'

The voice was whispering and sounded very agitated.

'Sis, it's me. Patrick.'

'Patrick? Where the hell are you?'

'That friend of yours, sis.'

He sounded hoarse, almost as if he'd been crying.

'She's a *maniac*.'

'Oh,' I said. I was becoming more awake now. 'Who, Lydia?'

'Keep your voice down! I don't know where she is.'

'Where are you?'

'That's the problem. I don't know. She took me back to her hotel and tied me up and . . . did *things* to me.'

'Patrick. Have you been interfered with? Did somebody touch your special area?'

'Well, I liked it to start with, but . . . she just went on and on. And *on*.'

'She's been holding herself back for the right person. I think it's all coming out in a flood.' I thought for a second. 'God, *that* explains the unchannelled aggression.'

'She said she's just going to get some whipped cream . . .' Patrick's voice was almost a sob. 'How do I get out of here? She's going at it with an egg beater right now.'

'Just creep out very quietly,' I said. 'Forget about your pants. Then go through the courtyard, and just start down the hill. Everything here goes downhill. When you get to the sea-front go to the Metropole hotel and ask for JJ. He can look after you after that.'

'If I turn up at JJ's without my clothes he'll rip the piss.'

'Well, it sounds like someone's going to rip something.'

There was a gulp on the line.

'Bye.'

I couldn't get back to sleep after that. The sun was starting to creep over the horizon, I could tell, even in my dank little room. I felt a little buzzy still, the way you do when you've had adrenalin running round your system, no dinner and not enough sleep. So I ran a bath. It was that horrible French bath, but as long as I threw both my legs over the side I could just about lie back. What could I do? Today was the last chance to have a shot at it – my flight home was tomorrow. Without a job, without a friend, without anything. And that bloodstained boat would be sailing straight out to sea.

Well, not if I could help it. If I only had one day, I could give it my best shot. I leaned out of the uncomfortable bath and grabbed my phone. One last shot.

'Did I wake you?'

'Oddly enough, no,' said Wilf, who did actually sound wide awake.

'Good,' I said. 'What were you doing?'

'Just thinking about things.'

'What things?'

There was a pause.

'You ask a lot of questions, Evie.'

'I know,' I said. 'You'd think I'd be a better spy than I am.'

I could hear him smile down the phone. 'Don't tell me. This isn't a good news phone call. Or have you called me to tell me you *don't* want to do something completely stupid?'

'What do we have to lose?' I said. 'We've already lost our jobs, our trip . . .'

'Our dignity . . .'

'Dignity's overrated,' I said.

'Right,' he said. 'And what's with the "we"?'

'Listen,' I said. 'You don't have to go near the boat, or Philippe. You just need to talk to Kelly. Put on your best serious doctor voice,' I said. 'You know you can do it. Pretend you're breaking bad news. It will be, to her.'

It felt oddly intimate, lying in the bath naked, talking to Wilf. He didn't even know where I was.

'Are you splashing?' came the voice. 'Are you in the bath?'

'No!' I said, inadvertently making an even bigger splash in surprise.

'You are! You're calling me from in the bath!'

'Shh,' I said. 'We've got important plans to discuss.'

'Well, it's hard to discuss them when I'm picturing you in the bath.'

'Well, don't then. Picture me wearing a snow suit or something.'

There was a pause.

'Break the bad news,' I said.

'Uh-huh,' said Wilf reluctantly.

There was a silence on the end of the phone. I could hear him breathing. The room was still dark, with only the solitary tap dripping at the end of the bath. I felt like we were the only two people on earth. Sometimes things are more intimate over the telephone.

He took a deep breath. 'I don't like breaking bad news,' he said. There was another long pause. Then it all came out.

'When I was a young surgeon – well, hardly a surgeon at all, a senior house officer, I had to tell two parents that their six-month-old baby— The child had been shot. Drive by. No reason. I was assisting. Anyway. It doesn't matter. They . . .

she . . . didn't make it. The consultant had a six-month-old himself. He couldn't face it. He got me to do it because "I had to learn sometime", and I didn't have children.'

There was a long pause after that. I wasn't sure, but I think from the tenor of his breaths he was crying.

'Well, I can tell you it doesn't matter if you have children or not.'

There was another long pause as he got control of himself.

'And that was it for me, really. I mean, I finished my training and everything . . . but telling people that their life – their world, everything they had ever had – was completely fucked, as from today . . . I mean, that's not a job. Or, it wasn't a job I could do.'

'All doctors learn to, though, don't they?' I said timidly. 'They just have to get on with the job.'

'I know,' he said. 'But not me. I couldn't. I just couldn't.'

'So you went somewhere where you wouldn't have to,' I said.

Finally I understood. All the skills, wasted in the wrong place.

'Because I'm a wimp,' said Wilf. He half laughed. 'I'm not up to the job.'

'But you're a wonderful doctor,' I told him simply. 'Wonderful.'

'And a coward,' he said.

'You're not a coward, are you?' I said. 'Look at you, up at all hours, preparing to help me. A coward wouldn't have decided to make a stand, would he? A coward wouldn't have confronted Dr Bennet. A coward wouldn't have fronted up to him with that card game the way you did. You were even going to take on my brother.'

'Oh, yes,' said Wilf, remembering. 'I wasn't, really. If he'd raised a hand I was going to run for it.'

'Shh!' I said. I was on a roll. 'A coward wouldn't be going down right now to talk Kelly out of this dangerous surgery, not with John Jr on the loose. You're a lion! A lion! Grr.'

'Am I?' he asked faintly.

'Of course you are.' I reached over for a towel. 'You've got over your fears without even trying! Watch you go! Grr!'

'Of course I am!' he said. I heard some warmth come back into his voice, and the sound of him jumping up. 'What are you doing?'

'Me?' I said. 'Well, once I get out of the bath—'

'Aha,' he said. 'I knew it.'

Busted.

'Uh, I mean . . .'

I was about to explain the plan I'd come up with walking home the night before. Then I figured that he'd try and stop me, particularly in his newly invigorated state, so I didn't.

'I think you'll manage it all fine by yourself,' I said. 'Nothing. I'm going to stay here and order breakfast in bed.'

I took a look round my grubby cell and laughed hollowly to myself.

'OK,' said Wilf. 'I'll come and get you when I know what's happening. If we can get your sister—'

'Sister-in-law.'

'Off that boat . . . well, I think that's as much as we can do.'

'I agree,' I said, and hung up the phone. I didn't agree in the slightest.

Chapter Fourteen

Even at first light, when the whole of Cannes looked like an army of pixies had been up all night scrubbing it clean (hey, maybe they had, they're all rich round here), there were lots of people down by the docks – some early fishermen, coming in with the morning's catch, then there were bakers' shops open for early trade, and lots of yachties. I'd learned to recognise them; young men and women with very clean polo shirts, identical shorts, brown legs and nice teeth, who looked after the ships that lined the shore. They looked like their lives were pretty fun, as they loped on and off the gangplank, hailing their friends on other boats. The girls were getting on with shopping, the men were washing down the blue and white sides of the boats, or hosing the decks. I idly wondered if they had better lives than mine. Hey, who was I kidding? One of those lab rats that gets given electric shocks all day has a better life than mine.

I marched down to the big quay again; the one reserved for the largest boats. Behemoth after behemoth loomed out of the oily depths. Near the end I drew to a halt. *Operation Sunshine*. Here she was.

This boat wasn't a shimmering city of lights, like the party boat had been. It wasn't full of fun people having a fun time. It was sleek, and grey – grey all over, like pewter. The portholes were small, and the front of the boat sharpened to a point, as if it was designed for cutting through something. It was huge, but looked like it had more in common with a warship than a pleasure boat. She looked sinister, even at dawn with the golden rays of another perfect day breaking over her bow.

I didn't have a good plan about sneaking on board. I realised I had imagined something out of an old Laurel and Hardy movie, like a laundry van driving up that I could jump into, so I tried to hover inconspicuously.

Suddenly a friendly-looking girl was standing in front of me.

'G'day!' she said cheerfully. 'Are you looking for die work?'

I was so shocked for a second I couldn't speak, until I realised she was Antipodean, and had actually said 'day work'.

I had no idea what day work was either, but it sounded a lot better than 'die' work, and she was wearing a polo shirt with 'Operation Sunshine' embroidered on the pocket, so I decided to say yes, in lieu of a better idea, and see what happened.

'You're first,' she said. 'Die workers normally don't start queuing till seven.'

'Actually, this is my first day-work job,' I said, hoping she'd give me at least the tiniest clue as to what a day worker was.

'Oh, will done you,' she said. 'Will, you're just in time for breakfast if you like.'

And she turned round and indicated that I follow her on board. It was as simple as that.

Having been in two minds about this 'day work' charade, suddenly, from the bottom of a very steep set of stairs I smelt bacon frying . . . with tomatoes, and was that mushrooms? And that was definitely toast. I hadn't eaten since my plate of ice cream yesterday about lunchtime.

'Great!' I said truthfully.

'I'm Dibs, by the way.'

'Hiya, Debs . . . I'm . . .'

I couldn't think of a fake name straight away. 'Wow, I'm Debs too,' I said.

'*Wow!*' said Debs. She was quite smiley. 'That's *amazing.*'

She led me down the steep staircase. At the bottom was a large, low room with lots of doors leading off it. A large TV played in the corner, next to other screens that monitored locations around the ship. Around two large tables sat a host of healthy-looking boys and girls – well, in their early twenties, I supposed – who had the sheen of people who eat a lot of good food and get plenty of fresh air and sunshine. They just looked gleamy. I felt shockingly haggard in comparison.

'Hey, everyone,' said Dibs. 'This is Dibs – amazing, eh? I'm going to put her on as a day worker. Remember it's a big day today.'

There was general muttering. Obviously getting a day worker wasn't a particularly unusual occurrence, and a few of the boys (mostly good-looking) rather annoyingly tilted up their heads then went straight back to their bacon sandwiches. I ordered myself sternly to keep my mind on the task. It was *good* that no one was looking at me. I was a top secret agent.

I squeezed myself round the table and found space for my vast plate of food and, despite my nerves, managed to eat every scrap, keeping my ears open for gossip. Debs was mentioning the large party of people who were coming on board that day and how everyone had to stay away from the basement. My ears pricked up. The basement, huh? I filed that away as extremely useful information. I suppose it would make more sense to put an operating theatre in the basement, rather than, say, an upper-floor conservatory.

She also warned everyone again to keep security tight on the gates. I loved the fact that I didn't look like I needed security. Hooray for James Bond and her out of *Alias*; everyone obviously thought infiltrators would arrive looking attractive and well dressed.

Dibs passed me a clean polo shirt and shorts of my very own and ordered me to go and get changed. I was delighted. As soon as I did so (if I put my hair in a very perky pony tail), I would look just like one of these guys. Effectively, I hoped, I'd become invisible.

Just as I'd finished changing, a young guy pushed past the curtain. He was thin and bald and had a friendly face.

'Excuse me,' I said.

He stared at me. 'Who are you?' he said rudely.

'I'm the new day worker.'

'Day worker? Bloody Debs; nobody's allowed on the boat today.'

My heart started to pound. I was about to be unmasked and thrown off – or worse. I thought of Tom's black eye, and gulped.

The man gave me an appraising look then furtively glanced outside. He leant towards me.

'You don't look like a yachtie,' he said.

'Well, that's where you're wrong.'

'Which side is port, then?'

Shit. Shit. Shit. Rumbled.

The man took a deep breath. 'Earth Friends?' he whispered.

My heart leapt in shock. 'What do you mean?'

'Are you Earth Friends?'

'Why?'

Was he going to dob me in?

He winked and held out his hand. 'Kizza. Earth Friends' man on the inside.'

Oh my God. As I looked at his open face I realised that word obviously hadn't yet filtered down to the rank and file that Earth Friends had, in fact, turned.

'I'm here to help you any way I can,' said Kizza. For a second I thought he was going to salute. 'But whatever you're doing . . . it's got to be *fast*. We have to leave the port tonight.'

I found my voice again. 'Can you get me to the operating theatre? When the docs come?'

He nodded. 'Yes.' Then he slipped behind the curtain as fast as he'd appeared.

First, I followed Dibs. The thrill of being undercover lasted about as long as it took to comb out the first rug so that all the woollen strands were facing the same way. It's true. This is the kind of job people do on yachts.

'You wouldn't *think* pipple would notice,' said Dibs. 'But they rilly, rilly do.'

So here I was, bent over, combing through tiny strands of presumably priceless Persian rugs along miles and miles of corridor, constantly looking at my phone to see if Wilf had called. He hadn't, and I didn't want to call him in case he was in the middle of something. I knew he'd get in touch the second anything was happening. I thought back to our conversation this morning. I'd been touched by how much he'd confided in me. The more I got to know him, the more I liked him. Not that history had proven my skills in that department.

Once I'd finished with the rugs, Dibs set me to polishing

anything brass I came across. I wondered how much I'd get paid for this then remembered that, actually, as soon as word came from Wilf that he'd talked Kelly out of it I was scarpering, so it didn't actually matter. But still. This certainly felt far more like work than sitting behind a nice warm desk in London. If the air con hadn't been so fierce I'd have been on the verge of sweating.

Finally, after what seemed like hours and hours, I heard a bit of general kerfuffle going on outside. Dibs poked her head into the main cabin, where I'd just finished up. It had been bedecked by the other girls with huge, towering flower arrangements that gave the air a heady scent.

'Lit me look at you,' she said. 'OK. Grab a pair of white slip-ons and come and join us.'

There was a big box of very clean white shoes by the crew door and I found a pair that fitted. But then, I didn't really have any choice in the matter as I was drafted in, with all the others, to the back of the boat near the gangplank. Half of the crew – the senior half, I assumed, including Kizza – had changed into formal naval-looking uniforms, complete with epaulettes and hats. The rest of us were in our polo shirt outfits. Dibs got us all into position so that we fanned out from the gangplank on either side, uniforms in front, polo shirts in the back, to welcome the visitors on board.

My heart sank into my shoes. Oh my God. Now I realised. We were going to stand here like some royal-receiving line whilst Philippe, Dr Bennet and, Christ, probably Lydia as well, all marched past. At least I was in the second row, but oh my GOD.

'I have to go to the bathroom,' I muttered to Dibs.

'You cin't,' she muttered back, resplendent in her crisp white shirt. 'They're arriving. Stand still.'

And she pushed me into line, shaking, as the huge shiny cars drew up on the jetty.

If my heart could have stopped, it would have. Every cell in my body was flattened with the mental effort of me trying to turn myself into a two-dimensional object, as close to the far side of the ship as possible. I took a deep breath. Sure enough, first to emerge was Philippe, looking as smooth as he had the previous evening, with two of his omnipresent goons. Then from the second car slithered Dr Bennet, next to him, Lydia. So, she had taken my place after all. Well, it was what she'd always wanted.

Lydia looked, and I suppose was, utterly shagged out. It was mesmerising; for a second I almost forgot to be frightened for my life. Her normally shiny straight hair was mussed and a complete fright at the back. Her eyes were ringed with dark shadows and her normally pale and perfect skin was flushed, like the blood vessels had expanded in her face. If this was what *she* was like, I really didn't want to see Patrick. Then, to my complete and utter horror, out of the other side of the car, got Wilf.

I felt like someone had punched me in the chest and I involuntarily took a step backward, then steadied myself in case I drew attention. Both doctors wore their white coats, which somehow removed them from being normal people; it was like a suit of armour. If you wanted to look stern and responsible – stick the white coats on.

They mounted the gangplank. Dr Bennet's and Wilf's – Dr Maitland's – heads were close together. He must have sought him out last night after I'd gone. No. Not after our conversation, surely? After everything we'd said – he must have thought he was a coward after all; that a safe job and a cushy salary was good enough really. And why would he want to give it up, anyway? Not for me. Oh my God, the filthy, lying ... I strained to hear their conversation.

'I'm just so sorry,' Wilf was saying.

'It's all right,' said Dr Bennet. 'These things happen. You got carried away with a girl. But *that* girl though ...'

I bit my lip. Yuri shook his head.

'Anyway,' went on Dr Bennet. 'I'm very glad to have you with us today. It's a tricky operation, this.'

'Looking forward to it,' said Dr Maitland.

Inside I was boiling. I couldn't believe it. That rat had betrayed me. After our conversation this morning. He must have thought about it then decided that he absolutely wasn't going into charity medicine, or travelling abroad or anything he'd talked about after all, because he was still just a big crawling coward. He'd thought about it then scrambled back like a rat to his regular pay cheque. He probably thought I was still in my hotel room, waiting patiently for him like a dog. Well, was he going to get a shock . . .

I kept my head down, blushing furiously. I was sure that at any moment Philippe, who was at the front of the group, was going to lean over and grab me by the shoulders but, as I held my breath, he strode along the line of waiting staff with barely a grunt for the captain. Lydia followed, nose in the air, though I don't think she'd have looked quite so snotty if she'd known that it clearly displayed the stubble rash on her chin. Then I darted my eyes up just a little, in time to see Dr Bennet whispering in Dr Maitland's ear, close as you like. I wondered how much Dr Bennet had made him grovel. Loads, probably. Arse-licking extraordinaire. I thought of how much I'd started to like him, and sighed. Suddenly, I felt very, very alone. And furious with my stupid bloody sister-in-law.

I stayed stock still as it seemed to take them for ever to parade up the line, deep in conversation. At least Bailey wasn't coming on, he'd have cracked immediately. But finally they passed by into the main body of the ship and I could let out a sigh of relief.

Or could I? As I straightened up, my brain spinning from Dr Maitland's deception, I spied a whole group of people coming up the pier. It was the docs. They looked happy and excited to be finally witnessing what they'd come for. Real operating conditions, and a real boat to work on. They must all be seeing the pound signs in front of their eyes as they imagined flying out only their richest, their most *exclusive* clients for a week or so of sun, sea and surgery. They were like a group of overexcitable schoolboys. The money men were there too, looking graver. And behind them, another car was pulling up. This time, a pure white limo, the sun glinting off its roof like a mirror. Hmm. I wonder who was in that.

The doctors coalesced round the limo as it drew to a halt, and a chauffeur jumped out to open the back door. They actually started to applaud. I rolled my eyes. No way. Here was Kelly, a pretty girl who got lucky, or unlucky depending on your tolerance for JJ, stepping onto a Riviera yacht and being hailed as a conquering hero. The only time I'd ever had a round of applause was when I'd walked across that entire nightclub dance floor with my skirt tucked in my knickers.

Well, obviously Dr Maitland hadn't worked very hard to convince her. I wondered if he'd even tried. He'd thought about his mortgage, and his sports car, and what side his bread was buttered on, and he'd caved in like the yellow-bellied snake he was, crawling back to Dr Bennet, begging forgiveness. Which of course he'd gotten – Dr Bennet knew he needed him; knew he was the better surgeon by miles. Maitland would have spun some line about falling under my spell – ha – and they'd all have been big boy mates together again in no time. Men. All the bloody same.

Kelly was acknowledging the claps gracefully, which was good of her, then let JJ, who'd heaved himself out of the other side of the limo, and was looking particularly scarlet that morning, escort her up the gangplank, as if she were a fine piece of bone china. I couldn't help wishing for a second that someone treated me like that. They weren't such a bad couple, those two.

I steeled myself, ready for the inevitable howl of recognition – I was wondering if I could write it off as coincidence; tell them that this really was my new job. Philippe and Dr Bennet had already disappeared into the bowels of the ship. But, to my complete amazement, they stalked right past the line. Well, my goodness. That shows how long it takes to think you're better than everyone else – about two minutes, obviously. We might all have been mice living down a hole for all the attention JJ and Kelly gave us.

After the doctors had been herded on, them, too, not giving any of us a second glance, we were told to stand down and head back to work. I wasn't 100 per cent sure what to do. Being on the receiving line had proven that I had a very good disguise. But now Wilf had gone back to the enemy, I was on my own.

'DIBS!' shouted Dibs, interrupting my train of thought. 'Kizza says he needs you down in the garage to valet the cars.'

Valet the *what*? There were cars driving on here? But I didn't mind. I knew where the garage was; it was down. And that was the way I needed to go.

'So what's your plan then?' said Kizza. It was dark and warm in the garage, and it smelled (quite reassuringly) of petrol. His face looked amused in the half-light, but wary too. I didn't blame him.

'I don't know,' I said. 'I just know I've got to get my sister-in-law off this boat. And stop the operation.'

'Right,' said Kizza. Then he paused. 'But you know we're going out to sea.'

Suddenly I heard the ominous hum of the huge engines starting up. It wasn't a roar; just a low and very definite vibration.

'I left my second in the engine room,' said Kizza, which didn't mean a thing to me. I was suddenly terrified. Up until now it had all been a bit of a lark, but this was it, no turning back now. It was me against this entire boat. Bruce Willis in a polo shirt. What the hell was I going to do? I stared at the car I was meant to be polishing (something called a 'Maybach'; it looked like it weighed 95 tonnes) and wondered what it would be like to feel the clanging bars of a prison cell.

Chapter Fifteen

'The thing is,' Kizza was talking, but I could hardly hear him. 'Just so as you know . . . when we stop . . .'

I forced myself to look at him. My hands were all soapy, holding a large damp sponge. They were shaking.

Kizza looked uneasy.

'You know, the tender's at the back.'

'What?'

'The tender.'

I shook my head.

'A little boat. That goes inside the big boat,' he explained patiently. 'To take people into land when we're anchored at sea.'

'Oh,' I said.

'Anyway.' He looked around, as if there might be a goon

hiding behind a fire extinguisher. 'Well, it has to make a run to the coastguard's office. At two o'clock.'

'Uh-huh.'

Kizza scratched his head.

'I've seen a lot of things go on on board ship,' he said. 'I've been doing this for a long time. But *this*. Cutting people open at sea. I don't like it. I really don't like it. I wouldn't like it to happen to my sister.'

'Sister-in-law,' I murmured, but it didn't seem to matter any more.

'Anyway,' Kizza said again. 'It'll be out the back in about an hour. Probably. The tender can't wait, though, it has to leave on time. If someone wasn't there, well . . . it would have to leave without them.'

'Thanks,' I said.

Suddenly I heard a noise. It was a very distinctive noise. It was the ping of a lift.

'There's a lift on this ship?' I asked.

'There's three,' said Kizza.

'And one goes down to the operating theatre?'

He nodded. 'Do you know the way?'

I shook my head. Oh my God. This was it.

'Level minus four. Past the engine room on the right-hand side. Over the metal grille. I've unlocked the door. It leads to the back of the anaethetist's cupboard. It's a sterile area, OK? I could get shot for leaving it open.'

'Right,' I said.

'Then you're in the theatre.'

'As easy as that?'

My heart felt like a pack of galloping horses.

'As easy as that.'

Kizza patted me on the arm. 'You must be used to these undercover operations, eh? Must be pretty shit hot for Earth Friends to send you on your own. What do you do – karate? Ju-jitsu?'

'Something like that,' I muttered. I couldn't take my hand off the car door, I was shaking too much.

'Well, good luck! Better get a move on; I'll go lower the tender.'

I wiped my hands down once more on my new shorts as I crouched listening to the muffled voices. I could tell there was Dr Bennet, Dr Maitland, a couple of other people I didn't know, the anaesthetist, I supposed, a nurse. A growl that sounded like Philippe. And, squeaking excitedly, Kelly. If I was to get to Kelly before the anaesthetic did I was going to have to move now. I had to get going, however much my legs were telling me to run away as fast as I could. Oh, God. How could I do this? I had no idea what I was doing. This was just stupid, surely. I couldn't . . .

I looked around for something to take in with me – a weapon? Was that a good idea? What was I going to threaten them with? A pounding from a fire extinguisher? What if I hurt someone? What if they already had Kelly on the table? I thought about it, still wiping down my sweaty hands. Then I stopped.

What was it doctors hated and feared more than anything else? What was it they couldn't bear anywhere near them when they were working? What we had to watch for every second of every day? I looked around the basement. And here there was *loads* of it.

Dirt. Dirt and grime. Infection. MRSA. Septicaemia. The one thing that couldn't be tolerated under any circumstances.

Of course, this was probably the cleanest basement on earth. But it was still a basement.

I rushed over to the corner. Sure enough I found a pile of swept-up dirt and motor-oil spills. I took handfuls and rubbed the dirt liberally all over my face, arms and hands until I was black. I must have looked shocking, but I didn't care. I even ran bits through my hair, until I felt like I was camouflaged up for the jungle. Then I approached the door again. This was the best I could do. If I could just hold up the operation for long enough and make them have to sterilise their instruments again – well, if the boat had to leave at sundown, they wouldn't have long enough. I checked my watch. Twenty minutes till Kizza's tender left. It was now or never. I twisted open the handle of the watertight door. Well, I had wanted change in my life.

I was in a disinfected area. It looked like the pristine new bottles of steriliser had been opened and used. That meant that everyone was soaped up and ready to go. I read the big red sign on the door again, the one that said absolutely no entry except to authorised personnel. I was so not authorised personnel.

The voices were clearer now. I could hear the two doctors. They rarely operated together unless it was a big job, but their murmurings showed how practised they were at working together. A Frenchwoman's voice – she must be the anaesthetist.

I took a deep breath. OK. I may be rubbish at holidays, and family, and holding onto jobs and spotting what blokes were actually like. But I absolutely did not QUIT. And I knew when you had to fight dirty. I burst through the heavy door.

'Jesus Christ!' said Dr Maitland. He was the first to see me. Dr Bennet looked up and swore and dropped his scalpel. Good. Kelly was lying on the table, blinking warily. She'd obviously had her first injection to relax her, but not yet the second to knock her out cold.

'Who *is* this bitch?' yelled Philippe. Glancing above his head I could see a bank of windows with the doctors looking in. Some of them already had cocktails in their hands.

I ran to the bank of instruments and wiped my filthy fingers all over them.

'Don't do that!' squeaked Dr Bennet. 'You're contaminating the sterile area!'

'Am I?' I said, running over to Dr Bennet and touching his

face and hair. He jumped back like I was poisonous, which I was.

'Kelly!' I shouted. 'Wake up!'

'Whas going on?' she slurred.

I pulled the venflon out of her arm as gently as I could, careful not to touch her skin at any point.

'We need to go!'

'You do *not* need to go,' said Dr Bennet. 'What you're doing is dangerous and completely illegal.'

I danced out of his reach and spat on the operating table. The doctors now were all crowding round. I spotted Mrs Bennet.

'Hey, Mrs Bennet!' I shouted. 'Your husband knocked off the Earth Friends woman! I saw them!'

'*Stop this immediately*,' said Philippe. He grabbed me from behind, and his grip was strong and painful.

'Let her go!' shouted Dr Maitland. He'd pulled down his mask.

'I don't need help from you, jelly legs!' I shouted. I kicked out using Philippe as support and, amazing myself, managed to kick over a whole tray of instruments. They made a tremendous noise on the floor. 'Scared of losing your pension, were you?'

Thinking of Wilf's betrayal made me a wildcat. I stomped down on Philippe's foot (expensive loafers – nice soft leather) and he howled. 'Didn't want to give up the sports car?'

'No, it wasn't . . .' said Wilf, looking at me unhappily. Kelly was sitting up on the table.

'Wot's going on? Are you trying to ruin this for me?'

'Yes, I am,' I said. 'Now hurry up, we have to get a move on.'

'I don't want to get a move on. I want my operation.'

'You can't have it. I've contaminated the area. So come on, move, before they inject you with something that's been banned from every bloody country on earth.'

'Well, it hasn't been banned from France, 'as it?'

'We're not in France, you plank! We're nowhere! We're out in the middle of the ocean where you let them knock you unconscious so they can stuff you with bloody seals just to see what would happen! You pricks!'

Suddenly, Philippe released me, and I realised that he'd actually had my feet off the ground. I dropped heavily, winded. He pulled me round to face him.

'You're ruining my investment,' he said menacingly. 'Now I am going to ruin your life.'

'How?' I said. There was so much adrenalin coursing through me I didn't feel in the slightest bit afraid.

'I will find out where you live, where you work, where you sleep and I will make sure it becomes a living hell.'

'My life already sucks,' I said. 'And anyway, you won't. I'm not that pretty. You've never even looked me in the eye. You completely ignore anyone who isn't blown up like a big, blonde, inflatable doll. So I bet you –' and I pointed at him – 'don't even know my name. Because I look normal.'

He paused and caught his breath. Everyone went silent. The seconds passed like days. Finally Dr Bennet stepped forward.

'It's—' he started. I turned my face towards him, just as Dr Maitland grabbed his arm. He stared at me for one minute. Then he lowered his eyes and didn't say any more.

'*Evie!*' screamed Kelly. 'What the hell are you doing?'

'Oh, for fuck's sake!' I yelled. Then, as Philippe made a strange growling noise, and a lunge straight towards me, I grabbed her arm. 'RUN!'

I pulled her back through the door to the disinfected room, picking up a bottle of steriliser.

'BLEACH!' I yelled as Philippe pulled open the door behind us, squirting as much of it as I could over his Jermyn Street suit. He staggered backwards, covering his eyes, as I ran, half supporting Kelly, who was a little wobbly on her feet (probably because she wasn't wearing stilettos, like a Barbie doll), through the garage and towards the stairs.

We burst out onto the deck just as the doctors came swarming out of the salon towards us.

'Run!' I said. 'Don't touch us! Don't TOUCH US!'

Oh, God, I must have looked unbelievably crazy, because they all stood back! They must have remembered me from the other party as a dangerous maniac. We pounded down to the back of the boat where, sure enough, and thank God, Kizza was standing, his hand on the tiller of a beautiful wooden speedboat. I've never been so pleased to see anything in my life. He helped Kelly down the stairs at the back and got her sitting down and comfortable. I prepared to follow her when I heard my name called again.

'Evie!'

It was Wilf. He was standing on the highest aft deck. He must have caught the lift all the way up. He looked immeasurably sad and was holding up two vials. It must have been the last of the Radoflux – well, bugger him. As I watched him, he threw both vials far, far away into the sea, as I threw myself into the tender.

Kizza was frantically untying ropes as Philippe pounded up the deck towards us, his handsome face completely transformed by a huge snarl. He was brandishing something at us. It couldn't be a gun, could it? Oh my God, was it a gun? I'd never seen a gun. Shit, was he going to shoot? Were we going to die? Was I going to die single without a man to throw himself onto my coffin, howling, 'It should have been me'?

Well, it wasn't to be my time to find out. With a grunting roar, John Jr leapt forward out of the crowd and did what John Jr does best – picking people up and throwing them in the water.

Philippe was swallowing, shouting and cursing us desperately as the rest of the doctors peered over the side, eyes wide. Some of them were laughing. Maybe they hadn't seen the gun. If it was a gun. Maybe it was just a very big syringe.

More importantly, as I clung onto Kelly, struggling to catch my breath as Kizza accelerated away, I could make out the bankers in their formal suits, huddled together, desperately trying to get signals on their mobile phones. And I don't think they were calling to increase their stakes.

Chapter Sixteen

It was morning. My bags were packed. I'd slipped out of the hotel without settling my bill – they could charge bloody Maitland and Bennet, I wasn't paying for it, those bastards. I'd dragged my bags down with me to the beach. My flight didn't leave for another six hours. Theoretically I supposed Philippe could track me down and come and find me there, but I didn't think he would. I'm not sure bad people really do go around killing people willy-nilly like they do on TV. I think they're as rational as the rest of us; they weigh up the best thing for them in any given circumstance and go ahead and do it. So storming the beach and knifing me just probably wasn't worth his time. I fervently hoped.

So I went back down to the beach – I had my bikini on under my clothes, but I was pretty well wrapped against the sun this time. I had the paperback I hadn't picked up the entire trip, and I had decided to sit, look at the sea and not let a single thought cloud my mind. Not one. Not the fact that we had left John Jr behind on the boat with an angry mob (though that had interesting possibilities) or that Kelly had actually been a bit pissed off with me, at least for a bit, till I explained what was really going on. Certainly not Wilf's betrayal – well, there was just too much betrayal going on at the moment even to consider it.

Nope, I was going to stare at the sea, maybe have a swim and a snooze and think about a big fat white nothing until it absolutely was time to go home and start picking up my life again with, I reckoned, a lot of help from my mum's shepherd's pie.

It was in this state of mind – not exactly made worse by buying an ice cream every time the seller came round – that I sat, gazing at the sun on the water. I didn't even notice two figures, slightly out of focus, appear in my peripheral vision.

'*There* you are,' said Lydia. 'Everyone's going nuts.'

She was dragging Patrick behind her. He looked a broken man. I think he'd lost weight in twenty-four hours. But weirdly, he was smiling.

'Go away,' I said. 'I never have to speak to you again. So, go away. You're horrible.'

She pouted. 'Well, you *might* have to speak to me again,' she said, 'if I become part of your family.'

Patrick whimpered a bit at that. Well, maybe it was time he was taken in hand.

'The boat's gone,' she said. 'It went last night. The bankers decided not to invest. They're going to dismantle the operating theatre and use it as a cinema. Too at risk from terrorism apparently.'

'I'm a terrorist?' I said. 'Cool.' Then I worried about the police. But I'd been invited on the boat. I hadn't really done anything wrong. I didn't think.

'They dumped us all off last night,' she said. 'They got us as pissed as farts on Cristal as long as we promised not to mention it.'

'Ah, plastic surgeons,' I said. 'Nature's incorruptibles.'

'Your "friend" Bailey pulled a supermodel they'd brought in for promotional pictures. Oh, *sorry*. Did I hurt your feelings?'

I shook my head. 'Not really.'

And I half watched as Lydia dragged Patrick up the beach, whispering something about love under the dunes.

After that I must have dozed off, because when I woke the sun was low in the sky. At least I was covered up this time. As I gradually opened my eyes I became aware that someone was standing over me; standing very still, as if they'd been there for some time. I jumped out of my skin, throwing myself upwards off the sunbed. My heart tried to get up before I did. I had to blink a hundred times before realising that it wasn't

Philippe and his henchmen come to kill me; it was Dr Maitland.

'Christ,' I said. 'I thought you'd come to kill me. Have you?'

'No!' said Dr Maitland. 'No.'

He shuffled and looked at the sand.

'Well, you can fuck off then,' I said. 'I'm fired, remember? I never have to talk to you again.'

I took a slug of Sprite to clear my sandy mouth. I wanted to tell him a thing or two. Then I realised I didn't. I was sick of being outraged and angry. I was tired of it all. I was relaxing, remember? And then I was going home.

'You were very brave on the boat,' he said. 'Very brave.'

'You weren't.'

'You looked very cute covered in engine oil.'

'I'm glad you think so. Now fuck off back to your MG, will you?'

His face looked pained. 'I wasn't going to tell you this . . .' He tailed off. 'Some idea of nobility, I don't know. Stupid. Anyway.'

He swallowed hard.

'I can't stop thinking about you, and I can't help it.'

I blinked in the sun.

'Your sister.'

'In law.'

'Yes . . . anyway. I, em, I did a bit of switching on board.'

'You did what?'

'I switched. I switched the Radoflux with saline. It

303

wouldn't have done anything at all. She'd probably have thought she looked better or something – crap, she's only thirty-one – but it would have been harmless. I thought that was the best way of helping.'

'But you made up with Dr Bennet!'

'I had to, didn't I? How else would he let me in the operating theatre?'

I thought about it.

'Why didn't you tell me?'

'I told you I was going to do what I could. I thought you'd trust me to come up with something. I didn't want you to worry until it was all over.'

I shrugged. 'You know, trusting men hasn't seemed to get me very far recently.'

He moved towards me. 'Your plan worked better anyway.'

'Yours would probably have been less messy.'

'Maybe life is messy.'

'Oh, it is,' I said.

'I know,' he said. 'I think I've been avoiding the messy bits of it for too long.'

'So what are you going to do?' I said.

He shrugged. 'I thought I might go look at hospital practice – maybe not abroad, but there's a lot of great reconstructive work going on in the UK. There's a face transplantation team that might be recruiting.'

'That'd be great,' I said. 'Good for you. I think I'm going to amass a private army and take over the world.'

'I bet you could too.'

He paused, and pushed his feet in the sand.

'You know . . . I think you've made me braver too.'

'Neh,' I said. 'It must have always been there.'

'Well, maybe . . .' he said. 'Uh, Evie . . . back in London.
Do you want to get a cup of coffee sometime?'

I stared at him. 'You are joking.'

'What do you mean?'

'Well . . .'

Everything that had happened spun through my mind.
Tom, Bailey, the boat, and now Wilf . . . I think I had trust issues.

'It won't work,' I said. 'I don't think so. I have men problems and you have . . . well, just general problems.'

'As solved by me being very brave,' he said. 'Haven't you
seen *The Wizard of Oz*?'

I smiled. He really was lovely once you got to know him.

'I'm sorry,' I said. 'I think I need some R&R on my own
for a while.'

'What the doctor ordered,' he said wryly, then came over
and gave me a very sweet, very gentle kiss on the forehead. I
almost changed my mind right there and then but for once
was going for a bit of dignity.

'Bye,' I said. He looked defeated and a little clumsy,
stomping up the beach. The sand must be getting in his
brogues. I'd never asked him why he dressed like that. I think
I'd got to like it, then stopped noticing. Oh, well.

*

The airport was mobbed again, but this time I strode through it confidently. I didn't need a helicopter or a business-class seat. I was Evie Kennedy, fighter for seal rights, and I didn't need to be anyone else at all. In the queue I stood behind Lydia and Patrick, but they were snogging too hard to notice me and I didn't really feel like chatting. Bailey had squeezed through too on his way to business class. He'd given me a big hug and asked if I wanted to go to Wagamama when we got back, as if nothing had ever happened. Typical. I told him Wagamama was really no good for geeks like him, the soup steamed up his glasses too much. He was also talking excitedly about some underground project in Dubai that I reckoned I'd better keep a close eye on.

As we were chatting, Kelly and John Jr got out of their chauffeur-driven limo. John Jr was shouting at the driver about something. I looked at Bailey and he looked at me.

'Oh, no,' he said.

'He saved my life!' I said. 'We have to.'

And we hoisted our bags and went towards them.

'JJ,' I started. 'I know we think you're an oaf . . .'

'And you were really mean to me when I was small,' added Bailey.

JJ's face contorted. 'And?'

'Thanks,' I said. 'Thank you for everything. You're a good brother.'

'Better than Patrick?'

'Of course.'

'Better than Cassandro?'

'He bloody started all this,' I mused, briefly. 'Stupid over-romanticised holidays.'

'Aren't they all?' said Bailey.

I gave JJ a hug. 'See you at Mum's,' I said.

'I'm not hugging you,' said Bailey.

'I'd break your arms if you tried,' said JJ. But then he smiled.

Back in the queue, out of the corner of my eye, I noticed two familiar figures skulking in. They didn't see me. I was shocked as they headed for the first-class desk. Oooh, those charlatans! Someone was behind them, carrying all their bags. She saw me and broke away.

It was Janey's helper, poor old Judy. She ran across to me when she saw me and grabbed me by the hand.

'You saved those seals,' she said, as if I'd raised them from the dead. 'You did it!'

'Not really,' I said, trying to look modest. But it was too late. The noise had attracted attention.

'I love seals,' Judy was saying. 'That's why I work so hard to save them. I love seals.'

'Oh, it's you,' said Lydia, turning round in the queue. 'You'd better ask for extra rolls on the plane. Keep you going for a while now you're unemployed.'

I ignored her, tried to ignore everyone, and kept my head down.

*

'What do you mean, customs want to see me?' I'd just heard Lydia say. 'Well, yes, I do work for Dr Yuri Bennet . . . what do you mean, you're holding him? No, I don't want to answer any enquiries . . . Rado what?'

I realised that there were two security guards standing right next to her. Oh my God! Oh, they'd find out she was clueless, surely. Not before she spent a little time cooling her heels, though, I should think. And not in business class either.

Then there was a commotion across the departures hall. Someone was pushing their way through, with a bold, confident stride. I ignored it, until the tumult stopped right under my nose. I looked up. There, right in front of me, was Wilf.

'Courage,' he said, when he was as close as he could get. Then he grabbed my face in his hands and gave me the best kiss of my life.

I was gasping when we came up for air. Now there was a hubbub all around us.

'I'm sorry, ma'am, but you definitely cannot board this aircraft,' I heard the BA woman say to Lydia.

Then everything faded away as Wilf kissed me again. A few people even clapped, which shows you how much there is to do waiting in a long departure queue at an airport.

'Come on!' he said loudly.

'Where? I'm waiting for a flight.'

'I've got you a flight,' he said, brandishing two vouchers in his hand. I knew what they were. They were helicopter passes. Lydia gave me a filthy look. She knew what they were too.

'My darling girl. I'm not letting you go. Come with me. You haven't even had a holiday yet. You haven't seen anything of Cannes . . . or Antibes, or Mougins. There are art galleries, and walks, and bars, and sunsets and lots and lots of things for us to do with the money I won at the casino. But first, there's a helicopter taking us away to a quite appallingly decadent lunch. Absolutely no seal on the menu. Coming?'

'How did you win that money again?' I asked him. 'It's been bugging me.'

'Bored medical student,' he said. 'Docs have great memories. We can all count cards. I'm surprised Yuri didn't figure it out. Anyway. Lunch?'

I couldn't help it. I grinned a grin that threatened to burst my face, then stretched out my hand and put it in his.

'Well,' I said. 'I do believe I need a holiday . . .'

Keep in touch with

Jenny

www.jennycolgan.com

**For more information on all Jenny's books,
latest news and mouth-watering recipes**

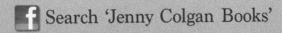 Search 'Jenny Colgan Books'

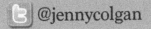 @jennycolgan

LOVE TO READ?

Sign up for early sneak peeks of our
hot new books, exclusive competitions and more

www.littlebrownbooks.net/newsletters